PARANORMAL HUNTERS EPISODE 2

BLACK MOON
rising

MILA NICKS

First paperback edition April 2021

Book cover design by Red Leaf Design

When we are asleep in this world, we are awake in another.
-Salvador Dalí

PROLOGUE

HALLOWEEN 1961

Cordelia Dunn stood in the hall and stared at the many pretty things. The door was half ajar, offering a sneak peek at the soft, rosily lit room. The sleek golden tubes of lipstick and sweet-smelling perfume called to her. She didn't give it a second thought. Her feet began to move and her hand stretched out. She pushed the door open with a slow creak and wandered inside.

Rhonda's room was like heaven. From the dream closet full of clothes to the bouquet of fresh flowers, everything felt chic and expensive. Cordelia sat down at the vanity and ran her fingers over the glass of the shapely perfume bottles. She picked up one of the makeup brushes and smiled in the mirror as she pretended to swipe rouge onto her brown skin. She'd watched Mom and Rhonda do it a thousand times before.

But pretending wasn't enough. One tiny sample couldn't hurt. Cordelia glanced over her shoulder and then reached for a lipstick. The shade was a fire engine red called Cherie Amore. She applied the tube to her lips and her heart raced. She felt a thousand times prettier.

Next she reached for an eyebrow pencil. A small giggle rolled off her tongue as she leaned in close to the mirror and posed. Now she really looked like—

"What in the world are you doing?" shrieked Rhonda from the doorway.

Cordelia yelped, dropped the eyebrow pencil, and clumsily moved to get up. She bumped into the vanity table, knocking over several of the perfume bottles. They crashed to the floor and shattered into tiny glass shards. Her mouth fell open as horror struck her.

Rhonda flocked over like a bird on the attack. "Look what you've done now! Do you know how much this Lancôme perfume cost? I saved up for months!"

"I'm sorry, Rhonda!"

"I can't leave my room without you sniffing around! Why do you always have to be so nosy?" Rhonda ranted as she salvaged whatever hadn't broken or been knocked over. "I agreed to babysit you and this is how you repay me—I could've been out having a swell night with my friends!"

Cordelia's heart was still beating fast as she tried to explain. "I just wanted to try your lipstick, Rhonda. I…I just wanted to look as pretty as you."

"There's not enough lipstick in the world, Cordelia! GET OUT!"

Rhonda chased Cordelia from the room and slammed the door shut. Cordelia stood staring at the door for a couple more seconds in the vain hope her older sister would change her mind and open up again. When nothing happened, she sighed and turned away. She hadn't meant to break Rhonda's things, but she'd been bored. Mom and Dad were out to dinner with Mr. Poe. The twins, Ernie and Dick, were downstairs watching *The Twilight Zone*. Was it wrong of her to want to spend some time in her big sister's room?

Cordelia didn't think so. The night was boring and there was nothing else to do. When she asked Mom and Dad about trick-or-treating, they said it was too dangerous for their five-year-old daughter. That left her without anything to do but wander the premises seeking out a pastime.

It had been one week since they moved to Maresburg, Virginia and bought the Poe Hotel. The property had been around for over a century, but it was originally a hospital that treated wounded soldiers. A decade or two after the Civil War ended, Mr. Poe's grandfather had the bright idea to the buy the land and refashion the place into a luxury hotel.

Dad had similar ideas except he wanted to turn the Poe Hotel into accommodations for colored folks passing through. There weren't many towns in the area where colored folks could stop when traveling and safely rest their heads overnight. He sold Mom on the idea and they packed up their things and headed to Maresburg.

Cordelia wasn't sure how she felt about living at the hotel. The floorboards creaked and the paint was peeling. Odd noises echoed on the large property in the silence of the night and the plumbing needed some work. The only room Cordelia liked was Rhonda's. At least her room was pretty and smelled nice.

Rhonda dreamed of being a big-time singer someday, like her favorite, Etta James. She had a beautiful voice, both bluesy and heartfelt, oftentimes filling up their home with her crooning. Everybody said she had the looks and talent for it, but stardom wasn't always so simple for young women like Rhonda. Cordelia hoped her dream of stardom didn't come true. Was it selfish of her to want her big sister to stick around Maresburg forever?

Before she realized where she was going, Cordelia looked up and noticed she'd gone down a forbidden hallway. Dad said the area needed a lot of repair work and it wasn't safe for the kids, though the twins claimed he was lying. The real reason was a lot grimmer. Mrs. Poe used to live down this hall before she passed away. She was unwell for some time and had been rumored to experience funny thoughts.

But as Cordelia remembered something else the twins had told her, she slowly smiled. Mr. Poe had kept his late wife's things stored just as she left them. Cordelia had seen photos of her hanging downstairs. The woman was beautiful with skin like honey and her figure svelte and elegant.

Cordelia wanted to be glamorous too. If she snuck down the hall and crept into Mrs. Poe's old room, she could rummage through her belongings. Mrs. Poe looked like she had been the type of woman to have a selection of things like floral perfumes and high heels. Even a couple minutes browsing her closet would help her stop feeling like such an ugly duckling.

After a glance over her shoulder, Cordelia headed for the door at the end of the hall. The door loomed over her. The dark oak was scratched in different places as if someone had taken their long nails and sank them into the wooden surface. She reached out with a shaky hand and touched the large brass handle. Second thoughts floated into her head, but she pushed them aside.

A few minutes looking around and then she would leave. It was too risky otherwise. Rhonda could find her at any minute and Mom and Dad would eventually be home from dinner with Mr. Poe. She had to be quick.

At first it appeared the door was locked. Cordelia pressed down as hard as she could on the handle, and the heavy door cracked open. She crossed the threshold and blindly reached for the light switch. As the ceiling light flickered on, the door thudded closed.

Cordelia jumped at the unexpected sound, but then turned her gaze on the rest of the room. Ernie and Dick had been right about Mr. Poe. The room might've smelled like dust and the carpet was spongy, but he had left it exactly as Mrs. Poe had kept it—or at least it looked that way. The bed in the center of the room was neat and made. The nightstand had a book Mrs. Poe must've been reading and an empty vase Cordelia supposed used to be filled with flowers. She padded over to the window and glanced at the streets below.

Tonight was an unusually murky one, especially for Virginia. A haze of mist hovered in the air, its thick clouds swallowing up whatever it touched. Trick-or-treaters couldn't be seen so much as they were heard; children's giggles and footsteps echoed in the dark. It might've been the spot by the window, or maybe the heat didn't reach this room, but there seemed to be a permanent draft.

Cordelia rubbed her arms with either hand to warm up. Her eyes widened when she spotted the large trunk and vanity in the other corner of the room. She was on her knees digging into the trunk within seconds. Mrs. Poe really was a woman with good taste. The trunk was full of silk scarves and fashionable hats. She wrapped a scarf around her neck and pushed on a pair of sunglasses and then rose to her feet for a strut around the room.

Mrs. Poe's makeup selection was also impressive. Cordelia spritzed on perfume and swiped lipstick on the back of her hand. She coughed when she opened a jar of some type of makeup powder. Time got away from her as she discovered a leather-bound book with impressive stitched trimming and bold letters imprinted on the front:

Journal of Maya G. Poe

Mom said it was inconsiderate to peek at people's private diaries. People jotted down their innermost thoughts and secrets in their diaries and it wasn't meant for prying eyes. Cordelia moved to put the journal back as Mom's stern, syrupy lecture replayed in her head, but then she stopped. Mrs. Poe had passed away some time ago. Was it really intruding if she was no longer around?

She flipped through the ink-heavy pages of the journal. The beginning entries were mundane. Daily accounts of Mrs. Poe's marriage to a much older Mr. Poe. At the midpoint, the tone shifted. Her entries detailed how horribly lonely she felt. The later the date inked in the corner of the journal, the darker the entries became. Cordelia clapped shut the book with a squeak when Mrs. Poe mentioned witchcraft and spell work. No wonder Mr. Poe claimed she had been unwell.

Cordelia shuddered and stuffed the journal back into the drawer. It was time to go before she grew too greedy and got caught. She returned the scarf and sunglasses to the trunk, noticing a few new items buried at the bottom. One of them was a gold-plated hand mirror that looked like an expensive family heirloom. She picked it up and held it in front of her. The hand mirror didn't show her reflection. The glass was empty, as though nothing were in its line of sight.

She frowned and whispered, "What sort of funny mirror is this?"

A cold sense of foreboding filled Cordelia's lungs, making it so that her next breath was difficult. Something was wrong with this mirror. Even holding it felt off. In the distance, trick-or-treaters giggled and screamed out to each other. Cordelia flinched and the handheld mirror slipped from her grasp. She fumbled to catch it, but she was too late. The mirror hit the floor, cracking down the middle.

The room itself was upended. As Cordelia gasped, the light above started blinking. The temperature in the room plummeted and the giggles from the children outside faded far out of reach. The broken mirror was no longer empty, clouding with what looked like black fog. Cordelia scrambled to get up, tripping over the chair and colliding face-first with the spongy carpet.

The light gave up and went out—or maybe whatever was in the mirror chased it away. Darkness filled every corner of the room. Even the half-moon itself, once a silvery glow visible in the bedroom window, went dark, as if switched off by a higher force. Cordelia opened her mouth to scream but her throat closed up and she coughed instead. She was no longer alone. Something else was in the room with her; she could feel its presence, *sense* its movements.

Cordelia crawled for the first hiding spot available. She rolled under the bed and peeked out into the dark. Her eyes were starting to adjust. It was a shrouded figure—an inky shadow with a life of its own. It glided through material objects like the chair and the trunk and then the door, leaving droplets of ink in its wake.

She waited a few seconds before she inhaled a sharp breath. Quick relief swept over her. She was alright. It was gone and she was tucked away safe. She crawled out from under the bed as another dreadful realization sunk in. The shadow might've been gone from the room, but now it was loose in the hotel!

Cordelia fled from the room screaming. Rhonda or Mom and Dad catching her was no longer a concern. The more frightening prospect was that thing on the prowl. Her heart thudded erratically, like it would burst from her chest, as she dashed down the hall. She rounded the corner and collided with someone taller and stockier.

Dad wrapped his arms around her and said, "Cordelia, *Cordelia*! Calm down. I come home and find you spooked. You're shaking."

"T-the shadow! It's…it's on the loose!"

He frowned, his kind face etched with concern. "What shadow? This is the last time I let you watch *The Twilight Zone* with Ernie and Dick. That show always gets you all worked up—"

"Dad, it was *REAL*!"

He escorted her away from the section of the hall that was off-limits. Cordelia didn't protest, walking alongside him feeling dizzy and confused. Maybe she had been imagining the shadow. It was a figment of her imagination, which would explain why it had disappeared. It had never existed in the first place.

They passed by Rhonda's door on their walk to Cordelia's bedroom. She glanced at the door that had transfixed her earlier and then did a double take. The soft rosy light was no more. Rhonda's door was ajar, but now it was dark inside—as dark and ominous as Mrs. Poe's room had been. Horror flooded Cordelia in an instant cold sweat.

She shrugged off Dad's arm and started for Rhonda's room. "RHONDA!"

"What's the matter with you?" Dad asked. He grabbed her before she could get far, plucking her off her feet with ease. "You're acting delirious. Do you have a fever?"

"The light! It's gone!" she shrieked helplessly.

"You know how your sister feels about you barging into her room. You'll see her in the morning. It's time for bed."

That night Cordelia tossed and turned. She struggled through a fitful sleep and woke still exhausted. The sun blinded her, pouring through the part in the curtains. She crawled out of bed, breathing out a relieved sigh. Even despite her achy eyes, she had never been more grateful for morning light. Where there was light, there was no darkness. No strange shadows.

Her relief was cut short. A horrified, ear-splitting scream tore through the morning silence. It belonged to Mom, and it was coming from the room down the hall.

Last night Rhonda had gone to bed, never to wake up again.

CHAPTER ONE

PRESENT DAY

"I can't sleep."

Selene Blackstone twisted from her left side onto her right and let out a frustrated groan. She was cold and itchy, uncomfortable, and cranky tucked deep inside the sleeping bag, serenaded by the pesky chirp of what could only be crickets. She rolled onto her back and glared up at the ceiling of the Dodge Caravan affectionately dubbed Ghost.

"Aiden," she whispered and then prodded him hard in his side. "*Aiden!*"

"Hmmm?"

Aiden O'Hare lay beside her in his own sleeping bag, drifting off to dreamland, seconds away from snoring loudly.

"Did you hear me? I can't sleep."

"What's wrong?" he mumbled, eyes still closed.

"I'm cold."

"C'mere."

He was still awake enough to open his arms to her, beckoning her closer. Selene stayed put, however. She folded her own arms and continued glaring up at the van ceiling. She couldn't sleep and when she couldn't sleep she lost all pretenses.

"Aiden, this is ridiculous. We need to do something about this setup."

"Hmmm?"

"Aiden," she repeated in another whine. She sprang up in her sleeping bag and curled her knees up to her chest, arms resting atop. "How have you and Eddie survived like this?"

Now, finally, Aiden seemed to be stirring. His eyes opened and he scratched his head. "Like what, Selene? What do you mean?"

"I mean, *this*—the van—these sleeping bags."

"We've always camped out in the van when on the road. It's all the show budget can afford. At least we get to do hotels when we're in town investigating."

Selene glanced around the roomy open space that was the back of the caravan. It was enough to fit two more rows of seating and a whole trunk section if they wanted—*or* something more practical to their needs, like installing a real bed and even a kitchenette.

"Why can't we give Ghost a makeover?"

"We've gone over this," he replied. He also glanced around, his gaze following hers as it eyed the open space. "Eddie and I were originally going to transform Ghost into a van you could live out of. Ghost was supposed to become a full up campervan. We even had a plan to install a water tank."

"*And*? What happened?"

"Eddie didn't think it was important. We spent that part of the budget on new paranormal equipment," he explained. He slipped an arm around her and brought her against his side. Her head automatically fell onto his shoulder. "I hate that you hate sleeping in Ghost. I'm sorry it's not comfortable for you. How about we do another hotel tomorrow when we get to DC?"

Selene sighed. Aiden's hard shoulder was a surprisingly cozy place to rest her head. She burrowed closer, his body heat warming her smaller frame. "Every time we stay in a hotel between filming, it's out of pocket. You can't keep affording them, and I know I can't. Miriam paid me pennies. I don't want you to keep charging your card because you feel bad for me."

"I don't mind if it means you're comfortable," he said, running a hand up and down her arm to warm her up. "We'll be on location in the next few days anyway. Then it's the show footing the bill."

"But you've taken me to so many cities. The last month has been nothing but us on vacation," said Selene. She tilted her head so that she could look up at him, and she smiled. "I don't want you to think I haven't been having a good time."

Because she had been.

For the first time in her twenty-six years, Selene Black-stone had crossed the border of the small New England town Brimrock. After spending years trapped within the town borders, she was now free to go anywhere and do anything. The curse placed on her family was finally broken.

It was once again an example of the impossible being the possible. She had grown up convinced it would never happen; she would forever be doomed to an existence of misery, just like her mother and grandmother Luna before her. Like them, she was a *witch*.

All of that changed when Aiden O'Hare stepped into the picture. At first the prickly, sarcastic paranormal investigator had confused her, but they promptly formed an inseparable bond. No matter what an evil, vengeful, succubus witch had to say about it.

Now, here they were—boyfriend and girlfriend, partners in their paranormal investigations for a show called *Paranormal Hunters*. She was excited, filled to the brim with curiosity for what the future held, but in the moment, she was also frustrated and cranky. She wanted sleep.

"We'll figure it out," said Aiden. His deep timbre softened for her, his hand finding hers and taking hold. Their fingers laced, his longer ones between her shorter ones. "I'll demand Paulina give us another van budget. What can she say? Our show is in the top ten for most gained subscribers on YouTv. We're doing big numbers."

Selene kissed Aiden on the mouth, pushing him backward. They lowered to the van floor with her on top of him and his hands holding her face. She spread both legs so that she entrapped him between her thighs in a straddle. Aiden loved when she pinned him like this, when he was under her and the curves of her body.

He wasted no time communicating this. His hands drifted from her face, traveling lower, down her neck, outlining the sides of her breasts and the slight cinch of her waist and then the swell of her hips. They landed on the undersides of her fleshy thighs and stayed there, gripping the skin as though he couldn't help himself; she was too tempting.

"This is how you get your way," Aiden teased between kisses. "You can convince me to do anything."

Selene smiled against his lips, rocking against him. His hard-on was fast on the way. "It's almost like magic…"

The February drizzle couldn't bring the mood down if it tried. Selene hopped off the tour bus and gasped at what awaited her. For as dull and damp as the afternoon was, color now bloomed on the scene in ivory whites and blush pinks. It would be another few weeks before the cherry blossoms reached the full extent of their beauty, but the flowery trees around the Tidal Basin were breathtaking regardless.

Washington, DC, was everything she had imagined.

She fumbled in her leather book bag for her Polaroid camera, snapping her first of many photos to come. Aiden made fun of her for carrying around a camera from the nineties, but it worked as well as any camera on a smartphone. Plus, it had once belonged to Mom.

"*And* I get my photos printed right into my hand," Selene had boasted to him. "Does your fancy iPhone camera do that?"

Her mouth fell open in a smile as she clicked away at the historic scenery. She had nabbed some good shots of the Tidal Basin with the Jefferson Memorial in the background, and even some artsy ones of her fellow tourists strolling along the water banks. *Finally* she had an excuse to take up scrapbooking. Photos of places like the Brimrock library and park grounds weren't too exciting after twenty-six years. But places like Washington, DC? Definitely scrapbook-worthy.

The drizzle continued to fall, showing no signs of slowing down anytime soon. One particularly pesky drop plunked down onto the slope of Selene's nose, a cold and slippery bead that dangled off the round tip. She ignored it, along with the rest of the sprinkles, clicking away with zealous tourist abandon.

A black canopy floated above her head, blocking out any more drizzle. She paused, lifting her gaze from behind the camera and turning it upward. Aiden stood half a step behind her, holding his giant umbrella over them. He smiled when she met his glowing hazel eyes. They had changed colors, now a green one or two tones off from emerald.

Warmth quickly radiated in her chest that had nothing to do with the fuzzy sweater she wore and everything to do with his thoughtfulness. She twisted around, balancing on tiptoe, and planted a kiss on his chin. Classic short girl problems.

Fortunately, Aiden had enough height for them both. He plucked her off her feet for a real kiss, his arm banded around her waist. They traded laughs between pecks on the lips, indifferent to their rainy day surroundings.

"Gather around, gather around!" Mrs. Francis, the tour guide, screeched in the distance. "No time for dillydallying!"

Selene pulled away from Aiden. Why did she feel like a misbehaving student scalded by her schoolteacher whenever Mrs. Francis spoke?

"C'mon, or we'll get left behind!" She grabbed Aiden's free hand and rushed after the gaggle of tourists.

"Would that be such a bad thing, though?" Aiden asked with a waggle of his brow. "I'm sure we'd manage just fine without Mrs. Francis."

"Shhh, or she'll hear you!"

"And what? Give us detention? Put us in time-out?"

Selene shushed him again, though a grin fought its way onto her face. Aiden's sarcasm no longer surprised her, but it was still difficult to resist its humorous effects.

"I said everybody hush up!" Mrs. Francis shrieked as if she'd overheard. The group of tourists shuffled to an ill-timed stop, clumsily knocking into each other. She waited at the front with her clipboard hugged to her chest, eyes narrowing in a severe stare. She vaguely resembled a bird, beakish nose in the air and her thick fur-lined coat like plumage. "I'm sure by now you've noticed the trees all around you. Who knows what these are called?"

Eager hands shot up into the air, but Mrs. Francis ignored each one. She scanned the crowd in typical suspicious-teacher fashion, determined to catch the rule-breaking student. She used the rolled-up tour pamphlet in her hand as a pointer, picking Aiden out of the group.

"You," she said, squinting at the badge pinned to his chest. She'd made all of the tourists wear one with their names scrawled across the front. "Adam, is it?"

Aiden's reddish-brown brows rose. "Actually, it's Aiden."

"Close enough," she dismissed. She gestured to the trees around them. "What are these called?"

Several of the tourists half turned for a glance at Aiden. Selene clapped a hand to her mouth and ducked behind the man in front of her. The look of offense on Aiden's face was one worth capturing with her camera. Aiden hated being condescended to.

"The tour is called DC Cherry Blossom Tour," he answered at a slow pace, baffled by the obvious question.

"They're called cherry blossom trees," she went on as though he had guessed incorrectly. She turned to the nearest tree, pointing out the white petals on a flower. "They don't truly bloom until early spring, but even now, they're quite lovely. You'll notice they're a variation of shades between ivory white and pale pink. Who can tell me what year they date back to?"

More hands darted up, but Mrs. Francis skipped them. Her eyes were so beady they were smaller than pinholes. It didn't occur to Selene until a second too late that she was squinting at Aiden again.

"Well?" Mrs. Francis quizzed. A flicker of satisfaction passed across her birdish features, as though she was certain she had stumped him this time. "Do you know what year these trees were planted?"

"1912," said Aiden with ease, one hand stowed in his pants pocket. His volume increased. "In fact, the first person to plant one along this Tidal Basin was First Lady Helen Taft herself."

The crowd made impressed sounds of *ooh*s and *aah*s and nodded their heads at the fun fact. Only Selene and Mrs. Francis didn't. Selene because she was busy smirking proudly at Aiden. Mrs. Francis because she looked like a bird about to explode in squawks at any second.

"Mrs. Taft planted it on her own?" one tourist in the group asked Aiden.

He nodded. "That's right. Mrs. Taft and the wife of the Japanese ambassador, Iwa Chinda, planted the first two. The idea was a symbol of national friendship between the United States and Japan."

"How many trees did they end up planting?" another tourist asked him. The crowd had turned away from Mrs. Francis.

"More than three thousand at the time, but Japan later gifted more cherry trees in 1956 as another sign of good will," Aiden explained.

Mrs. Francis stuck two fingers in her mouth and whistled, alarming everyone and forcing their attention. With a more disgruntled expression on her face than ever, she scolded, "I already mentioned no more dillydallying, didn't I? Time to continue with the tour!"

Aiden and Selene hung back from the rest of the group as they obediently trudged behind Mrs. Francis. Selene turned to him wearing a small smirk. "You can't just behave yourself, can you?"

"I was trying to help the tour. If anything, Mrs. Francis should be thanking me," he replied innocently.

"Uh-huh. Whatever you say. If you had gone on another second, pretty sure she would've flung her clipboard at your head."

"It would've made the tour more interesting, wouldn't it?"

They ditched the rest of the tour to wander the edges of the Tidal Basin. The drizzle had let up, though the gray skies and weighty clouds remained. Selene ventured on her own to snap another few photos for her much anticipated new scrapbooking hobby. She was stowing her Polaroid camera back into her book bag when an arm slipped around her waist from behind.

"I saw this one and knew it was yours."

She looked down and found the cherry blossom he'd eased into her hand. "Aiden…where did you…?"

"I didn't pick it if that's what you're asking. It fell from a tree and was floating in the air." He eased her around so she was facing him, taking the flower and tucking it behind her ear. "You look beautiful."

Selene couldn't resist leaning upward for another kiss. The February showers started once more, falling in thin sheets across the area, making puncture marks in the water of the Tidal Basin. When they pulled apart and stood hugged at each other's side, they stared across the silvery-blue water at the architectural masterpiece that was the Jefferson Memorial.

Wonder filled Selene's heart in a slow, appreciative thump. To think months ago she had been convinced she would be stuck in Brimrock for the rest of her life. She had been so sure she'd be miserable and alone, doomed to suffer 'til her dying day.

And now here she was, exploring the world she had dreamed for years of seeing. She was at Aiden's side, embarking on a new, adventurous life. In a few short days, they'd be in Virginia, starting their first case as paranormal investigative partners. The sleep she was losing out on didn't matter; in that moment, the specter of it all weighed on her and she smiled brightly.

The impossible was possible and it was better than she'd ever imagined.

———

"Are you nervous?" Aiden asked later that night. They were preparing for bed. Aiden with his usual pre-bed reading and Selene with her skin and haircare routine.

Selene's deft fingers paused midbraid and she aimed a curious glance in his direction. Her face was slathered in moisturizing avocado goodness. The few minutes spent looking like a green Martian were worth it if the mask left her skin feeling baby-bottom smooth.

"Nervous about what?"

"The case," he said. He held his open book in his hands, his long legs stretched across the van floor. "It's a pretty big day—your first paranormal case."

"Maybe a little. I'm just going to channel my inner Nancy Drew."

He chuckled. "I don't know, Nance handled some kid glove type cases. She didn't handle anything dangerous like the Hardy Boys."

"Not this again. *Everyone* knows Nancy is superior. And you haven't forgotten I'm a witch, right?"

"Being a witch makes you immune to anything spooky?"

"Haunted hotel," said Selene with a mock arrogant scoff. "Piece of cake. Not spooky at all."

"Well, to be fair, we don't know if the Mhoon Hotel is actually haunted."

Selene rolled her eyes, forgetting about her skin and hair-care. She twisted around to face him and said, "Here we go again. Haven't you learned your lesson about being a skeptic?"

"All I'm saying is, I've spent the last five years of my life investigating these cases. Almost all of them have turned out to be false alarms," he answered with a shrug. "I wouldn't be surprised if there's a logical explanation for what's going on."

"And *what* is it do they say that's going on at the Mhoon?"

"Nobody knows for sure, but it's speculated some type of sleep monster is disturbing the guests. There hasn't been a consistent story throughout the years. The real issue is a few guests have passed away in their sleep. Like I said, it could be a terrible coincidence. Either way, Mr. Mhoon, the owner, wrote to the show and asked us to investigate." Aiden clapped shut his book and took off his glasses, rubbing his eyes. "We should probably get some sleep. Long day ahead of us driving into Maresburg."

Selene hadn't moved an inch. Her thoughts had drifted to Aiden's experience as an investigator. "Aiden, have you ever been afraid? You know, on an investigation?"

"Afraid?" Aiden repeated the word like it perplexed him.

"Yeah, like when ghost hunting or investigating Big Foot or something."

"Selene, you know I don't get scared by that stuff. Now, Eddie, he's a different story. Especially if it involved spiders of any kind."

"*Everyone's* afraid of something," said Selene. She

crawled over to his side by their sleeping bags and peered at him with a curious brow arched. "You're telling me if you investigated Bloody Mary you wouldn't be spooked?"

Aiden considered her question for a second. "I guess…if I had to choose, I'm not the fondest of huskies."

"You? Afraid of dogs? I thought you had one. Ruby—"

"Ruby's a French bulldog," he interrupted. He tugged on the sleeve of his hooded sweatshirt, pulling it up and pointing at a bite mark on his forearm. "My uncle's husky bit me when I was six. You can hardly see it now."

"Because of your hairy arms," teased Selene. She glided her fingers over the mark, her touch gentle and cautious on his ivory skin. "I'm sorry, Aiden. I didn't mean to bring up anything traumatic."

He shrugged and then rolled down his sleeve. "I barely remember it. Except pretty sure I cried."

"That seems like a reaction most would have."

"Right. Anyway, bedtime," he said, moving in for a kiss on her brow. He caught himself at the last second and let out a laugh. "Maybe I'll wait 'til you wash off that avocado stuff."

Selene smiled and rolled her eyes. "It's called a face mask."

She played along with his change of subject without protest. It was par for the course for Aiden, who grew uncomfortable anytime the subject required talking about feelings or showing emotion. She had learned to accept this about him, but at other times questioned if maybe he'd never truly open up. Not even to her.

They gathered their toiletry bags and then headed together to the campground's designated restrooms. Other RVs and campervans littered the vast outdoor space. Some travelers sat around fires and toasted marshmallows for s'mores while the low hum of TV could be heard from other open windows. The women's restroom was vacant except for a mother and her twin daughters washing their hands.

Selene ensured her bladder was empty, her teeth were squeaky clean, and not a glob of her avocado face mask remained. Normally by the time she emerged, Aiden was already done. He was standing outside waiting for her, but tonight was different. For once, she'd finished before him. She wrapped her arms around herself as a particularly strong gust of wind blew through the campgrounds.

The forecast called for more rain and even lower temperatures than last night. They'd have to keep the space heater on high.

The howl from the wind died out and left a silence in its wake. Selene peered at the dark campgrounds only sparsely lit by lamp posts here and there. Where had the other campers gone? Had everyone turned in for the night at the same time?

She shivered in the cold breeze and glanced at the men's restrooms. Aiden never took this long. She half debated marching up to the door and peeking inside. Drop by drop drizzle began to fall and storm clouds migrated into one giant cluster. It really was about to pour tonight.

Her gaze skimmed the blanket of purple sky and even purpler clouds, searching for the moon. It had begun to recede beyond the clouds. The ethereal silver glow normally shining from its depth had gone out, no longer decorating the night sky. Almost as though someone had flicked it off with a light switch. She stared at the ever-darkening moon with brows knitted, forgetting about the campgrounds. The moon had never been so dark, so *black*...

"Ready?" Aiden asked, coming up on her side.

Selene flinched, startled by his sudden appearance. "Where have you been?"

He frowned. "Restroom? I ran out of toothpaste and Jerry
—he's from one of the RVs—had to lend me some. What's
wrong? You look uneasy."

"I'm fine. Let's get back to Ghost. It's started to drizzle."

Aiden put his arm around her and they set off across the
campgrounds, but not without Selene turning her gaze up to
the black moonless sky along the way.

CHAPTER TWO

G host moved like a caravan half his age. The Dodge
Caravan with headlights redolent of a pair of eyes,
round and emotive, vaulted down the highway
lined by thick brush. DC was a long-forgotten memory as the
landscape filled out with lush green for miles. For hours, it
was going to be nothing but open road, pine trees, and the
overcast sky.

That didn't make the journey any less enjoyable.

Aiden sat behind the wheel, steering lazily, one arm
propped up on the ledge of the driver-side window. Every so
often he snuck a sideways glance at Selene. She was always
doing something different, which made him shake his head
and burst into a laugh.

On one glance, she was fiddling with the spirit box,
twisting knobs and holding it up to her ear to catch the low
crackles. On another glance, she was cross-legged in the
passenger seat, face glued to the window, keeping count of
cars' state license plates as they passed them by.

It was an understatement to say Selene wasn't a natural
on the road. She didn't care for being cooped up in the van

for hours at a time and reading while on the move made her nauseous. She hated the sleeping arrangement and preferred their touristy destinations to the woodsy terrains in between.

But Aiden would be a liar if he said he wasn't enjoying himself. Even during the moments Selene seemed less than enthused, he couldn't help being smitten with her *for* her quirks, not in spite of them. Silly things he never would've imagined like her penchant to break out in song at any moment or how she got snacky while on the road, prompting him to keep a supply of kettle chips and sugary candies on hand. Other silly things like how she didn't bother folding up her sleeping bag in the morning or how she took up more space than her sixty-two inches warranted by the end of the night. Usually he woke to her body swathed halfway across his at the most perplexing angles.

These quirks of hers were unexpected but special. Since embarking on their travels, he had learned a lot about the woman he fondly called his girlfriend.

It had been a month since their departure from Brimrock, and he sometimes still marveled at how much had changed over the last two and a half months. The Aiden O'Hare who first set foot in Brimrock back in December was a Grinch, as his best friend Eddie called him. He wasn't coming to the cozy New England town for holiday cheer; he was there to investigate the paranormal and film the fiftieth episode of their YouTV show, *Paranormal Hunters*.

Falling for Selene was *not* part of the plan.

Also not part of the plan was Selene being a witch. Witches weren't real. Neither were ghost witches. The ever-skeptic in Aiden was out to prove as much, but unfortunately, he got the opposite. Instead he discovered the paranormal was real—*witches* were real. Selene was living proof of that.

They were not only boyfriend and girlfriend, they were

now investigative partners as they set out to film for *Paranormal Hunters*. The turn of events was something Aiden never would have predicted and yet as his heart drummed in light beats, he could no longer imagine any other outcome.

Selene referenced the maps app on her phone. "Two hours down. Two more to go."

"And then two weeks of investigating," he finished.

"The closer we get to Maresburg, the more I'm wondering if maybe I underestimated how nervous I'd be," she confessed.

"Don't be. You're going to do great. You're resourceful and quick-witted. You'll have no problem getting to the bottom of our cases."

"I do have big shoes to fill taking over for Eddie, but it's not just the investigating part I'm nervous about. Aiden, I'm a *witch*."

He mock gasped, dropping his jaw open. "You *are*? This changes everything!"

"You just can't resist the sarcasm, can you?"

"It's a lovable quirk."

"Says who?" she bantered back. Her left brow rose on its own, though the beginnings of a smirk were playing on her lips. "You know what I mean—I'm a witch. I do paranormal. I *am* paranormal."

"It's a lovable quirk," he repeated. He didn't dare glance her way.

Selene gave a shake of her head. "I'm talking about the audience. My personality's not the most popular."

"You have to be kidding."

"Aiden, have you forgotten I was an outcast in Brimrock? Half the town hated me. The other half feared me. I wasn't going to win any Miss Congeniality contests."

"I haven't forgotten Brimrock. But have you forgotten the

evil curse placed on you and your family?" he asked back. "It was beyond your control. Nothing you could've done to make them like you. Besides, the people in Brimrock were lame."

"*Lame*?"

The right corner of his lip ticked upward. "You heard me."

"Oh, I heard you. Just never imagined the word *lame* would come out of Aiden O'Hare's mouth," she said, snickering.

"It's fitting, though, isn't it? You're amazing, and it's Brimrock's loss for not appreciating you."

"Aiden—"

"*Selene*, our audience is going to love you," he said. "You give it a couple episodes. They're going to all love you more than me. It'll be Eddie who? Aiden who?"

A small moment passed between them in which Aiden finished speaking and Selene stared thoughtfully out the van window. The wind crowed, filling up the blank space they left quiet. The soughing matched the leaden sky, its ashen gray stubborn and gloomy.

After another few seconds, Selene's lips spread into a maybe smile and her tone softened. "Thanks."

"For what?"

"Believing in me."

"Everything I've said is the truth." He reached over the cab of the van, the large palm of his hand landing on her thigh. He gave her a reassuring smile and thigh squeeze. Consoling people wasn't his forte, but for Selene, he tried his best.

It was the downside of growing up in a family that prized logic over empathy. The brain over the heart. Facts over feelings. It meant he was quite unprepared to deal with how he felt about Selene. The racing heartbeats and quivers in his stomach and the flushed heat that burned the tips of his ears —all things he couldn't control whenever thinking about her.

He had never been afraid of emotion before. Probably because he had never allowed emotion to take over. But with Selene…

"Did you see that?" Selene cried out suddenly. She clapped her hands together, her whole face brightening. She sat up straighter, legs still crisscrossed. "*Another* Delaware! Second in an hour—what are the odds?"

Aiden laughed, the loud sound starting in his belly, traveling upward, and bursting from his throat.

"You laugh but it's rare!" Selene huffed. She straightened her glasses with an indignant air. "We've been seeing nonstop Virginia and West Virginia, District of Columbia, Maryland, even Pennsylvania and New York—but *Delaware*? It's the unicorn of license plates."

"Maybe we need to take a trip to Delaware next. Something tells me you would see more than two."

"I should start collecting them. Don't people do that? Collect license plates?"

"We have plenty of space to store them in Ghost." He regretted his sarcastic remark a second later as Selene snagged the chance for another complaint about the van.

"We really need to do something about the interior. It's like sleeping on a pile of rocks."

"I know, I know. You've told me."

"I'm really not trying to be a Debbie Downer. I know you and Eddie were okay with it, but…but it's been hard for me to get some sleep." Selene started picking at the wooly ends of her mustard-yellow sweater. "I haven't had a good night's sleep for days now. Since Philly."

"When we stayed in a hotel. I get it." Aiden kept his eyes on the road, but grabbed hold of her hand, entwining his fingers with hers in a show of affection. "We'll be in a hotel in Maresburg. Hopefully you'll be able to get some rest."

Ghost traversed the wide open rural roads. The last vestiges of snow melted into slosh and then puddles. Soon the forecasted drizzle tinkled down, deepening the pools of muddied rainwater. Storm clouds floated into larger formations, signaling what was to come by dusk.

By that time, they'd be in Maresburg.

"So about this haunted hotel," said Selene with eyes on her phone screen. "It's supposed to be one of the biggest tourist attractions in Virginia."

"*Because* it's rumored to be haunted."

"By sleep demons."

Aiden's hazel eyes twinkled with humor. "You say that as if you don't believe it. Are you the new skeptic? Does that make me the new believer?"

"We both know you'll always be the skeptic." Selene scrolled through the webpage open on her phone. The lower down the page she scrolled, the higher her brows climbed on her forehead. "Did you know Mr. Mhoon has a whole merch store on the hotel website? He sells everything—T-shirts, hats, mugs, even tacky jewelry I'm assuming is made of fake gold. They're all branded with the phrase 'Most Haunted Hotel in Virginia.' He sure loves to use the paranormal rumors to market his hotel."

"Welcome to skepticism," Aiden teased. "Something tells me you're going to be lead on this case."

"I mean, it's strange, isn't it?" Selene asked. Her face filled out with that deep-in-concentration look she always developed. Behind her bold-framed glasses, her eyes sharpened and she raked teeth over her bottom lip. "According to any report I've found, the hotel was already rumored to be haunted when Mr. Mhoon bought it. The Dunn family sold it to him after their daughter passed away."

"Marketing your hotel as haunted after people have passed away seems…"

"Morbid?" Selene offered.

He grinned at her. "I'd say morbid is right."

"Well, the odd occurrences have been going on for decades now. Some people claim they've seen a specter wandering the premises. Others report nightmares that leave them more frightened than they've ever been in their life."

"And then there's been the most recent incident."

"Correct. Freddie Koffman. He passed away in his sleep. This is going to be a fascinating first case."

As though affirming Selene's statement, the highway sign advertising forty miles until Maresburg sprang up on the righthand shoulder of the road. Aiden and Selene shared in smirks, their eyes shining, and Aiden pressed his boot harder on the gas pedal. They would be arriving in Maresburg in no time.

———

Maresburg, Virginia, materialized before their very eyes. The quaint town unraveled, revealing squat brown stone buildings and pleasant tree-lined sidewalks. The historic clocktower stood tall in the backdrop along with the distant peaks of the Appalachian Mountains.

Selene rolled down the passenger-side window and basked in the cool air whipping her jet-black coils back. Aiden loved watching her reactions to whatever new destination they set foot in. The pure joy that broke out across her face was more than enough to make the trip worth it. To think this was his new reality—his job was to travel with his girlfriend and witness the wonder lighting up her warm brown eyes.

The Mhoon Hotel boasted a waterfront view, located near the Maresburg River and woodland. The large home possessed a timeless charm about it, originally built in the mid-nineteenth century, fronted by a grand veranda and generous green lawn. It was three-stories tall, each level featuring a neat row of shuttered windows and white trimming, and lastly topped off by twin brick chimneys. The hotel was picturesque, like the kind of landmark perfect for a magazine photoshoot or a movie setting.

Aiden parked Ghost across the road and he and Selene hopped out of the van to stare at the allegedly haunted hotel. The wind hadn't let up, if anything it was blowing harder, sending errant damp leaves scuttling at their boot-clad feet. The storm clouds had finished moving in, thick, gray, and angry. It would start raining any minute now.

"Ready?" he asked.

The corners of Selene's mouth curled and she nodded. "More than ready. *Excited.*"

CHAPTER THREE

"We simply don't have the room," said Mrs. Mhoon. She was in her sixties, skin a rich brown barely touched by wrinkles, hair feathery and soft gray. Instead of a smile in greeting, she wore a pinched expression with her mouth a straight line and her eyes narrowed. "You'll have to try somewhere else. I hear the Oak Tree Motel off the highway has a room or two. Truckers love staying there…"

Aiden didn't budge an inch. "We booked over two weeks ago. I spoke to your husband, William Mhoon. He said we were welcome to stay as long as we needed—he signed off on filming for our show—"

"I don't care if he signed off on turning the Mhoon Hotel into a zoo. It's simply not possible," interrupted Mrs. Mhoon. The pursed-lipped manner in which she held her mouth reminded Selene of Miriam Hofstetter, her former boss at the Brimrock library. "I'm happy to provide you two the number and address to the Oak Tree. Now, it's had a known flea infestation, but I've heard it's gotten considerably better."

"What's all this I'm hearing?"

The Southern baritone belonged to a man big and tall enough to make any room feel undersized for him. He ducked his head under the door frame through which he entered, towering head and shoulders above everyone, including Aiden's seventy-five inches. He joined Mrs. Mhoon at her side, his countenance unreadable.

Aiden cleared his throat uncertainly, still stubbornly immobile. "We have a reservation. It should be under the name O'Hare. I'm from the YouTV show *Paranormal Hunters*. I spoke to the owner about an investigation we're going to be conducting. He said—"

"You're welcome for as long as you like," finished the burly man. He surprised them with a howl of a laugh. "Aiden O'Hare—should've known but you look shorter in person."

Mr. Mhoon held out his titan-sized hand for Aiden to shake. Aiden hesitated for half a second, visibly stunned by the abrupt pivot in Mr. Mhoon's temperament. Selene elbowed him and he snapped out of it. The two men shook hands and laughed off the brief misunderstanding.

"Willy, we have no room," muttered Mrs. Mhoon. Though she tried to speak in a low tone without moving her lips, every word was perfectly audible.

"Nonsense. We have plenty of vacancies right now. Isn't that why we've called them?"

"*I* never called them. That was *your* decision."

"Potato, potahto. Point is, business has been down and it's time to solve the shenanigans on going around here. We need professional help."

Mrs. Mhoon's unimpressed gaze flicked over Aiden and Selene from head to toe. "Professional feels relative."

"Now, honey, no need to be judgy! You have your afternoon tea with the ladies from your book club for that," said Mr. Mhoon, chuckling heartily. He rounded the corner of the reception desk and offered Selene a more delicate handshake than he'd afforded Aiden. His massive hand enveloped hers as he smiled. "And this must be your partner in crime. You didn't mention he was a she. I've watched your show and this certainly doesn't look like Eddie."

"That's because this is Selene Blackstone, my new investigative partner."

"Selene, huh? Beautiful name for a beautiful young lady. Very unique."

"Thanks…" Selene trailed off, uncertain of what else to say. Her cheeks were warm, and so was Mr. Mhoon's hand.

His wife cleared her throat. Her cold stare had turned into a glare. "Can we get back to the matter at hand? If you insist they investigate the hotel, I don't see why they still can't stay at the Oak Tree—"

"Nothing but the finest accommodations for the *Paranormal Hunters* crew!" Mr. Mhoon exclaimed, looming over them like a skyscraper on a city street. "You know, this won't be the first time the Mhoon Hotel will be featured on a television show. We've been on the local news several times over the years. Of course I was the one interviewed. I have them recorded on the DVR. Maybe I'll play them for you sometime."

"I think it's time to show our guests to their rooms," said Mrs. Mhoon, sighing. She aimed a venomous look at her husband as she strode past him and toward a wide hall that stretched on to the back of the house. "If you get to book the hotel to be filmed on another TV show, I get to decide where they sleep. Follow me."

Selene and Aiden glanced at each other and then did as told. The Mhoon Hotel was as spacious on the inside as it was on the outside. The halls ran deep and the staircases climbed high. Each room they passed had a timeless charm about it, filled with pieces of antique mahogany furniture, decades-old portraits of landmarks like the Appalachian Mountains, and even vases of fresh flowers.

In the strangest, most unexpected way, it reminded Selene of home. 1221 Gifford Lane was a hunter-green Victorian house with a third-floor turret and stained glass windows. Spooky to the others in Brimrock, it was the place she had called home every day of her twenty-six years. The Mhoon Hotel looked like a relic from the past just like 1221 Gifford. Its halls and its rooms, each and every corner, felt like a story itching to be told.

On the second-floor landing, Mrs. Mhoon issued a warning. "I'm not familiar with whatever show you claim you're from, but I'll tell you one thing—you're not the first folks to investigate our hotel. I do hope you know this is not only a place of business, it's a *home*. We don't take kindly to anyone trying to exploit us for financial gain, nor do we welcome anyone who is looking to tarnish our reputation."

"Mrs. Mhoon, we wouldn't do that," said Selene, but the woman ignored her.

"Willy has a heart of gold. He invites just anybody under our roof, but I'm more discerning. I'm more watchful. So please know I'll pick up on anything unsavory." Mrs. Mhoon stopped so abruptly, Selene stepped into her and then stumbled back. Either she didn't notice or she decided Selene's clumsiness was too pitiful to address, because she spun around and eyed them with more suspicion. "I don't mean to seem like the bad guy. I'm only trying to establish ground rules."

"Of course," Aiden choked out. He had grabbed Selene to keep her from tipping over. "We understand. We're on your turf."

That seemed to please Mrs. Mhoon. Her severe demeanor

lessened some and she gave a nod. "Good. Now I'll show you to your rooms."

"One room should be fine," said Selene, thinking she was being helpful. Her remark had the opposite effect.

Mrs. Mhoon reacted as though she had bitten into rotten fruit. Her face screwed up in distaste and she led them farther down the hall. "Oh, no. There will be no sinful premarital relations with any guests I book. We're a wholesome, family-oriented hotel. You'll have a room and Mr. O'Hare will have a room."

Selene and Aiden fell a couple steps behind Mrs. Mhoon, looking at each other with equally stunned faces. Neither worked up the nerve to counter her when it seemed like their stay was already on shaky ground. They trailed behind her as she showed them their rooms. She chose to put several rooms between them.

"And this will be you," said Mrs. Mhoon, gesturing to the second room. She flashed her first smile of the day at Aiden. "It's next to the staircase that leads into the back side of the house. Right by the kitchen."

"Err, right," stuttered Aiden. His ears were glowing red. "Thank you."

"I'll leave you be so you can unpack and get settled. Dinner is at six."

With that, Mrs. Mhoon pivoted on her heel and strode back down the hall, leaving a baffled pair of paranormal investigators in her wake.

———

Selene had never seen so many doilies. They were every-where. Under the lamps. Hanging as curtains from the windows. Strewn across the foot of the bed as a decorative throw. Even on the wooden floorboards as a small rug. Was there such a thing as doily fatigue?

She waved her hand and many of the doilies rose up off their pieces of furniture and flooring. She sent them flying into the closet with another sweep of her hand. Far, *far* out of view where they could never hurt anyone's eyesight with their hideousness ever again.

"That's better," she breathed. She glanced around the room that would be hers for the next two weeks.

The walls were a powdery blue and the huge window afforded her a view of the woodland at the back of the house. She walked over to the vase on the dresser and inhaled a whiff of the fresh flowers. Maybe the Mhoon Hotel wasn't so bad after all.

And then there was the bed—it was *queen-size*!

Selene tossed herself backward onto the bed and moaned in delight as she sunk into cushiony mattress heaven. After weeks of a sleeping bag, the bed was pure luxury. Sleeping at night without Aiden to snuggle with was going to be strange, but at least she had a bed! She could finally catch up on sleep.

Her phone started buzzing from within her leather book bag. She bounced off the bed and snatched it up to answer. As soon as she pressed the answer button, a voice that was like home shrieked in her ear.

"Selly!" Noelle Banks screamed.

"Noe!" Selene gasped, just as excited.

The two best friends spent the next sixty seconds gushing over each other. Noelle had always been the one person in Brimrock who understood Selene, who stuck by her side and fiercely had her back. If honest, while traveling with Aiden had been a fun adventure so far, being separated from Noelle was the hardest part. She missed her sister-like best friend and cherished any minute they talked.

"Tell me you finally made it to Virginia!" Noelle said. "It feels like you and Fudgeboy have been traveling for fifty-eleven years."

"Are you *ever* going to call him by his name?"

"The guy who took my bestie away? Why the hell would I do that? Yukie doesn't like him either. Tell her, Yukes," said Noelle. She must've held the phone closer to Selene's Yorkshire terrier, because a string of little yips filled Selene's ear. "Did you hear that? Yukie says, 'Dump him, girl.'"

Selene laughed at the teasing. "What if I told you I've been buying you souvenirs from everywhere we've gone? I've dedicated an entire small suitcase to you."

"You know just how to bribe me—buy me lots of shit," said Noelle bluntly. "Anyway, how are you? Tell me *everything*! I got time today."

The next half hour was spent detailing the latest. Selene told Noelle about their trip to Washington, DC, and then their drive into Maresburg, Virginia. Halfway through she decided to multitask, lazily swatting her hand and wiggling her fingers, magicking her luggage to unpack itself. Soon her clothes were hung up and her toiletry items were perched neatly on the bathroom counter and she hadn't broken a single bead of sweat.

She threw herself back onto her bed, phone tucked into the crook of her neck. "Supposedly this place is haunted by some type of sleep monster...or demon...or whatever you want to call it."

"A sleep monster, huh? That's different," said Noelle. "I'll have to ask Aunt Bibi. She might have some ideas."

"How is Bibi? Everything good at the Magic Bean?"

"You know Bibi. She's the same ol' same ol'. Just yesterday she scolded Mr. Higgley, the mailman, about leaving pastry crumbs all over her floor—almost had him in tears. Can't wait 'til I reach my sixties and have no fucks left to give."

They hung up when Noelle mentioned she had to get ready for dinner with her girlfriend, Shayla. Selene smirked and snatched up the opportunity to tease Noelle back. "Sounds romantic! Glad you finally stopped playing games and put a title on it."

"Shut up, Selly!"

In the quiet aftermath of their phone conversation, Selene relaxed against the bed pillows. The forecasted drizzle had started up, speckling the window with tiny droplets in a rhythmic pitter-patter. If she lay like this and closed her eyes, listening to the tinny sound of the rain, burrowed between pillows on a comfy mattress, she'd slip off to sleep in no time. Sleep trouble or no sleep trouble...

BANG!

The portrait hanging across the bed slipped off its hook and crashed to the floor. The wooden frame colliding with the wooden flooring produced a loud thud that almost stopped Selene's heart. She sprang up in bed and scanned the room in drowsy confusion. The relaxation melting over her evaporated, replaced by the uncomfortable prick of pins and needles.

She slipped off the bed and dropped to her knees. Thankfully the portrait hadn't broken, but picking it up off the ground, she was no closer to figuring out how it had fallen in the first place. The hook could've been faulty. The portrait could've been too heavy. Maybe even her magic had done it.

Knuckles tapped against the door and then a second later, Aiden called, "Everything okay in there?"

Selene snapped out of her reverie. "Huh?"

"I heard a loud thud. Are you okay? Can I come in?"

Instead of a real answer, she substituted with a throaty

hum. Aiden noticed the fallen portrait in her hands. He moved over and eased the portrait from her hands, using his height advantage to hang it up.

"How did it fall?"

"I'm not sure. It just sorta…slipped off the hook."

"That's strange. I was coming by to see if you were done unpacking."

"Hmm? Oh, yeah…" Selene straightened her glasses and then gestured to her empty luggage. "I unpacked earlier while on the phone with Noe. After I finished, I started falling asleep. That's when the portrait fell. It was probably me. My powers get wonky when I'm tired."

Aiden's hands landed on either shoulder and she closed her eyes as he gave her an impromptu massage. His thumbs rubbed circles on her skin, the pressure he applied enough to melt any tension and stress in her muscles. She tipped her head and leaned back against him. Her lips parted for a throaty, relaxed moan.

His breath tickled the nape of her neck as his massage continued. "I like that sound from you. It's music to my ears."

She smiled, her mood mellow and calm. "Maybe you'll get to hear more later."

"Something to look forward to."

Aiden bent his head and his lips skimmed the side of her neck, kissing his way up its length. His hands bracketed her waist, holding her in place for his affection. Eventually, he turned her around and dropped a soft kiss on her lips.

"How about some dinner?" he asked afterward. The afternoon light changed his hazel eyes to an amber shade that gleamed as he looked at her.

Selene perked up. "Food is good."

"I figured you would say that." Aiden's hand reached for hers and they started for the door. "We could use it as an excuse to explore downtown Maresburg. We'll tell the Mhoons we lost track of time and forgot about their dinner. Anything's better than listening to Mrs. Mhoon talk about sin again."

She giggled and quipped, "I'm surprised you didn't burst into flames on the spot."

CHAPTER FOUR

The rain-soaked streets of Maresburg was the setting of every cozy mystery book Aiden had ever read. The streetlamps had flickered on early and passersby rushed past with umbrellas open or hoods up. Cars splashed down the single lane, puddle-ridden road, probably headed home. It wasn't getting any lighter out. The storm clouds made sure of that.

Aiden dutifully held the umbrella above them as Selene pressed into his side for warmth. Their silence was a calm one, companionable in tone, taking in their surroundings. They stopped in front of the town library and noticed the lights off and Closed sign in the window. As they carried on with their rainy day stroll through Maresburg, it became the running theme—*everything* was either already closed or minutes away from locking up.

"There's a bookshop. Want to check it out?"

Selene shook her head, her tight curls springing side to side. "If I buy any more books, I'll need yet another suitcase."

"Point taken. Some other time. Should we start looking for a dinner place? Somewhere has to be open."

They crossed the slick street at a light trot before the next car passed. Once their boots touched the sidewalk's pavement, Selene held back, staring at the shops down the block. Aiden followed her gaze with a wrinkle in his brow, searching for the source of what caught her attention.

"There's a new age spirituality shop," she said and she pulled on his hand. "The light's still on inside."

"I didn't realize you had a thing for that kind of store."

"Sometimes they have an interesting item or two."

As they approached the shop called Hidden Senses, with its advertisement for your first palm reading free and its crystal ball selection perched in the front window, the lights inside flicked off. They stopped short of the door and peered through the glass. Shadows engulfed the shop interior as a solitary figure moved through the aisles.

The door swung open and a woman emerged with keys in hand. Her copper brown skin transitioned into copper red hair combed into a beehive. She wore a matted, thrift store chic fur coat and a blue velvet sweater, paired unfathomably with polka-dot leggings. Sunglasses covered her eyes despite the fast-approaching dusk and glowing streetlights. Locking the door as if Aiden and Selene were invisible, she stashed the keys in her purse and started down the sidewalk.

Selene called after her. "Excuse me, are you closed for the night?"

The woman doubled back, sliding her glasses into her hair and peering at Selene with interest. "You're early."

"Early? I thought we were late…which is why the shop is closed."

"Early to town," the woman clarified in a slow, dreamy voice. "I didn't expect you so soon."

"I didn't know you were expecting us at all," said Aiden, bemused.

The woman slid her glasses onto her face, still looking at Selene. "I wish you luck investigating at the hotel. Time will tell if you have more success than the others."

Before either of them made sense of what the woman meant, she was gone. They stared after her in silent confusion, roused only by more tinkling drizzle. Aiden readjusted his grip on the umbrella and looked up and down the street.

"Moving on from that strange interaction. It looks like we only have one option—this Ms. Coco's Coffee and Cookies is the only place still open."

"Skip dinner for dessert. That's a pretty us thing to do," joked Selene. Several rain-soaking seconds later, they arrived at the sweet-smelling cafe. The door dinged and cold air whipped into the otherwise warm establishment as Selene wandered inside first. Aiden paused at the entrance and struggled closing the dripping wet umbrella.

"That's okay, baby. Just leave it out to dry," came a voice as sugary sweet as many of the cafe treats on the menu. The woman behind the counter smiled at them with the kind of warm affection redolent of a grandmother. She resembled one too, with smoke white poodle curls and an apron swathed over her front. She beckoned them closer and then grabbed a set of tongs. "How about you sit down and I'll help you to some cookies? Any preferences?"

Selene scurried over to the glass case with undeniable interest. She gasped. "What are these?"

"Snickerdoodles. They're my specialty. Want one?"

"One. Sure. One's good."

The woman smiled. "I'll grab you a plateful. You look like you've had a long day. Coffee's probably not a good idea, but hot cocoa might do you well."

"Thanks, ma'am."

"Call me Ms. Coco."

"Coco…like Coco Chanel?" Selene asked.

Ms. Coco smiled, amused. "Something like that."

"Or hot cocoa," said Aiden, joining Selene at the counter. His fight with the stubborn umbrella had left him winded. "I'll take a mug of that hot cocoa you mentioned if you don't mind. We'd hate to hold you up if you were about to close."

"No rush at all. I've got nowhere to be. When you're sixty-three, you learn there's no need to rush time going by."

"You look much younger than sixty-three," Aiden complimented. In his periphery, he noticed the small smirk Selene gave him.

"Well, thank you, baby. I'll be sixty-four in two weeks. How about you come to my birthday party? You can jump outta the cake!"

Surprise widened Aiden's eyes as he stared flustered and flattered at the older woman. Selene was at his side holding in a snicker. He stumbled his way into a response. "Oh…uh…I don't think—"

"Kidding! I'm kidding, babies. Go have a seat and I'll bring your goodies over."

The only ones in the cafe, Aiden and Selene nabbed seats under the heating vents. It was a few more seconds before Aiden calmed down from Ms. Coco's birthday remark. She delivered a tray of goodies, including hot cocoa and snicker-doodles among other cookies.

"If you need anything else, I'm a holler away, babies," simpered Ms. Coco.

Aiden waited until the cafe owner was out of earshot before he said, "Ms. Coco is night and day from Mrs. Mhoon."

"Ms. Coco is like the grandma who sneaks you sweets."

"That must mean Mrs. Mhoon is the grandma who makes you stand in the corner with a phonebook on your head for five hours."

Selene lifted a brow, dunking her first snickerdoodle in her hot cocoa before biting into the cookie. "Why do I feel like that was a personal anecdote?"

"Probably because it is. The O'Hare family is one of a kind." He spent a second sipping from his mug, reveling in the delectable taste of melted chocolate on his tongue. Their chatter about grandmas and families prompted his next remark. "I guess we should probably go over what we think about the Mhoons so far."

"The hotel's nice. The Mhoons...not so much."

Aiden folded his arms on the table. "You mean you don't think Mrs. Mhoon is the beacon of hospitality?"

"I'd almost rather sleep in Ghost—if not for the comfortable queen-size bed."

"Mr. Mhoon did say his finest accommodations," he said, ruminating over their earlier conversation. "It is interesting that he contacted us when his wife had no idea."

"Something is definitely off about the situation." Selene stared thoughtfully out the rain-streaked window, her mug of cocoa cupped in her hands. "Where should we start?"

"Freddie Koffman," said Aiden. "The Maresburg PD investigation is still going on."

"*Such* a tragedy," said Ms. Coco. Both Aiden and Selene glanced up in surprise at the cafe owner. She had drifted over to their table without either noticing. She untied her apron and pulled it off, folding it in neat halves. "Freddie Koffman was only a traveler passing through, but it's a shame what happened to a bright, talented man."

"I read he was a science professor on his way to a symposium," said Selene.

"That's right. Where he was expected to be recognized for his contributions." Ms. Coco shook her head with grave sadness settling on her face. "I don't know what else it's going to take for them to realize that hotel is no good."

Selene perked up in her seat as though the magic phrase had been uttered. "Do you know about the haunting at the Mhoon Hotel?"

"I know enough to never set foot on the premises ever again—and the Mhoons should do the right thing and shut the place down. Sadly, if they haven't learned a thing after what happened to the Dunns and Mrs. Poe, I'm afraid they'll never learn."

"What happened to Mrs. Poe?"

Her face drained of its coloring. "The same thing that's happened to everyone. She died."

Ms. Coco mentioned it was finally time to close up, but without her previous sunniness. Aiden and Selene drained the last of their cocoa and nibbled on their remaining cookies. The streets outside the cafe had puddled deeper the more raindrops pelted down. Aiden held up the umbrella to shield them, but a spontaneous blast of wind twisted its black canopy inside out.

"We might as well run for it," said Selene, shivering in the cold rain. "Ghost is right across the street."

They broke out in a fast scurry across the slippery street. No other cars were on the horizon except for one—a boat-sized bronze Cadillac with the headlights on. It blared its horn as Aiden and Selene made it onto the opposite sidewalk.

At first Aiden hardly paid the angry driver any mind, assuming he would drive by and they would never see him again. But as Aiden unlocked the van doors and they scram-bled inside, the bronze Cadillac screeched to a halt in the middle of the street. The driver's side popped open and a man

with a steel-cut jaw and gaze got out, indifferent as his trench
coat quickly dampened in the downpour.

"I haven't seen you two around Maresburg before," he
said in an authoritative tone. He held his mouth in an unnatural tight, thin line, barely moving his lips when he spoke.

Aiden stared back, unfazed. "That's typically the case
when someone's traveling through."

"Traveling through, huh? I don't suppose it's unreason-
able to expect someone traveling through to know what
jaywalking is?" he asked. The wind blew against him,
ruffling his long trench coat, revealing a gold badge pinned to
his chest.

Of course. Aiden almost rolled his eyes in exasperation.
He should've guessed it. The man carried himself like a cop
eager to catch any and all wrongdoers, no matter how small.
He had seen them rushing across the street and decided a
torrential downpour was the perfect time to harass them.

"You and your girlfriend watch out," he warned
ominously. His stormy gaze drifted to the van, where Selene
was seated on the passenger side. He walked backward to his
open car door. "I'd hate to have to fine you for breaking the
law."

Aiden returned his chilly warning with a glare equal in
measure. He stood outside the van like a guard dog, soaked to
the bone, until the man disappeared into the Cadillac and
drove off. Of the many people he had met throughout the day
—from the Mhoons to the Hidden Senses shop owner to Ms.
Coco's sweetness—*something* about the police officer rubbed
him the wrong way. Selene recaptured his attention by
tapping her knuckles on the van glass and pushing open the
driver side door.

"Get in!" she called with brows knitted in concern.
"You'll catch a cold."

"Better than letting whoever that guy was intimidate us."

"He was a cop?"

Aiden slicked his once neat and tapered, now drenched auburn hair with an impatient hand. He stuck the key in the ignition and said, "Yeah, but something tells me not a very good one."

CHAPTER FIVE

The rain pelted them with bullet-sized droplets all the way to the Mhoon Hotel. Aiden reached the door first, holding it open for Selene to dash through. They stopped in the foyer, shivering and dripping wet, trying to catch their breath. The afternoon had quickly gone from investigating Maresburg to being run off by torrential weather. They'd have to wait 'til tomorrow.

Selene tugged off her peacoat and beanie. "So much for scoping out the town. I feel like a chihuahua after a bath."

"If you're a Chihuahua, then I'm a Doberman," quipped Aiden, a tinge of amusement in his tone. He wiped rain droplets from his brow with one hand and grabbed hers with the other. "We should probably get out of these clothes."

They turned to head for the staircase, but jumped backward when they almost ran into a wall. Or rather, Mrs. Mhoon. She stood tall and billowy, her face sharp with judgment. Neither had heard her approach. She must've been working behind the check-in counter. She took their soggy coats off their hands and clucked her tongue in the "I told you so" manner most mothers mastered.

"Didn't you check the weather forecast?" she asked. "You're dripping everywhere."

"Good thing neither of us are allergic to water like the Wicked Witch of the West," said Aiden. Selene shot him a glance with a brow quirked. He picked up on her hint—any witchy-related topic was a little too close to home. He cleared his throat and added, "We're sorry about the mess. You don't have to worry. We'll clean it up."

"No need. You've done enough. I'll handle it. Go ahead and dry yourselves off. Dinner is at six."

Mrs. Mhoon shooed them away before they could protest. They climbed the stairs with their boots squelching, feeling like children sent to a timeout. When safely out of earshot on the second-floor landing, they stopped down the hall and faced each other. Selene swatted Aiden on the arm.

"What was that Wicked Witch mention for?" she whispered. "You forget I'm a you-know-what?"

"They don't know that," he whispered back. Then a slow grin started to form at the corners of his lips. "Besides, it's true what I said—you really *don't* melt under water."

Selene rolled her eyes. "You're impossible. But we better get to our rooms before she pops up out of nowhere."

"Our separate rooms. And who can forget the dinner we didn't ask to go to?"

"At least it's another opportunity to get info," said Selene as she moved to her door, pausing with her hand on the knob. "Let's just hope it goes better than this afternoon!"

———

The table in the formal dining room was already full by the time Aiden and Selene made it downstairs for dinner. Only two empty chairs remained on opposite sides of the table.

Neither of them moved, hovering in the doorway like outsiders as everyone chatted.

The table fell silent when Mr. Mhoon noticed them. He threw his arms into the air and beckoned them forward. "There you are—guests of the hour! Come in, sit down, and get grubbing!"

Selene nodded and offered a polite smile, though she barely moved an inch. Mr. Mhoon sat at the head of the table, his wide and tall frame eclipsing the others. Mrs. Mhoon was on his right, wearing a different outfit than earlier; she'd changed into a midlength button-down dress that looked suited for special occasions. Did she really feel their arrival was cause for celebration?

There were two other men seated at the table, both unfamiliar. The one across from Mrs. Mhoon had already started eating, his mouth in a permanent frown, wire-framed glasses low on his nose and his salt-and-pepper hair neat and cropped. The other man was younger, wearing a shirt tight enough for his muscles to bulge, his hair a sandy color. He didn't wait long before he shot up and forced a clenching handshake out of Aiden.

"Tom Lester," he said in a gruff voice. "Manager at the local coal mine."

Aiden glanced at Selene and then back at Tom. "Aiden O'Hare. Guest for dinner."

Selene smirked. Mr. Mhoon barked out a laugh while Mrs. Mhoon raised a brow. The man with the wire-framed glasses kept eating as though alone in the room. And the woman in the last chair, who Selene hadn't noticed 'til now, was actually familiar—

"The Hidden Senses psychic!" Selene exclaimed.

"Phoebe Mhoon." She sniffled, picking lint from her off-the-shoulder blue velvet sweater. "And I'm *not* a psychic. I'm a seer of the tangible world and the great unknown. There are many complex forces the average person off the street simply cannot comprehend, and yet their very lives are shaped by them! You'd be surprised to learn."

"Enough, Phee. None of that gibberish at the dinner table. You'll scare our investigators away," grunted Mr. Mhoon. He turned to them and said, "Sit."

Aiden and Selene dropped into chairs. Selene claimed the seat between Mrs. Mhoon and Tom. Aiden snagged the chair between the quiet man and Phoebe. In seconds, dishes were passed around the table like a game of hot potato. Before Selene knew it, her plate was loaded with pot roast, an assortment of veggies, mac 'n' cheese, mashed potatoes, and an oven-baked dinner roll. Mrs. Mhoon said grace and they dug in.

Aiden was content scarfing down his food and staying silent like the wire-framed glasses man, but Selene saw the dinner as a chance for intel. She turned to Mr. Mhoon and said, "I'd love to know more about what happened with Freddie Koffman. You mentioned he checked into the hotel alone."

"Tragic what happened to Freddie!" Mr. Mhoon replied without missing a beat. He forgot about his dinner plate, though a speck of mashed potatoes clung to his grizzly beard. "The man was divorced. No children or next of kin. Brilliant science professor on his way to collect an award. Let me tell you, it was the last thing I expected to find that morning—it's been years since! But you have to be ready at a moment's notice. You'll never catch *me* off guard."

"Willy, this isn't exactly great dinner conversation, is it?" asked Mrs. Mhoon. She gazed around the table. "Selene, why don't you tell us how you met Aiden?"

Selene choked on her bite of pot roast, clapping a hand to

her chest. The piece of savory meat slipped down the wrong pipe and she coughed against the burning ache in her throat. The others sat and stared as she wiped her mouth on her dinner napkin and failed at a graceful recovery smile. "I'm sorry, what was the question?"

"You and Aiden—you two are such an unexpected pair—how did you meet?"

Her eyes caught Aiden's and she skimmed her thoughts for what to say. Their first meeting wasn't ideal like in the movies or some adorable meet cute like in the books she sometimes read. They had met when the URide app on their phones malfunctioned and they fought over who the ride share car belonged to. Her first impression of Aiden hadn't been the best and she was assuming the same on his end.

And then there was that whole investigation into her witchy grandma thing. That wasn't a part of the story she could divulge to the Mhoons as they sat around the table and waited on her answer.

Selene cleared her still-sore throat and said, "We met at the library. I used to work as a librarian and he reads a lot. He asked me to help him find a book and we…we sort of hit it off from there."

"I was expecting something more exciting for two para-normal investigators!" Mr. Mhoon barked out a loud laugh that made several of them jump. "Me and the missus might look like a couple of old sixty-four-year-olds, but even our story is better than that. It was 1981. We were twenty-five and I entered this pen pal program for—"

"*Willy*!" Mrs. Mhoon squeaked.

"Honey, no need to be shy about your age. There's nothing to be ashamed of. I'm simply saying I figured they'd have a better story, like meeting in an abandoned mine inves-tigating ghosts or out on the hunt for Big Foot."

"No one wants to think about Big Foot as we eat our dinner," lectured Mrs. Mhoon icily. She seemed to decide a safer topic was needed, directing her attention to Tom. "Why don't you tell us more about your luncheon with Mayor Breen."

Over the course of the next ten minutes, Tom recounted how the mayor had sat at his table and asked him to pass the salt shaker. In his gruff voice, he made it sound like he'd achieved an impressive feat. More than once, Selene caught him throwing boastful glances at Aiden.

"Very impressive," Mrs. Mhoon said, nodding along. "We've sent him a wedding invite. Let's hope him and his wife Wilhelmina accept. Just imagine—the mayor himself attending our wedding!"

"My and Tom's wedding, mother," interjected Phoebe in a tone both airy and genteel.

"Of course, you know what I meant."

"Oh, you're getting married?" Selene asked, casting Phoebe a congratulatory smile. "That's so exciting!"

"This upcoming Saturday. Here at the hotel," piped up Mr. Mhoon. "As much of a beaut as my property is— wouldn't host it anywhere else. Ain't that right, Tom?"

The muscles in Tom's face worked harder as he clenched his jaw. "That's right, Willy. And thanks to my mingling with heavy hitters in town, we'll have some important guests attending the wedding."

It was like watching two alpha dogs growl and snipe at each other at the park. Selene hovered somewhere between the two competitive men as they traded passive aggressive words across the dinner table. It wouldn't have been surprising if they each tracked down a fire hydrant and started marking it as territory. Thankfully Phoebe, being the flighty mystical woman she was, cleared the tension.

"Your charts predicted this, Tom," said Phoebe. She reached across the table and grabbed his hand. "Remember what I told you about your sun being in the eighth house?"

"If only Freddie's charts could've predicted what happened to him!" Mr. Mhoon shook his head and tossed his dinner napkin onto his empty plate. "Maybe he'd still be alive."

Phoebe's eyes widened. "Natal charts do not predict death, father. How many times do I—"

"Exactly my point. Nobody could've predicted what happened to Freddie," Mr. Mhoon said, bulldozing over what she had to say. "It's part of the downside of owning a hotel like this. I didn't like all the media attention at first. It felt a little unnatural to be billed as the most haunted hotel in the state, but somebody's got to have the duty. I make the place as safe as possible. I'm sure you agree."

"You can't make it safe enough to escape death," said Phoebe gloomily. "If death has marked you, then your existence in this realm is over."

"For heaven's sake!" cried Mrs. Mhoon. She scooted back her chair, her dinner plate in hand. The faintest touch of red blotched her light brown complexion. "I've already told you about this kind of grim talk. *Not at dinner*!"

Selene's gaze snapped to Aiden. He had a similar idea. Over the past few months of their relationship, they had grown skilled at communicating without words. Now was one of those times as they wordlessly agreed. Something was up with the Mhoon family.

Mr. Mhoon waited for his wife to leave the room before he rolled his eyes and muttered something under his breath. Tom sighed and returned to his food. Phoebe fussed with her blue velvet sweater some more, sniffling with an air of haughtiness. The silent man next to Mr. Mhoon dropped his fork on his plate, the metal clanging against the porcelain, and he got up to go.

"Turning in for the night, Omar?" Mr. Mhoon asked.

Omar nodded. "Early morning."

Silence hung in the room as Omar shuffled out the door. The others seemed too stubborn to say much else after the blowup. Selene searched for a lighter topic. Before she could find one, Mr. Mhoon gave a husky clearing of his throat and wished them good-night. As everyone rose to leave, he pulled Aiden and Selene aside.

"I'm sorry about how dinner turned out," he said, tugging on his suspenders. "Koffman's death is a touchy topic around here. As you know, he's our first accident in a few years. Best keep any discussion about what happened more private. Of course, we can sit down for more details later. I'm a busy man, but I'll make time in my schedule to help the investigation any way I can."

On that note, without waiting for them to respond, Mr. Mhoon left the room.

———

The hotel was so silent, Selene's thoughts were loud. She padded over to the window in her room and peered at the empty street below. It felt like the whole town of Maresburg was in deep slumber. Everyone except her. Her eyes flicked up to the inky sky, searching for the moon. The cluster of clouds obscured it from view. She'd need to sneak out for a lunar ritual, and soon. Her powers were already waning.

Tomorrow was their first full day of investigations. A point of no return as she officially transitioned from cursed witch stuck in a small New England town to a roaming, adventurous witch who investigated paranormal mysteries across the country. Even weeks after her initial exit from Brimrock, none of it felt real. At times it still felt like a dream she'd wake from.

She inhaled a slow, steady breath in hopes of chasing away the twitchy butterflies loose in her stomach. Aiden believed in her. He was confident, so sure she'd excel at their investigations. That the audience would love her and she could fill Eddie's shoes. That she would be a valuable member of the *Paranormal Hunters* team.

More importantly, she believed in herself. She inhaled another breath and reaffirmed this declaration with a nod of her head. Overthinking was her weakness. If she stopped analyzing every minute detail and focused on solving the case, she'd likely succeed. Together she and Aiden were a force to be reckoned with. In her core she had no doubt about that.

A small smile tugged her lips apart as she moved to the mirror and began twisting her freshly conditioned curls. As the dark and quiet of night settled around the hotel, the prospect of her queen-size bed wasn't enticing enough anymore. For weeks she'd slept snuggled with Aiden, warmed by his body heat and fitted in his arms.

Yes, he snored. Yes, he was always hot while she was always cold. Yes, he could sleep through WWIII. But it wasn't the same sleeping without him. Even despite her recent difficulty sleeping.

Maybe a late-night visit to Aiden's room would be more fun. She had been okay with the idea of separate rooms only to stay on Mrs. Mhoon's good side. At least as much as possible 'til she learned more about the Mhoon Hotel. Pissing off the matriarch wasn't the smartest idea.

But it seemed silly not to go visit him. Besides, she thought, twisting the last section of her hair, she was feeling playful. Mrs. Mhoon would have to understand. If she even found out at all. As the clock ticked toward midnight, she was probably sound asleep.

Selene pulled on a robe over her chemise and opened the bedroom door. She slunk down the dark hall as silent and unseen as a black cat in the night.

CHAPTER SIX

nock. Knock.

Aiden tore his gaze away from the book in his lap and stared at his hotel room door. The gentle tap had interrupted the otherwise silent night. He had collapsed in the armchair by the floor lamp for some light reading before bed, but hadn't expected any visitors. His mind jumped to the likeliest culprit and he tried to keep an amused grin from forming. He opened the door, discovering he was right. Selene stood on the other side, a smirk of her own on her face.

"Do I have the wrong room?" she teased. "I could've sworn this one was mine."

He stopped fighting his grin. "It's yours if you want it to be."

He let Selene pass through the open door before gingerly closing it shut. Though no one could dictate what they chose to do, it was best they kept as quiet as possible. Neither wanted to spur the ire of Mrs. Mhoon and her strict cohabitation rules. Their stay in Maresburg would be easiest if they avoided drama altogether and focused on the investigation.

"I'm guessing you couldn't sleep?" Aiden asked as Selene parked herself on the edge of his bed.

"I was getting ready to go to bed and realized I've gotten used to having you around."

"But I thought my snoring kept you up," he said, amused, raising both brows.

Selene's eyes twinkled from behind her bold-framed glasses. "Maybe this time I *want* to be kept up."

There was an irresistible element about Selene. She possessed a quiet, understated sexiness that always drove him wild. To the untrained eye, she looked sweet and unassuming, but he knew better. When alone, she was playful and mischievous, a sensual undercurrent he couldn't put into words as his brain powered off and his caveman alter ego stirred.

Aiden stowed his hands in his sweatpants pockets—mostly to keep from touching her—and let the grin spread on his lips. "I brought a decent reading selection. Everything from Tolstoy to Tolkien. Take your pick."

Selene rose from the bed and stopped in front of him. Her gaze had pinned his, still twinkling. "Aiden…are you talking nerdy to me?"

They both laughed. His arms slowly encircled her as they drifted closer and he found himself concentrating on those soft, heart-shaped lips of hers. He muttered, "It fits us, doesn't it?"

He kissed her before she could answer, but she did anyway, with a small sigh. They walked backward toward the bed, lips still locked, hands starting to wander. Selene wasted no time slipping hers down the waistband of his sweatpants. His hand caught her wrist and he smiled against her lips.

"This isn't about me tonight," he said between kisses. "Let's get you relaxed for bed."

Selene let out a small gasp of surprise as he untied the

belt of her robe. It fell to her ankles on the floor and he moved in for more kisses, taking advantage of the newly exposed skin of her neck and shoulders. His mouth explored her throat as he inhaled her familiar sweet and floral scent. A mix of lilac and vanilla that left him dizzy in the most arousing way.

She was a sight to behold in that the satin chemise. The short nightdress with its plunging neckline and lace trimming stopped midthigh, accentuating her figure, loose but somehow also hugging her curves in the right places. He paused only to meet her eyes, his hands on the hem of the slinky fabric. She raised her arms and he pulled the satiny dress over her head.

Her body was his weakness. As soon as he let his gaze dip, traveling her every curve, he could hold back no longer.

A greedy man, Aiden filled his hands with her round, full breasts. The soft weight felt indescribably nice in his palms as he rubbed his thumbs across her nipples. They were dark and pebbly, hardening under his touch. He bent his head and sucked one into his mouth.

Selene threaded her fingers in his hair, holding him to her breast. She inhaled a sharp breath, the rest of her body trembling on the spot. He spared no expense paying tribute to her breasts, teasing one with his tongue and other with the knead of his hand. He switched off, eager to show them equal affection.

The first time he and Selene had been intimate, he had blown it—*literally*. It had been a disappointing experience for her. Ever since, he had made it his mission to pleasure her to the fullest extent possible. He saw it as his duty not only because he was her boyfriend, but because he genuinely enjoyed eliciting the moans, groans, and gasps of air out of her. Even the way her eyes rolled into the back of her head as she thrashed and orgasmed was a beautiful sight.

Aiden loved and wanted all of it out of her.

He eased her down, so she was sitting on the bed. He kneeled and hooked his fingers in the waistband of her panties. Plain, cotton, and lavender purple, they were practical—they were Selene, sexy and simple. She understood his request and lifted her hips, allowing him to peel them off of her. He pulled her to the edge of the bed, holding her legs by the calves, kissing his way upward.

His mouth blazed a trail across her skin, landing on the fleshy insides of her thighs. She was achingly soft and supple, like kissing and touching the most luxurious silk. He reached the apex of her thighs and greedily memorized the glorious sight in front of him. His dick hardened, twitching in his sweatpants, begging for a release, but he ignored it.

For now.

Selene was already glistening. His fingers teased her folds, the merest touch drawing a hiss from her. He hooked her legs over his shoulders and dove in, dipping his tongue into her wet, hot sex. Her soft moans followed like music to his ears as she clenched shut her eyes and arched off the bed.

Aiden couldn't stop once he started. He feasted on her like a man long starved, savoring her sweetness on his tongue. She responded with more moans, her hands balled in the comforter of his bed, her fleshy thighs squeezing his head.

The last straw was his thumb pressed down on her clit and another flick of his tongue. Selene came hard, shaking and shivering, unraveling in seconds. He lapped up every last drop of hers, inhaling her heady, addictive scent.

Her skin was hot and so was his. He couldn't last much longer. He needed to feel more of her. Her moans were still on her tongue when he moved up and kissed her full on the mouth. She welcomed his kiss, hooking an arm around his neck, drawing him closer.

They didn't make it far in their new kissing expedition. The long length of Aiden's body had covered hers, Selene's legs falling even wider apart. They were beginning to wrestle off his clothes when a distinctly loud bump interrupted them. Midkiss and midtug, they froze on the bed.

Another second passed and the bump sounded again, even louder. Aiden tore his lips away from Selene's and his eyes landed on the floor. Whatever it was, it was coming from downstairs, and it didn't sound like the harmless creaky noises of an old home.

Selene had a dazed look about her, still coming down from her orgasm. She propped herself up on her elbows and said, "It sounds like a body hitting the ground."

Their eyes met and it took only a second before they leapt off the bed. Aiden helped Selene gather her clothes. She slipped her satiny nightgown on and then tied her robe about her waist. Aiden paused at the door, his hand on the knob.

"Are you sure you want to come with me? I can check it out alone."

"We're partners, remember? We investigate together," answered Selene.

Aiden opened the door and the pitch-black shadows swallowed them up on step one. They slunk down the hall, sneaking over to the staircase. Aiden went first, each stair a slow descent. His ears were open for any sounds, picking up on the whispering wind and smatter of nocturnal rain.

The hall downstairs was spookily dark. He held his breath without realizing it, bracing himself for anything at any time. They drifted in the dark, following the mysterious noise they had heard. The hall ended and they reached the foyer, another giant space of shadows.

Aiden glanced over his shoulder at Selene. Even in the dark, he sensed her gaze was elsewhere. She was staring across the foyer. He promptly discovered what had caught her eye—there was a light coming from a room on the other side.

The wind squealed, its whistle harsh on the ears. They flinched without thinking, but then pressed on. Aiden skulked across the foyer, stopping outside the door with the light on. It was half ajar, the crack in the doorway offering a preview into the room. He put an arm around Selene and together they peeked from among the shrouding shadows.

From inside there was a scratching noise. It sounded like the claws of a cat, but as Aiden peered into the room, that proved incorrect. The silent man Mr. Mhoon had called Omar was seated at a desk, scribbling away on a piece of paper. Only a dim desk light was on, bright in the otherwise deep darkness of the hotel. His back was hunched, his hand moving furiously from one end of the paper to the other.

Aiden glanced at Selene, their faces half shadowed. Her brown eyes simply stared back before they both turned to the crack in the door again. Omar had stopped writing, sitting up in his chair as though he sensed something amiss.

At his side, Selene inhaled a sharp breath. Aiden's posture grew rigid, trying to anticipate what would come next. It was hard to tell what type of situation they had found themselves in. If this was just a case of Omar being up late at night or something more sinister.

Omar rolled his chair back, got up, and moved to a filing cabinet. He yanked it open and began rifling through the many documents inside. Under his breath he muttered, "Where is it? Where did it go? I know it's around here some-where—unless they're hiding things again."

They watched as Omar's search turned more frantic. He slammed shut a filing cabinet drawer and rounded on the desk. Aiden eased back from the edge of the doorway, holding out an arm to keep Selene behind him. Omar had started gathering a handful of papers from the desk, ranting more about missing documents.

"We better go," Aiden whispered so quietly only Selene heard.

They slunk back into the shadows of the foyer. They disappeared up the stairs as Omar emerged from the office. He stopped and peered into the darkness. Aiden wasn't sure if it was his imagination, but as he escaped up the steps behind Selene, he heard Omar hiss in the dark.

"I know you're there."

CHAPTER SEVEN

Selene snuck back to her room by sunrise. Mrs. Mhoon was none the wiser when they arrived for breakfast the next morning. She greeted them from the reception desk as they descended the staircase minutes before nine.

"Food is in the kitchen. Sit in the dining room. Eat as much as you'd like," she told them. "Anything we don't eat, we leave out for the stray dog that comes around."

Here and there other guests arrived for the hotel's advertised free breakfast. Rather than one larger table in the casual dining room, the Mhoons had set up half a dozen smaller tables with chairs. Guests piled on food from a buffet-style line in the kitchen and then shuffled into the dining room for their first meal of the day.

Aiden snagged the last available table. "You go up first," he urged with a paranoid glance over his shoulder. "If we both go, someone might steal our table."

Selene rolled her eyes as she tried to resist a smirk but failed. In the kitchen Mrs. Mhoon had cooked an assortment of breakfast favorites, including scrambled eggs, hash browns, and meats like smoked sausage and crispy bacon.

Selene drifted along the buffet-style setup with her plate, eyes on the selection. The food selection was so plentiful and distracting, she bumped into the woman on her left.

"Oops. I'm so sorry! I wasn't paying attention," said Selene, releasing a mini mortified gasp.

The woman was short and stubby with a long sheet of black hair and reddish-brown skin. It took her a second to react, casting a slow glance at Selene. She had bags under her eyes. Had she fallen asleep in the line for breakfast?

"It's okay," she replied in a low tone threaded with drowsiness. "I barely noticed. Really not noticing anything right now. Didn't get much sleep."

Selene frowned, instantly feeling a kinship with the fellow hotel guest. "I know how that goes—feels like you're sleepwalking through the day."

"And zoning out every five seconds." The woman shuddered out a deep yawn. "It's a shame this is the only place to stay in town. Except the Oak Tree...which has fleas."

"Are you unhappy at the Mhoon?" Selene asked, curiosity piqued.

The woman shrugged. "I haven't been sleeping well. My room's an igloo at night. I turned up the central heating and had a space heater blasting—didn't make a difference. Even had them move me to a different room. A few more days, then I'm gone. My car should be fixed by then. I haven't seen you around here. You new to the hotel?"

"Just got here yesterday. My name's Selene."

"Yvette. On my way to California. Bad breakup. But now I can do what I wanna do and make music."

Selene's face lit up. "Oh, you're a singer?"

"Mm-hmm, gonna audition for a female R&B group called Vibe. Google them," said Yvette tiredly. She speared a couple strips of bacon with a fork from the main platter and dropped them onto her plate. "Anyway, see you around."

Once Selene rounded off her plate of eggs, toast, and ham with some fruit, she returned to the table Aiden was guarding with his life. His stomach gave a loud and impatient grumble as she sat down across from him.

"Took you long enough. My intestines are eating each other. Food looks good."

"Mrs. Mhoon wasn't lying when she said there's plenty of it. I'm sure you'll have seconds."

"Maybe thirds." Aiden winked as he got up and disappeared into the kitchen.

She laughed because it was the truth. Aiden's appetite was unmatched. She supposed he needed a lot of fuel to keep his tall and athletic body running.

The rest of breakfast was uneventful. Aiden and Selene chatted over their scrambled eggs and orange juice as the tables around them emptied. In no time only one other table was occupied. A middle-aged couple seemingly on vacation who snapped at each other every second word. Selene accidentally learned their surname was Jackson when Mrs. Mhoon passed through and greeted them good morning.

After breakfast, Selene climbed the steps alongside Aiden. They were walking to their rooms to pick up their coats when Aiden brought up last night.

"Did you notice the missing face at breakfast?"

"To be honest, most of the faces I didn't recognize."

"I don't mean the other guests. I'm talking about everyone from last night's dinner. They all passed through except one."

"Omar?" Selene asked as they stopped halfway down the hall. "He did mention he had an early morning."

"After a late night…of snooping around. Meet you down-stairs in five?"

In her hotel room, Selene buttoned up her peacoat and yanked a beanie over her head; she had freed her curls from her twist out so that they appeared as fluffy clouds from underneath her beanie. She had her leather book bag and phone in hand walking back out the door.

The room two doors down caught her eye. A woman with a pin curl updo had poked her head out of her open doorway. She quickly ducked back inside as if trying to go unseen, but it was too late. Curiosity piqued, Selene passed by at a slow stroll. The woman wore a floral robe that stopped at the knees as she stood and fiddled with the thermostat.

"Do you need help?" Selene asked.

She paused, eyes landing on Selene before a gracious smile formed. "I do. I've been fussing with this thing for half an hour now."

"I had some issues with mine too. There's a trick to it. Here," said Selene, moving forward to take over.

The woman stepped back to give her space. "I called the front desk and they said they'd send someone, but that was twenty minutes ago. I've been poking my head out like a gopher in a hole ever since."

"Hopefully that's better."

"I feel the heat already. Thank you," said the woman in a deli-cate voice. She was pretty, with her honey-brown skin carrying a dewy glow. It seemed she had been in the middle of getting ready for the day as she wore a full face of makeup in her robe, her nails freshly painted red. She gave Selene a head-to-toe once-over. "You must be a new guest. I haven't seen you around."

"Just got here yesterday."

"I'm Grace."

"Selene. How long have you been staying here?"

"Long enough to witness what happened to poor Freddie," answered Grace with a rueful shake of her head. She put a hand to her cheek, her nails a shiny cherry apple red. "The town police haven't been much help."

"Why do you say that?"

"Isn't it obvious? Freddie's been dead for two whole weeks and nothing's been done. It's like nothing happened. The poor man didn't have much family."

"The Mhoons seem to have very different reactions to what happened," said Selene, fishing for more info. "Are they cooperating with the police investigation?"

Grace frowned. "A better effort could be made. This isn't the first time something like this has happened in Maresburg. I'm sure you've heard all about this hotel. It's been going on since the 1960s. I haven't been able to sleep much myself. I can't wait to be on my way."

"Sleep definitely seems to be an issue around here," muttered Selene, thoughts on yesterday's strange experience as she tried to nap. She thanked Grace for answering her questions and then headed downstairs.

Aiden was already waiting on her. He pointed at his watch. "Five minutes turn to ten?"

"Let's go," said Selene, hooking her arm with his as she walked toward the door. "I've got something to tell you."

―――――

The morning in Maresburg was a gloomy gray one full of frequent drizzle and wind. Aiden and Selene hopped in Ghost and drove to the town park. Before they dove into the day's investigation, they needed to film the intro for the episode. Since Dale, the show's usual cameraman, wasn't available, Selene used her magic to levitate the camcorder for them.

She smirked at Aiden and said, "Perks of being a witch. You nonwitches wouldn't understand."

He answered her with a chuckle before clearing his throat and focusing on the camcorder. They hit record.

"Aiden and Selene here. Checking in as we start our first full day of our investigation at the Mhoon Hotel," said Aiden to the camera. "A lot of mysterious goings-on at this place. It's been rumored since the 1960s to be haunted by some sort of night creature. No one knows for sure what it is, but we're here in Maresburg, Virginia, to find out."

Aiden stopped recording and played back the short footage. Selene sat down on the top of one of the park's picnic tables, watching over his shoulder.

"That seems good enough," she said.

"You're not familiar with our executive producer, Paulina, yet. She would categorize that as dumpster-worthy," replied Aiden.

"It sounds like Paulina needs a chill pill."

"She would have to put down the kombucha first. Are you going to tell me what interesting stuff you discovered?"

"I met one of the hotel guests after breakfast," explained Selene without missing a beat. "She thinks the Mhoons aren't cooperating with the police investigation."

"Is this the sleepy one you mentioned? Yvette?"

"No. Grace. She wasn't at breakfast."

"Then why would they reach out to the show?"

"Good question. Mr. Mhoon seems eager to help."

Aiden stopped playing the footage on the camcorder and looked up, his expression thoughtful. "It's possible Mr. Mhoon contacted the show for the notoriety. A regular small town police investigation isn't going to give him that."

"Because our show is so famous." She giggled.

"You laugh, but we have almost a million subscribers—people from all over the world. All publicity is good publicity."

"Okay," she said, resting her hands on her kneecaps, "but what does that have to do with Freddie? He *died*, Aiden. Most people don't just drop dead in their sleep. Add on the fact that this isn't the first time this has happened at the Mhoon Hotel. Something's fishy."

"Fishy as in plausible in the real world or fishy as in mole people and Sasquatch?"

Selene's normally warm brown eyes narrowed. "How many times do we have to go over this? You're the boyfriend of a witch and you *still* question what is and isn't plausible?"

"You're easy to believe in," he said, swooping in with a save. He gave her a peck on the lips and then smiled. "I can touch and hold you, which is always a treat, might I add. But some imaginary monster prowling in the night?"

"Not just any monster—"

"A dream monster. A sleep demon. A night crawler," he finished for her dramatically. "Selene, even you have to admit, it's a little out there."

She glanced up at the murky sky with shades of swirling, angry gray and said, "We better go. It's about to start drizzling again."

"The library's two blocks away. We can stop by there to dig up old news articles about the other incidents at the Mhoon Hotel."

"Maybe they'll *actually* be open this time."

They pulled away from the curb as the first droplets fell. The library in Maresburg matched the rest of the town. It was made up of brown stone on the outside. On the inside, it was cramped and dusty with as many bookshelves shoved into the small space as possible. The study area consisted of two long tables and a few chairs and there wasn't a computer lab.

Selene glanced at the abysmal section for children's books and said, "This library makes the one in Brimrock look luxurious."

"No kidding. Did you see the nonfiction aisle?" Aiden asked as they turned down the periodicals section. He stopped in front of the selection of town newspapers and began rummaging. "Do you miss it?"

"Being a librarian in Brimrock? Not really," replied Selene, shrugging. "I miss the books. I miss the library itself —I miss Noelle and Aunt Bibi and Yukie. But I don't miss Miriam or the other ladies, and I don't miss being stuck in town. It was time to move on."

Aiden threw her a glance from over his shoulder. "It's selfish, but I'm glad you did."

"I'm glad too. Except I'm trying to fill Eddie's shoes."

"No need to try. You're not Eddie, but that's a good thing —you're Selene and viewers are going to appreciate that."

She smiled. "Thanks. How's Eddie doing, by the way? Have you talked to him?"

Aiden used his discovery to change the subject. He pulled out a few different newspapers from years past and walked them over to one of the study tables. Selene followed, but only after releasing a short sigh. Aiden and Eddie had met in college and had started *Paranormal Hunters* together. They had spent years as investigative partners and best friends until they came to Brimrock. When Eddie's aunt turned out to be an evil succubus witch out for revenge against Selene, they had a falling out. Their friendship still hadn't fully recovered. Anytime she brought up Eddie, Aiden miraculously became hard of hearing.

"I haven't been able to find much on the Poes, but here's

the article from the incident in 1961 with the Dunns' daughter," said Aiden, laying the yellowed newspaper onto the table.

"Her name was Rhonda. She passed away in her sleep," said Selene, leaning closer. "She was only seventeen and perfectly healthy. Tell me that doesn't sound strange."

"I'll concede it's unusual. The Dunns sold the hotel a few years after this."

"I can't say I blame them. We should make copies of these articles. Then we can pore over them in our rooms." Selene blew dust off of the plastic laminate the article was sheathed inside.

They left the library and stopped at Ms. Coco's Coffee and Cookies. Since it had stopped sprinkling again, they sat down at one of the tables outside. They sipped their coffee, nibbled on snickerdoodles, and read through the copies of articles they had made from the library.

At first Selene was concentrating on the words in front of her, swallowing small mouthfuls of her hazelnut latte. She looked up and forgot about the article altogether. Standing outside the storefront of Hidden Senses was Phoebe Mhoon and another man Selene quickly recognized. She lightly kicked Aiden from under the table.

"Is that the…?" he asked.

"Mean cop from yesterday? It looks like him."

The man was middle-aged but handsome, his chiseled jaw and smoldering gaze adding to his appeal. He wore a long trench coat that hung open and showed off a shiny gold badge pinned to his chest. Despite the pristine glint of his badge, his half untucked shirt and wrinkled pants ruined the imagery of the sharp, clever detective.

"I'm assuming he's talking to Phoebe about Koffman."

"They look awful…chummy."

The police officer leaned closer and touched Phoebe's arm. The move was strangely intimate, as if it wasn't the first time. Phoebe had no real reaction. She merely nodded along and said something else. They were too far away to hear.

Aiden sipped more of his coffee and said, "Who would've thought Phoebe would be in the middle of a love triangle?"

"She *does* wear the hell out of those leopard print leggings. I wonder what Tom thinks about this detective being so touchy with his fiancée?"

"Probably itching to mention he's manager at the coal mine again."

Selene giggled at his quip as the detective seemed to sense someone was watching him. He tore his gaze from Phoebe and stared down the sidewalk. His intense gray eyes fell on them. He mumbled parting words to Phoebe and then started in their direction.

"Uh-oh. Detective at ten o'clock. Is it even worth hiding the articles?" Selene asked.

Aiden didn't have a chance to reply. The man came up to their table and surveyed the scene in front of him, his sharp jaw clenched.

"I didn't put two and two together yesterday. You must be the paranormal investigators," he said in monotone. He held out his hand and shook Aiden's first before moving onto Selene. "I'm Detective Humbolt, lead on the Koffman case. I'm assuming you're in Maresburg to poke around the Mhoon Hotel."

"Actually, we're on vacation," said Aiden sarcastically. "Though we were hoping for sunnier weather. Maybe we should've gone with Hawaii after all."

Detective Humbolt's left cheek twitched. "You'll find you're wasting your time here."

"What do you mean?" Selene asked, frowning.

He planted his hands flat on their tabletop and his piercing gray eyes bore into Selene. "There is no paranormal activity here. Nothing supernatural. Nothing that can't be explained by good ol'-fashioned police work. Whatever you're filming for your little show is a waste of time."

"Then what has your police work uncovered?" she asked simply. "Surely you've figured out what happened to Freddie Koffman."

"Even if I had, I'm not at liberty to say—certainly not to *paranormal* investigators." He sneered as if he'd told a joke worthy of a laugh.

Selene shrugged. "Then if you have it under control, I don't see why you're bothered by us."

"No one's bothered," he said, straightening up. "I just hope, for your own sakes, you stay out of an official police investigation. Maybe it's best you two really do head to Hawaii."

Aiden and Selene sat in silence as Detective Humbolt stalked off. He didn't head back to finish his conversation with Phoebe. Instead he disappeared down the opposite end of the street. Aiden released a sigh and shook his head.

"He woke up on the wrong side of the bed this morning," he said, sipping from his coffee. "But then again, something tells me that's the case every morning."

"Do you think Phoebe told him about us?"

"It doesn't matter. We're here to stay. We have an episode to film."

———

Later that evening, Aiden and Selene sat down for another dinner with the Mhoons. Everyone was present except for Tom. Phoebe mentioned he was working late at the coal mine. Selene couldn't help staring across the table at Omar. He sat as silent and stone faced as he had last night. He ate his dinner without a word, wiping his mouth with his napkin, and then excused himself.

Selene turned to Mr. Mhoon. "Is he a guest at the hotel?"

"Omar?" Mr. Mhoon asked with a hearty chuckle. "No, no...he's my brother! He's a man of few words. He's staying at the hotel 'til he's back on his feet."

"Hopefully soon," said Mrs. Mhoon stiffly.

Mr. Mhoon gave his wife a severe look. "After all we've done for *your* family, I don't think there's room to talk."

Aiden and Selene departed the dining room not long after. Mr. and Mrs. Mhoon started bickering. Anything Mr. Mhoon said, Mrs. Mhoon had a retort, and vice versa.

"A part of me feels bad for bringing up Omar," said Selene later on. They had gone up to Aiden's room. "If I'd known it'd cause an argument..."

"You shouldn't worry about it. They're married and miserable. Isn't that how it usually works?"

Selene paused for a second. The beginnings of a frown seeped onto her lips. "Is that what you think marriage is like?"

"You know what I mean," said Aiden hastily. He had taken out his contacts and put on his glasses, now rifling through their copies of the news articles. "At the O'Hare household, it's par for the course. I don't think a day went by without my mom and dad trying to bite each other's heads off."

"That doesn't sound too pleasant."

"It wasn't. Exactly why I don't go visit too often."

"And why you've avoided relationships," Selene finished on a slightly curious note.

Aiden looked up at her, surprise in his hazel gaze. "I

wouldn't say I've avoided relationships. I was with Delilah for six years."

"You've mentioned it was on and off and that you knew you were never in love with her."

"Where is this coming from?" he asked with an uneasy chuckle. "Why are you bringing this up now?"

Selene wasn't sure. She hadn't planned on it, but Aiden's comment about marriage and his parents had activated her curiosity. Aiden wasn't big on emotions. She had known that when they started dating. It wasn't like she was an expert on matters of the heart. Yet, sometimes, she found herself wondering if she was walking down the same path with Aiden as Delilah had. If they had been together for six years and he hadn't ever loved her…

Was she expecting too much emotion from a man like Aiden? Was she setting herself up for future failure?

"Forget I brought it up," said Selene after several seconds. She reached for another article they'd made copies of. "If the Dunn family sold the hotel in 1963, that means the hotel went unoccupied for two decades."

Aiden happily snatched up the subject change. "Then the Mhoons came along."

"In 1983. A year later there was another incident. A man by the name of Michael Yancy died in his sleep, but he was also in his fifties and had other health issues. It was ruled a natural death."

"Mr. Mhoon couldn't have been surprised when it happened. He had to have known what kind of property he was buying. A hunch tells me it's *why* he bought it in the first place."

"Possibly."

"We need to find a common link between the victims.

Aside from being guests at this hotel and dying in their sleep, they have to have something in common."

Selene could feel her concentration slipping. Exhaustion from lack of sleep and studying the small print on the old news articles was getting to her, making her eyes ache and lids heavy. She rose from the armchair in Aiden's room. "I'm going to head to bed. I'm exhausted and I still haven't gotten a full night's sleep."

"Sleep with me." Aiden blocked her path, his arms sliding over her hips. He bent down for a quick kiss to the mouth. "I promise no funny business keeping you up—though last night *was* your idea."

"We say that now, but you know how we are," she said, running a finger over the neckline of his sweater. "We can't help ourselves."

"Alright, alright. Then promise me you'll get some rest."

Aiden kissed her good-night before she left to her room. The caffeine she had earlier had worn off, leaving her body achy and her eyes itchy. She spent half an hour on her nightly routine and emerged from the bathroom craving her bed. The hotel had fallen into a heavy silence identical to last night. Even the light tapping of drizzle against the window was the same.

She crawled into bed, pulling the covers up, and turned off the lights. In recent weeks, no matter how comfortable she had gotten, she couldn't drift off to sleep. She'd spent hours upon hours tossing, turning, twisting as she tried to doze off.

Tonight, in minutes, her thoughts began to fall away from her. She started off mulling over why she'd asked Aiden about his view of relationships and marriage and moved onto earlier today with Detective Humbolt outside the cafe. Soon a yawn hit her, lids growing too weighty to fight, thoughts fuzzy as she finally gave in.

The scenery of her hotel room melted away as a more familiar setting materialized. Selene was back home at Brimrock, walking down the hall with her terrier, Yukie, at her heels. Yukie trotted along with her until she reached the doorway leading into the living room. The light was already on.

Selene entered the room to turn it off, but then stopped. Seated near the flickering flames in the fireplace was none other than her grandmother, Luna. She looked as regal as she always had in every photo Selene had seen of her, the flames reflecting in her dark brown eyes. She patted the seat next to her on the sofa.

"Well, what are you waiting for? Come and sit, Selly."

Selene was too shocked to move and choked out, "Grandma Luna?"

"The one and only. Is there another Grandma Luna you were looking for?" she simpered with a warm smile. Her brown skin glowed, her soft wrinkles adding to her timeless beauty. "I've been waiting to see you forever—and now, I finally can."

"I have so many questions to ask you. Where have you been all these years? Why have you stayed away so long?"

"We can talk about everything. Finally clear the air and give you some clarity. Come and sit with me."

A burst of energy shot through Selene and she rushed forward, excited. She made it only a few footsteps before the living room faded away. The flickering flames stopped and Luna vanished. She went from running to jerking awake, calling out, "Luna!"

But as her raspy, water-deprived throat cried out her grandmother's name, another scream pierced the hotel's air. It was coming from one of the other rooms. Selene leapt from her bed and bounded into the hall, almost crashing into a robe-clad Grace.

"What's the matter?!"

Grace clutched her face and said, "I'm not sure. I came out to see what the commotion was. It…it sounds like it was coming from over there."

Room nine. Selene raced down the hall as the other doors opened up and guests curiously poked their heads out. Aiden was one of them, joining her side as she stopped in front of room nine's door. She glanced at him before she knocked. A jolt of shock zapped her bones when the door flew open and a shaky, saucer-eyed Yvette answered.

"It…it was in my room. I saw the monster!"

CHAPTER EIGHT

Still in her pajamas, Yvette Howell stumbled into a chair as others poured into her hotel room. Aiden and Selene were among some of the first followed by a moody Mr. Mhoon. He still wore his flannel pajamas and bearpaw slippers. He wasted no time grousing about early morning noises. Yvette sobbed, her knee bouncing.

Selene knelt beside her and spoke in a soft tone. "Can you tell us what happened?"

Yvette shook her head, the tail end of her satin hair scarf swinging. "It's been difficult sleeping—tossing and turning through the night. Finally I fell asleep. I was dreaming about my car. It was time for me to go, for me to head to Los Angeles like I've wanted. Then it all changed. The car had a mind of its own. The engine revved up and it drove right at me. It…it tried to mow me down! I was screaming and running, but there was no escaping it. That's when a shadow fell over everything. I woke up in a cold sweat, thinking it was over…'til I saw it. It was real. It was in my room."

"Can you describe what you mean?" Aiden asked.

"It was dark in the room," Yvette answered, eyes glossy

with tears. "But I felt a sudden coldness. It's like the room turned into an icebox. Figured it must've been the central heating 'til I looked across the room. There was some kind of shadow moving."

"A shadow?" Aiden said, his brow creasing. "What did it belong to?"

Yvette dropped her face in her hands and mumbled, "Nothing! It was just a shadow by itself, growing bigger, coming closer."

"Oh dear, let's get you something warm to sip on," said Mrs. Mhoon. She nudged her way through the small crowd gathered at the doorway. She too wore a pajama robe she had paired with curlers in her gray hair. She put an arm around Yvette and guided her into the hall.

Aiden started to protest, but then he noticed the stain on the carpet. As the others in the room dispersed, he caught Selene's eye and jutted his chin in its direction. She quickly stepped in front of it, blocking it from view as Mr. Mhoon came up to them.

"It looks like now's a good time to start investigating," he grumbled. His usual boisterous nature was muted this early in the morning. "If you need me, I'll be in my office downstairs drinking half a pot of coffee."

Aiden and Selene waited for him to go before they turned to each other.

"Is this what I think it is?" Selene asked.

Aiden nodded, crouching low. Some sort of inky black substance had dribbled onto the carpet, shiny and still wet, but from where? His gaze flicked up to the vent on the ceiling.

Bingo.

Residual splotches of the mysterious ink had stained the slits in the vent. Whatever it was had leaked through and dribbled onto the carpet.

Selene waved both of her hands. One sent the door snapping shut and the other conjured an empty water bottle from the small trash bin near the desk. With another flick of her wrist, the plastic bottle soared through the air and straight into her hand. She knelt beside Aiden, eyes on the unidentified muck.

"We should take a sample of this," she said. "Whatever it is. Not sure what to call it."

"I'd say black ink seems apt enough. We just need a—"

Aiden cut himself off when he spotted it. He stood up and reached for the mug of cold tea on Yvette's bedside table. Plucking the spoon from the mug, he scooped up the gunky substance and funneled it into the water bottle as best as he could. It was no easy task, as the stubborn ink stretched like rubber, clinging to the fibers of the carpet even with the spoon lifting it off. He was handing Selene the bottle when the door burst open and Detective Humbolt barged into the room in his trench coat and wrinkled pants.

"What are you two doing in here?" he asked without preamble.

Aiden and Selene rose at the same time. Selene folded her arms behind her back, keeping the bottle hidden while Aiden stepped to the plate and addressed the detective.

"We've been asked to investigate," he replied calmly. "Is there a reason you're walking into guests' rooms unannounced, Detective?"

"Let's get one thing straight. *I'm* a police officer. I have authorization to search the crime scene."

"No crime has been committed here…unless you're aware of something we're not."

Humbolt's steel-gray eyes narrowed. "I was informed a guest potentially saw a suspect in her room. Where is she?"

"There was no suspect," said Selene. "She saw a shadow."

Humbolt looked over at Selene for the first time. "What are you hiding behind your back?"

"I'm not hiding anything."

"Is that evidence?"

As Humbolt strode over, Aiden stepped in the middle of his path. The bold move startled Humbolt for a brief second as he doubled back half a step. Once the surprise wore off, he resumed his tough-guy detective routine with an even deeper scowl. Aiden wasn't normally the type to get into pissing contests with other men. It wasn't his style. But it also wasn't his style to allow overly aggressive detectives to accost his girlfriend.

"Detective, I hope you were going to keep your hands to yourself. You have no right to touch anyone, particularly without probable cause."

Humbolt's already intense glare darkened. He started to draw himself up to full height—which was still several inches shorter than Aiden's seventy-five—before a loud crash outside of Yvette's room interrupted him.

"You two stay where you are! You've done enough damage," he ordered before rushing into the hall.

Selene came up on Aiden's left and whispered, "I magicked one of the portraits on the wall to fall from its nail."

Aiden smirked at her, always impressed by her cleverness. "Good thinking. Now where can we hide this bottle before he gets back?"

It turned out Detective Humbolt soon forgot about them. Phoebe approached him in the hall, batting her long lashes and smiling wide at every word he spoke. He seemed to forget about investigating the incident in Yvette's room. At least for the time being.

Aiden and Selene snuck by without challenge. They escaped into Selene's room since it was the closer one of the two, setting the latch on the door.

"If there was any doubt, I'm certain Humbolt and Phoebe have a thing going on," said Selene. She walked the plastic bottle with the mysterious black ink over to her desk. "Do you think she was the one who called him to the hotel?"

"I don't know, but he showed up pretty fast."

"Very fast. That couldn't have been more than five minutes. Maresburg is a small town, but even that's stretching it. Almost as if he was waiting for something to happen."

"*Or* already here knowing it had," Aiden said. He stroked his chin, giving the different possibilities some thought. "This weird goopy ink might be the clue we've been looking for. Kind of sloppy for the culprit to leave it behind."

"Yvette described a shadow. I don't know about you, but I've never seen a shadow drip ink."

"To be fair, she also admitted she was half asleep. People see shapes in the dark all the time. It doesn't mean it's the boogeyman."

"Something tells me this definitely isn't the boogeyman. I've never heard of the boogeyman bleeding ink onto carpets."

"This could be his younger, messier baby brother," he quipped.

"You joke, but you never know! Anything's possible when it comes to the—"

"Paranormal. Believe me, I've heard. How about we stick with the victims for now? Establish the pattern going on first?"

Selene pulled the curtains to her window apart. Today was the first day so far in Maresburg where the sun poked out from the dreary storm clouds. She began unraveling the twisted braids in her hair, her thick curls springing loose.

"And where should we start to do that?"

"Mr. Mhoon," said Aiden. "He's been the most cooperative so far. He's eager to tell us whatever we want to know about the case."

"We should probably give him a chance to drink that half a pot of coffee. Also, I'm using that as an excuse to buy myself time to get dressed." She moved to her closet and grabbed a sweater off a hanger.

Aiden got the hint, but not before he glanced at the bed. The comforter was strewn across the mattress and the sheets were wrinkled. A sense of relief filled him up as he said, "Judging by the look of your bed, you got some sleep last night."

"I did. Even dreamed a little too."

"Good. Look, Selene, about what happened before you left last night…" He drifted off as he pieced together what to say. She had played it cool as they exchanged good-nights, but it was an act. He had upset her with his cynicism without realizing it. "I didn't mean to come across as an insensitive jerk."

She smiled up at him. "Forget about it. I think sleep deprivation has been making me cranky."

"Otherwise known as the sleep version of hangry."

———

Aiden made it back to his room and was rummaging through his drawer for a pair of socks and boxers when his phone trilled.

It was a foreign sound. His phone never rang. Probably because nobody ever called him. Aside from the usual suspects like Selene and Eddie, his contact list was full of the most mundane numbers known to man. Local bookshops. Pizza parlors who delivered. 1-800 psychic lines when the urge to prank call struck him. Who could possibly be calling his number if not John Edward seeking revenge?

And then it hit him as he groaned and dread sank into his stomach. Paulina, their executive producer, was another real, and likely, possibility. It *had* been a few days since she last chewed him out.

He picked up his phone and braved a look at the caller ID.

Cara, his sister. He arched a brow as dread disappeared and confusion pooled in its place. The last time Cara had called him, it had been this past Christmas, and that was more of a hasty "happy-holidays-thanks-for-the-card-bye!" type of deal. He answered.

"The stranger's alive!" Cara shrieked in her brisk voice. "I was expecting a straight to voice mail."

Aiden took a second to blink away his surprise. "Cara, when have we ever been phone people?"

His sister paused and then sighed. "Okay, fine. You're right. We're not the chattiest bunch, are we?"

"Uh-huh. What's wrong?"

"Why do you assume something's wrong?"

"We *just* went over how we're not chatty and you're wondering why I'm asking what's wrong?"

"Alright, if you must know, it's Mom and Dad."

His chest tightened and he stopped breathing. "What about them? They're not hurt, are they? Did Dad blow his back out lifting air conditioners again?"

"Are you kidding? Dad's still drinking like a fish and Mom is as solid as ever. But they're divorcing."

"No, they're not," said Aiden automatically. He shook his head at no one, licking his suddenly dry lips. "They've always said they would, but they're not. It's meaningless talk when they're mad."

"Aiden," said Cara somberly. "They're divorcing. For real this time."

"But...why?"

"Mom's had her fill. She's tired of him. You know how he always promises he'll change and then never does. She's packed up and everything—she's moving back to Limerick."

"*Limerick*?!"

His parents had immigrated to the United States several decades ago after escaping their impoverished lives in Ireland. They had spent countless years working hard at dead-end jobs to make ends meets and put food on the table for him and Cara. It had been part of the friction growing up as sometimes they didn't have what they needed to survive. Still, he had never imagined they would ever divorce. Dad loved Mom. Mom loved Dad. Even for as often as they griped about each other—

"Limerick," repeated Cara, piercing through the fog of his thoughts. "Mom's going to stay with Aunt Imogen."

"I...I don't know what to say."

"I figured that'd be the case. You're not the most emotional guy. But I figured I'd call anyway."

Cara was right. Aiden wasn't one to be in tune with his feelings. Even during his six-year relationship with Delilah, he hadn't explored that side of himself. In fact, the most feeling he had shown had been recently. Selene drew a bit more than usual out of him, but he still wasn't a natural. He didn't tap into his heart often and he didn't articulate his feelings well—if he even acknowledged them at all.

"I didn't mean to ruin your day. Just thought you should know. You're filming in Virginia, right?"

"Uh…yeah…" The shock still consumed him, leaving him slow-witted and sluggish.

"With your new girlfriend," Cara went on. "The pics you posted on InstaPixel are cute. She's pretty."

"Right. Uh, thanks."

"Guess we'll have to see what happens. I'll keep you updated."

Aiden hung up and dropped down onto the end of his bed. He hadn't processed a word Cara said about Mom and Dad's divorce; it sounded like some absurd joke being played on him. His eyes fell on the bedside clock and it dawned on him he was already supposed to meet Selene downstairs. He forced the call with Cara from his mind and started getting dressed.

———

"Make yourselves comfortable. Coffee?" Mr. Mhoon asked them. His mood had done a one eighty from earlier in the morning. He had not only changed out of his flannel pajamas and bearpaw slippers, he had stopped scowling and grumbling. He was back to his loud, jovial, chatty self. He motioned for Aiden and Selene to nab seats in his office and then stippled his thick fingers together. "Did you two get a chance to look around Yvette's room? What did you find?"

"We didn't find much," said Aiden vaguely, omitting the black ink. They were there to extract info from Mr. Mhoon, not offer any prematurely. "Truth be told, we were interrupted by Detective Humbolt."

Mr. Mhoon glowered. "He's always poking his nose around here. Still thinks he's dating Phee."

"Oh?" Selene said, perking up with interest. "So they do have a history?"

"A brief one. They dated many years ago. Phee has moved on. Humbolt not so much. As you know, she and Tom are getting married in a few days, but he thinks he can drop by the hotel anytime. I've told Phee she needs to put her foot down."

Neither Aiden nor Selene mentioned what they had observed of the two—that for a woman about to marry, Phoebe seemed as friendly as Detective Humbolt. Aiden carefully circled back to Mr. Mhoon's clear dislike of the detective.

"He's mentioned he's the one investigating what happened to Freddie Koffman. Do you know how much headway he's made?"

"Not much at all. He'll rule it a natural death like he's ruled the others," replied Mr. Mhoon.

Aiden kept his face neutral, though his pulse spiked with interest. "I take it you don't agree?"

"I'll probably get in trouble if this ever gets back to the missus." He leaned forward on his desk, fingers still stippled, his large form slightly intimidating. "If you ask me, what we're dealing with has never been human."

Selene met him halfway, leaning forward herself. "You mean like the rumored sleep monster?"

"Monsters, ghosts, demons—whatever you want to call them, everybody's got a different theory. But I'm sure one of them is correct," he said with a grave expression on his face. "I've never been unlucky enough to encounter whatever it is, but I do know it's not a simple case of cardiac arrest like Humbolt and the Maresburg PD have always claimed it's been."

"And that's what they've cited for the other guests too, correct?"

A tick of discomfort flittered across Mr. Mhoon's face

before he picked up his coffee mug and chugged. "That's... that's what they've cited, yes."

"Can you tell us about some of the past victims?"

"Well, I don't know much. They were guests at my hotel. Fine people, each one of them, but we were hardly buddy-buddy."

"Any little bit helps," insisted Selene with an innocuous smile.

Mr. Mhoon's mouth twisted in unmistakable distaste, though he obliged. "There was Jamila Kerford in...in the early 2000s."

"You mean, 2003." Aiden referenced his notebook filled with case info.

"R-right. She was here with her husband visiting family. She was a very intelligent woman. She worked for the city council for many years and was making big plans to go into politics."

"There was another incident a few years after that, wasn't there?"

He inhaled a breath and gave a tight nod. "Quigley Oberman. Family man who just moved to Maresburg. He and his family were staying here as they house hunted. He was supposed to open up a big soul food restaurant."

"And then there's the first one," said Aiden, reading from his notebook. "Michael Yancy died a year into you owning the hotel. Did you know about the hotel's reputation when you bought it?"

"It's a complicated story, but that's one thing I'd prefer not to get into right now," said Mr. Mhoon, sighing. "When I bought this hotel, I had good intentions. I wanted to give people in Maresburg a place to stay—not unlike Darius Dunn all those years back. And I must say, I have. I've given thousands a comfy bed and soft pillow for the night. It hasn't been perfect with the incidents over the years, but I do my best. I keep the hotel in good standing. We've been ranked in Virginia's top twenty for hospitality despite all the goings-on. I'm damned proud of that."

Aiden and Selene wandered the courtyard at the back of the hotel after their meeting with Mr. Mhoon ended. He had received a phone call he couldn't delay and they had opted to excuse themselves. As they strolled in the garden among dewy leaves and bright flowers, Selene checked for any listening ears. They were completely alone.

"I know you don't agree," she said quietly, "but I really think we're dealing with the paranormal. Even Mr. Mhoon thinks so."

Aiden stuck by Selene's side as they browsed the garden. "Is that what you got from our meeting?"

"You didn't? Aiden, he's owned the hotel for over thirty years. He's seen his share of incidents here."

"And he's profited off of them too," said Aiden.

Selene stopped by a bushel of marigolds and glanced at him. "I have to hear this one. Spill."

"We've already established that he's happily billed this hotel as one of the most haunted in America. Remember the merch store on the hotel website? And then there's the hotel brochures—look." Aiden brandished the pamphlet for Selene to flip through. He waited for her to skim through its pages before he continued. "Mr. Mhoon is eager to tell us all about what's going on here. It's why he contacted us, a popular streaming show on YouTv, to feature him in an episode."

"I don't get where you're going with this. Are you saying Mr. Mhoon is behind what's going on?"

"I'm saying his intentions aren't as pure and noble as he's presenting them to be. He was excited to tell us about how he's some great protector of the hotel, but when we pressed him about the victims, he was uncomfortable."

Selene pushed the pamphlet into Aiden's chest and shook her head. "I'm not convinced. It almost sounds like you think Mr. Mhoon is behind the deaths themselves."

"Over the years I've investigated a lot of different paranormal claims, Selene. None of them have been true. It's always been something that's either a coincidence or something nefarious, explained by logic."

"*Except* for me—or have you forgotten?" she asked, meeting his eyes. Hers were brown and warm, full of spirit. He didn't look away, an electric shock zinging down his spine as if her doing. She was truly magical in more ways than one. "You investigated Luna and it turned out what was going on in Brimrock *was* real. It wasn't Luna or my family, but it turned out to be a succubus."

"No. No, I haven't forgotten," he said guiltily. He finally looked away.

Selene straightened her glasses and inhaled a sharp breath before releasing it again. "The ink's gone."

He stared in question. "What do you mean it's gone?"

"Gone as in gone. It evaporated from the bottle. I didn't have a chance to tell you before we sat down with Mr. Mhoon. After I finished changing, I checked the bottle, and it was empty."

"How's that possible? It was some pretty thick and ropey ink."

"We're going to have to keep an eye out tonight."

"Stakeout?" he asked.

She nodded. "Stakeout.. Hopefully an all-nighter will help us pick up on anything out of the ordinary. We can finally find out what Omar's up to and if Humbolt's lurking around.

It's a good chance for us to film more content for the episode."

"I'll bring the camcorder. You bring the snacks." His tease earned him a bright smile from her. The warmest, most pleasant feeling swelled up inside his chest when on the receiving end of one of those smiles. His brain was having none of it, shifting his thoughts to his earlier conversation with Cara about Mom and Dad's divorce. He pushed it away, refusing to spend time with Selene dwelling on it. He squeezed her hand and assured her with a return smile.

Though they had different theories about what was going on at the Mhoon Hotel, they would remain a united front no matter what. They still had many days left of digging deeper into the mysterious occurrences and would do so together. Their investigation had only just begun.

CHAPTER NINE

Staying up through the night *should've* been a piece of cake. Aiden and Selene waited until the hotel's evening ruckus died down and the lights flicked off before they set up for their stakeout. They snuck downstairs with their paranormal equipment and plodded down the first-floor halls cloaked by shadows. The century-old Virginian home possessed an ineffably spooky atmosphere at night. The creaks of floorboards and groans of pipes sounded louder, creepier in the stillness.

They tiptoed into the parlor and set up camp on a table and chairs. Aiden unfurled a large map and stretched it across the tabletop. Selene levitated her flashlight over the map, shining light on the excruciatingly detailed layout of the Mhoon Hotel.

Typical Aiden; he'd created his own map.

She looked up at him with a brow arched. "When did you have time to create an entire map of the hotel?"

"It wasn't that complicated," he replied nonchalantly. "I found the layout of the property online and then filled in some of the details."

"Why am I even surprised?"

Aiden looked amused, his long fingers drifting across the map and covering hers. Their gazes met as he moved in and captured her lips in what started as a light kiss. She hooked an arm around his neck and pressed her mouth against his. An electric tingle rippled through her body, almost tempting enough to fall deeper into his kiss.

She tore her mouth away with a shuddering breath, stepping back. "We probably shouldn't get distracted. Not in the middle of a ghost hunt."

"I thought it was a monster," he teased. Even in the dark, his hazel eyes gleamed.

"We'll never find out either way if we don't get started, Mr. Smartypants."

"Okay, okay fine. This is probably a good time to bring up what I found out about Yancy and other past victims."

Aiden dug up his notebook from his satchel full of supplies and delivered it into Selene's hands. She flipped to the last page with his borderline illegible writing and skimmed the bullet point notes. In true Aiden fashion, he had broken down each victim with excruciating detail, including information from their childhood.

"You really need to work on your penmanship."

"I write five pages of notes on the vics and *that's* what you take away from it?"

She arched a brow. "Joking. You're not the only one who kids around here. Nancy Drew can be just as fun as the Hardy Boys."

"Were either of them ever really fun? Maybe Joe. Definitely not Frank. I'm more of a Frank."

"Not surprising," she ribbed, leaning against the table with the map. "All of them were fairly different people. There doesn't seem to be much of a connection."

"I thought the same thing. Then I noticed they all had unfinished business."

"As in?"

"Koffman was on his way to a science symposium to collect an award. Jamila Kerford had plans to go into politics. Oberman was opening up a restaurant. After some digging, I found out Yancy was a playwright penning another play."

"Aiden, most people die with 'unfinished business'," said Selene, bending her index and middle fingers in air quotes. "I'm not sure that's much to go on, is it?"

"Maybe you're right. It just struck me as odd they all happened to be here with such specific plans for the future."

Selene pushed the notebook into his chest and stood up straight from the table. "Should we do a surveillance check of the house and start filming?"

"Good thinking."

He turned on the camcorder, its setting on night, and they launched into an explanation about their stakeout.

"I'm sure it's no surprise Selene and I disagree on what's going on here at the Mhoon Hotel," Aiden spoke to the camera in a low voice. "She's behind the tall tales about the place being haunted by some kind of paranormal entity."

Selene leaned into the video frame and whispered, "Rightfully so! People don't usually drop dead in their sleep —all at the same location!"

"There's a logical explanation. There always is," said Aiden. "Let's go take a look around, shall we? I'll admit, the hotel is a little spookier at night."

"Aiden O'Hare, loud and proud skeptic, admitting he's scared. I'm shocked." Selene smirked at the camera.

"Let's not get carried away. No one is scared."

After a few minutes, they moved on from filming in the parlor. The halls were long stretches of darkness. They explored the ground floor with their eyes peeled and ears perked, the camcorder shakily filming every step. On the second floor they repeated themselves. They perused the hallway for any signs of the paranormal, but the best they discovered was Mr. Jackson from room six snoring like an ogre with a head cold.

The third floor fared no better. They hiked up the staircase and flooded the empty hallway with bright light from their flashlights. No strange black ink. No unfathomable cold. No sightings of the bogeyman creeping among the shadows. Selene sighed while Aiden shrugged in a manner that was unmistakably *I told you so*.

They returned to the ground floor on an anticlimactic note. Aiden suggested they head to the parlor for another break. Selene trudged half a step behind him, but then stopped altogether. The oblong windows on the front door caught her eye. The night sky was changing.

It darkened from its typical plum to a purple hue tinged black, as though someone had spilled a jar of ink across the sky. Her feet moved on their own, carrying her to the hotel's double doors. She peered through the glass cutout and watched as a thousand stars blinked off. Gone without a trace.

Selene unlatched the lock on the left side door and rushed outside. The wind pushed against her with a brutal gust, but she pressed on, jumping down the hotel's stone steps. She tilted her head skyward as she jogged down the front path and her pulse thudded in her ears. The moon was next, the silvery orb losing its luster. The otherworldly glow she knew so intimately dimmed before her eyes, fading into the background. She raised a hand and reached for it, a frantic desperation seizing her.

"NO!" she cried out, but she was too late.

An unfathomable darkness eclipsed the moon. It vanished

from the night, like it had never hung in the sky in the first place.

"Selene!" Aiden shouted, grabbing hold of her.

She wrenched herself from his grasp and stumbled off-kilter. Her feet caught up on themselves and she tipped over, landing backside first with a painful thud. Another second passed before she shook her head and tried to orient herself.

"What's gotten into you?" Aiden asked. He extended both hands a second time, pulling her up to her feet. "You took off running."

"Look at the sky! The stars—the *moon*!" Selene rattled off.

Aiden's eyes, normally hazel but now dark emeralds in the night, flicked up to the sky. When his gaze returned to her, her insides knotted up tight. The look on his face said enough. He thought she was cuckoo for Cocoa Puffs…

"Why are you looking at me like that?" Selene snapped. She threw an impatient hand up in the air. "Don't you see it—don't you notice the sky's different?"

"Different how, Selene?"

She looked up, preparing to continue with her tirade, but then any nerve evaporated. Those tightly knotted insides twisted themselves further into a pretzel and a deep frown scrawled across her face. The sky was plum and the stars were twinkling. The moon shone brightly, as silver and ethereal as any other night.

"But just a second ago…" she whispered. Confusion washed over her. She knew what she saw was real, but now it was like it had never been.

"You're exhausted," said Aiden, putting an arm around her. "You haven't been sleeping well. It's time we call it a night. Besides, if we keep making a racket out here, the Mhoons will probably hear us."

Selene didn't protest as Aiden led her back inside the hotel. How could she? She couldn't even sort out if what had happened was real and not a figment of her imagination. If maybe her lack of sleep really *was* taking its toll. She needed a good night's sleep or else she'd lose her mind.

———

The next day, Selene suggested they pay Phoebe a visit at her new age shop, Hidden Senses. When Aiden asked why, she pointed out they had yet to interview Phoebe about the strange events at the hotel. What she left out was that she also wanted to ask Phoebe about dreams and hallucinations. She still hadn't made sense of what happened last night or the dream she'd had about Luna.

"She might point us in a new direction," she explained as they left the hotel and crossed the street to where Ghost was parked. "Phoebe is a common thread in a lot of what's going on. She's the Mhoons' daughter and she has personal involvement with Humbolt."

"Good point, but let's hope she cools it on the chart talk."

It was another windy day as they drove the Dodge Caravan to Mareburg's main street. Aiden seemed to be in his head again. She was in hers too, though she made a few half-hearted attempts at conversation. He provided a sarcastic answer or two, but it was without his usual glimmer of play-fulness. She gave up and let the conversations peter off.

There was a curtain of rainbow beads at the entrance to Hidden Senses. Selene passed through the decorative hanging beads and surveyed the shop. It was a cluster of anything and everything all at once. A wide selection of crystal balls and tattered books were perched on wall shelves. At the back of the shop crystals, gems, and stones glistened from within a glass case. Down different aisles were oils and sprays, decks of tarot cards, and other oddities like rabbits' feet.

The minty scent of sage was inescapable. It tickled Selene's nostrils as she wrinkled her nose and tried not to sneeze. Aiden followed in her footsteps as she started down the aisle with astral maps and charts. For being a small-town new age shop, Phoebe had amassed an extensive inventory.

"Selene Blackstone. I thought you'd be coming by today," said Phoebe softly, appearing from behind a second curtain of beads. She wore another pair of tight leggings in a polka-dot pattern. Her fried and dyed red hair was still piled into a beehive, if possible taller than the last time they'd seen her. "What are you interested in taking a look at? I bet you need a new cauldron."

The tiny hairs on the back of Selene's neck prickled. Phoebe Mhoon had no idea she already owned one—or did she? Selene stared at the seer and said, "We're here to chat if you have a free moment."

"The kettle's going if you'd like some tea. Follow me."

Selene and Aiden trailed behind her as she walked through the same beaded curtain she had emerged from. The back room of Hidden Senses was a lot less mystical, with piles of boxes everywhere. She strolled past the many boxes and into another smaller room. It must've been the place she did her readings from, because there was a table with a thick cloth strewn over it and tarot cards fanned out in the middle. Three chipped mugs waited for them along with a steaming kettle.

Phoebe gingerly picked up the kettle and poured piping-hot tea into each of the mugs. "What is it you'd like to know about Jude?"

Selene looked at Aiden, but neither answered.

"*Humbolt*. He hates his first name—with good reason, I

suppose," Phoebe said, nudging their tea mugs toward them. Tea sloshed over the rims and spilled onto the table. She didn't seem to care as she sat down and blew on her own. "You're suspicious and would like to know more about him."

Selene pulled out her chair and dropped into it. "I can't help but wonder if it's that obvious."

"I'm a good read of people, m'dear," said Phoebe.

"Then maybe you can give us more details about where he is with his investigation." Aiden was last to sit down and the only one who didn't touch his mug of tea. He looked a little ridiculous seated at her tiny table in her tiny foldable chair with the tiny teacup in front of him.

"I can't divulge details about a police investigation. You're already aware of that," said Phoebe flippantly. Her eyes were large as they rolled between Aiden and Selene. "If you'd like to know how Jude made it to the hotel so quickly yesterday morning, it's because he was already there."

Selene frowned. "There as in inside the hotel?"

"That's right, though he preferred no one to know."

"And why is that?" Aiden asked.

Phoebe fixed the neckline of her off-the-shoulder sweater and said rather demurely, "Because Tom wouldn't be happy if he knew Jude still visits me."

"Oh," said Selene. She stopped there, unable to think of anything else to say. It struck her as odd Phoebe was so forth-coming; she expected denials and circular talk. Instead the seer was flat-out admitting to some sort of love triangle with the men.

"Erm, if you don't mind me redirecting the topic of discussion," said Aiden on an awkward beat. "I'd like to talk about Freddie Koffman."

Phoebe smiled wryly. "You misunderstand, Aiden—*both* of you. The reason Jude was visiting me was personal. As you know, Tom and I will be married on Saturday. Jude is unhappy about it. But there's nothing romantic happening between us."

"I'd say that's an understatement. He hasn't made much ground on the Koffman case."

"He might be a little distracted by his heartbreak, yes," Phoebe admitted.

Selene kept to herself what she really wanted to say. Humbolt hadn't seemed heartbroken whenever she'd been around him; he'd seemed like an overly aggressive, cold asshole. She got to the point of what she really wanted to know.

"What do *you* think is going on at the hotel?"

"If you mean to ask if I believe it's a situation of natural death or something more supernatural, I don't know," she replied mysteriously. "But I will say, sometimes those can be one and the same. Maybe it's a case of both."

"Can you tell us what you know about Freddie Koffman?" Aiden asked, steering away from her supernatural mention. "Did you have any interactions with him before his death?"

"Only one. At breakfast. He was a nice man."

Aiden and Selene waited for her to expound, but when she didn't, they moved onto the next question.

"Have you witnessed anything out of the ordinary? Anything you find suspicious?"

"Well, I'm sure you've heard the tales about the whispers in the hall and the cold in the air." Phoebe placed her teacup onto the saucer and picked lint off of her sweater instead. "I may have felt a chill or two from time to time, but I've always slept soundly. Whatever supernatural entity is occupying the hotel, I've never encountered it."

Selene swallowed another tart mouthful of tea and then

steered the conversation to the topic most on her mind. "I noticed you do dream interpretation. I was wondering if I could ask you about that."

"Another time. I have a fitting appointment for my dress. Our wedding will be here before I know it. You understand." Phoebe rose and started collecting the teacups and kettle.

Selene and Aiden left Phoebe in the back room rinsing out her teacups. On their exit, Aiden led the way, eager to return to the wintry air outside. Selene stopped short when passing the glass case full of stones and crystals. Aiden turned to her with a curious expression but she pointed at the pale crystal in the corner. She'd recognize one of those anywhere after what she'd been through with Priscilla Myers in Brimrock.

"It's a lunar crystal," she whispered, gobsmacked. "How did Phoebe get her hands on one of these?"

"Who knows?" Aiden asked. "She seems to be a collector of everything."

The wind howled and brushed coolly against their skin as they entered the street outside. They strolled by the brown stone buildings and skipped over rainy puddles in tandem. Maresburg's sky-high clocktower served as a focal point no matter where in town you went, outshined only by the majestic peaks of the Appalachian Mountains themselves. Ghost awaited them at the curb where they had left him. They eagerly hopped in, happy to be relieved of the day's chill.

Selene buckled her seat belt. "What did you think?"

"Phoebe seemed to be suggesting Humbolt isn't in the right frame of mind to investigate what's going on at the hotel."

"It's a little strange for him to be put on the case," she said, mulling over their conversation. "But Phoebe was pretty confusing, wasn't she? What did she mean about natural death and the supernatural being the same sometimes?"

Aiden shrugged, starting up the caravan. His voice was distant despite his proximity. "Not sure."

"Is something on your mind? You've been distracted since yesterday."

"Why would I be?" he asked back as they hit the road. He tried to play it off with another roll of his shoulders, but Selene wasn't buying it.

Something was off about their conversation with Phoebe Mhoon. Something was off about Detective Humbolt. Most worrisome of all, something was off about Aiden. He was troubled about something and she didn't have the faintest clue what.

———

When they returned to the Mhoon Hotel later that afternoon, Aiden mentioned research and went up to his room. Selene grabbed a book and decided reading in the parlor would offer a change of scenery. The rest of the Mhoons were preoccupied. Mrs. Mhoon was working the front desk while Mr. Mhoon was in the back office. Phoebe was still at her new age shop. Omar was, as usual, nowhere to be found.

Selene spotted a tearful Yvette on her way up the stairs and called out to her to no avail. Yvette kept climbing the staircase with tears streaked down her cheeks, looking worn and sickly. She was struggling with the aftermath of what she had seen in her room.

In the parlor, Selene came across Grace seated at the piano, gliding her fingers over the keys, playing some light notes. She looked up and smiled at Selene as soon as she saw her.

"Did you see Yvette? She was crying," said Selene.

"Oh, yes. She's been upset since yesterday. I don't know her well, but I think the situation in her room really frightened her," said Grace with a regretful shake of her head. "It doesn't seem anyone's doing much about it, does it?"

"No...it doesn't." Selene's brows drew together as she walked over to the pair of armchairs by the window. She propped her book open and read only a sentence before she interrupted herself. "I'm starting to wonder if whatever creature is prowling around this hotel is working with someone."

Grace stared at her, alarmed. Her fingers forgot about the piano keys. "As in a living, breathing person?"

"There's too many strange people around. *Someone* knows something."

"Well, if anyone can figure it out, hopefully you can. Mr. Mhoon mentioned you and your partner are paranormal investigators. He's looking forward to appearing on your show."

"I bet he is," Selene muttered under her breath.

For another half hour she kept up the charade of reading her book in the parlor, but it was no use. She couldn't concentrate. She clapped shut her book, popped to her feet, and bid Grace adieu. Maybe a stop by Aiden's room would do her some good—*and* possibly him too. He'd been distant all morning and she hadn't a clue why. Whatever was bothering him he hadn't wanted to share; he'd decided to keep it to himself.

It was disappointing but not really surprising.

Faint cries from down the hall stole Selene's attention away from her thoughts. She stopped footsteps down the second-floor hallway and listened for the distraught noise. The cry sounded again, traveling from the last door on the left.

"Room nine," Selene whispered. "Yvette!"

She rushed over and thumped on the door. Yvette answered with a sniffle and mumbled, "Hmmm?"

"Yvette, it's…it's Selene. Are you okay in there? Do you want to talk?"

At first it seemed her offer had been rebuffed as Selene stood outside the hotel room door and stared at the brass number nine. Then the lock clicked and the knob turned and the door creaked open. Yvette peered at her through a crack, eyes even baggier and puffer than before. From what little of the room was viewable, the lights were off and the curtains were drawn.

Selene frowned and said, "Is everything okay? I know you've been struggling getting some rest and then after what happened yesterday morning."

"I still can't sleep. It looks like my car will be in the shop longer than I thought."

"Have you had any more of those nightmares?"

Yvette's nod was slight. "The car one all over again. Except the last time it mowed me down and left me to die. Then *it* comes. It takes over everything."

"What comes, Yvette? The shadow?"

"The last time I fell asleep, it felt like it was really happening. How could it be fake when it feels so real?"

"We need to get you out of here. What if we get you a ride share out of town? I'm sure there's a hotel a couple towns over—"

"It's f-freezing," Yvette interrupted, trembling. "It's like they never turn up the heat enough here."

"Yvette, the thermostat says it's seventy."

"Still too cold. And I'm letting the heat out with the door open. Bye, Selene."

Yvette slammed the door shut in Selene's face. Selene

stayed put, blinking and staring at the door an inch away from her face, trying to understand what had happened. How was Yvette shivering cold when the hotel temperature was a reasonable seventy degrees? What did she mean when she said 'it' comes and takes over everything? Did she mean the creature haunting her dreams?

Selene turned away from room number nine and headed for Aiden's room. She sighed and whispered to herself, "I don't have a good feeling about any of this."

CHAPTER TEN

Guilt ached in Aiden's stomach from shutting Selene out. She knew him well enough to tell he was hiding something. He had tried to go on about their investigation as usual, but his phone call with Cara kept replaying on repeat. Always a skeptic and realist, he hadn't thought of Mom and Dad's marriage as some fairy tale. In fact, sometimes they were more incompatible than compatible. Miserable even.

Yet, it still seemed like a reliable mainstay in their lives. For it to end after thirty years was a jarring shock to the system.

Selene deserved to know what was going on. Aiden asked Mr. Mhoon for romantic restaurant recommendations in the local area. The burly hotel owner suggested Chanler's Kitchen on the outskirts of town.

Aiden waited in the foyer for Selene to come down. He had pulled on a wool V-neck sweater and some slacks, opting to keep the reddish-brown stubble growing on his face. Mrs. Mhoon nagged at him, reminding him to bring coats and an umbrella.

"Another frosty one," she said, grabbing his and Selene's coats off the rack. She pushed them into his arms. "Don't stay out too late! The roads are dark and icy. If you get lost, just dial the hotel. I'll send Willy to come find you."

He didn't get a chance to thank her. Selene appeared at the top of the stairs and he became a man transfixed. She was beautiful, smiling at him from where she stood, biting down on her plush bottom lip. Her dizzying curls were gathered into two large puffs on either side of her head and her warm brown eyes twinkled from behind her glasses. She wore a chunky knit sweater and leggings with leather boots that climbed up her shins.

Her curves were tantalizing in those tights. The shape of her legs and thighs had him already fantasizing about what would come later, once they moved on from dinner to dessert, and he could finally touch the skin under that teasingly stretchy fabric.

When she reached the bottom stair, he pulled her in for a kiss, then separated for another reverent look at her. "I almost choked on my tongue."

She giggled. "Is that a good thing?"

"I'd say it should be a definite confidence boost."

"Be back at a reasonable hour!" Mrs. Mhoon called as they headed out the door.

Chanler's Kitchen turned out to be a great pick. The restaurant was a large open space with multiple fireplaces on the perimeter and tables and chairs in the middle, burning sweet-smelling candles. The atmosphere was as warm and romantic as Aiden hoped, pulling out Selene's chair so she could sit.

The waiter delivered their menus and a plate of flaky buns with butter. Selene picked hers up and eyed him from across the table.

"You're in a better mood than you've been lately," she said. "I've started to worry about you."

"That was the last thing I wanted you to do."

"So there is something going on." Her frown curved her lips downward.

Aiden sighed and knew it was time. "I've been in shock the past few days. My sister Cara called me and we talked."

"I'm guessing it's what you talked about that upset you?"

"My parents are divorcing," said Aiden dully. He grabbed a bun off the plate, though he was certain his glum interior was reflected on his exterior. "I've been trying to make sense of it. I've gotten nowhere. It's not something I saw coming."

Selene's eyes had widened, her hand traveling across the table to grab his. "Of course you wouldn't expect it—they're your parents."

"They've been married for thirty-one years."

"Oh, Aiden. I'm so sorry. I can't imagine what you're feeling."

"A lot of numbing shock," he replied candidly. He let out another sigh. "Their relationship wasn't perfect, but…but it was dependable. It might sound like a strange analogy to make, but it was like that old beater car you have. It might need a tune-up or might be an eyesore, but it still runs. It still gets you from point A to point B."

"Are you sure it's set in stone? Maybe they need some time."

"Cara says she thinks my mom is serious."

"I don't know what it's like to see my parents divorce, but I want to be here for you. Whatever's on your mind."

"I knew you'd say that, which is why I don't know why I kept it from you. Thanks, Selene." He weaved his fingers between hers and they sat sharing a fond stare.

A night out alone was exactly what they had needed. They

ordered a bottle of wine along with their entrees and soaked up the cozy vibe in the air. Soon their hearth-fired food arrived, and ruby wine flowed freely from their bottle into their glasses.

The heaviness in Aiden's chest, once weighing him down like an anchor, subsided and he found himself feeling lighter. Mom and Dad might've still been divorcing, but for tonight at least, he was enjoying himself.

"I'm so full I have a stomachache," he confessed an hour later. He leaned backward in his chair and stared at his abdomen. "Would you still like me if I had a gut?"

Selene giggled and said, "I think we're in the same boat. These leggings are feeling a little tight."

"Tight on you is good." He waggled his brows, his normally pale skin tinged pink from the wine.

"You are *such* a pervert," she whispered with another giggle. The wine had affected her in equal measure. Her brown skin was flushed and dewier under the light from the burning candles. "The problem is, I don't think anyone would believe me if I told them—not proper, straight-laced Aiden O'Hare! That's not possible."

"It's a great cover," he said with a laugh.

In Aiden's periphery he saw a man headed for their table. He assumed it was their waiter dropping off the check, but when he looked over, he discovered he was wrong. His brows squished together and a blank expression washed over his face. What was Detective Humbolt doing here?

"Aiden, Selene," said Humbolt, nodding at them. Again he wasn't without his wrinkled pants and long trench coat, his hands hidden in the pockets. Suspicion clouded his gray gaze as he eyed them. "It's a coincidence to run into you here tonight."

"Huge coincidence," Aiden answered with a sarcastic edge. "Almost as if you tracked our whereabouts down."

"Chanler's serves great food. That's why I'm here. I'd think a friendly hello wouldn't be a problem…unless you have something to hide."

"We're minding our business, having dinner," interjected Selene.

Humbolt ignored her. "But while I'm here, I would like to know if you've been tampering with evidence at the Mhoon Hotel."

"You've asked us this," said Aiden, his gaze trained on Humbolt. "The answer is no."

"I have reason to believe that answer is yes. What did you take from Yvette Howell's room?"

Aiden kept his cool. "I told you, the answer is no. You chasing us down to a restaurant to harass us and interrupt our dinner date isn't going to change that. Is there anything else we can do for you, Detective?"

A long moment passed where both men glared at each other. Humbolt leaned closer, biting down hard, making his already pronounced jawline sharp enough to cut. He spoke in a low tone for their ears only, carrying a smoky trace of what was whiskey on his breath.

"You came to Maresburg to film your little show. You're playing this trip to my town as all fun and games, but what you need to understand is that I'm onto you. You're inserting yourself in a matter that is above your pay grade. I don't know why or what you're trying to gain. Maybe it's nothing. Maybe it's something. But I'm watching you either way," he said with an intense flash of danger in his gaze. He stood up straighter and cast them one last stern look. "You two enjoy the rest of your evening. Good night."

Humbolt left them on that menacing note. He disappeared

through the door, leaving a frosty chill that wasn't in the air before. Selene picked up her wineglass and drained the last few drops of her merlot.

"He thinks we're the suspicious ones? He has some nerve," she said afterward. "I really think something's off about this entire investigation at the Mhoon."

Aiden stared at the restaurant door, where Humbolt had been seconds ago. "And if we keep poking around, we'll find out what."

————

Mrs. Mhoon was right about the roads driving home. By the time they left Chanler's Kitchen, it was well after ten. The evening showers had left the roads slippery. The streetlights were few and far between, particularly on the outskirts of Maresburg. Aiden drove them back to the hotel feeling lethargic after their large dinner. He turned up NPR on the radio to keep his brain preoccupied and focused on the dark roads ahead.

Selene had fallen asleep as soon as they buckled their seat belts. It was unlike her, but he didn't question it; if she was finally getting some rest after weeks of insomnia, he was relieved. He tried shaking her awake when he pulled up outside the hotel and turned off the ignition. She answered him in a sleepy moan, twisting her body into a more comfortable position.

"We're here. Time to get up," he said, but she didn't budge. He draped her arm over his shoulder and lifted her into his arms, carrying her down the passage leading into the hotel.

The foyer lights were already off except for the desk lamp at the reception counter. He staggered up the stairs, keeping his balance while holding a dozing Selene. He had no clue where her key card was and didn't have the energy to stop and search. Instead, he fumbled for his own, sliding it into the slot on his door handle. The lock clicked and the door swung open. He delivered Selene to his bed, figuring she would wake up once she realized they were no longer driving.

But she didn't. Aiden spent the next half hour showering and shaving. He emerged in his glasses, T-shirt, and pajama bottoms and discovered Selene was still deeply asleep. A frown curled itself onto his lips as he debated if he should try waking her again. He lowered himself at her side on the bed and gave her a gentle shake.

"Selene," he said. His insides knotted with a strange premonition. "Wake up. We're back at the hotel."

Selene was the lightest sleeper he knew. It was what made her insomnia that much worse; the slightest noise normally woke her. She needed a perfect temperature and often even the bed itself kept her up if not comfortable enough. She wasn't someone who fell into a deep hibernation type of sleep.

Her only answer to him was another sleepy moan. She rolled onto her side and snuggled one of the bed pillows. She really was knocked out.

"I didn't realize she was this tired," he said, sighing. He unzipped her boots, tugging them off, and then pulled the bed comforter over her.

He dimmed the lights and picked up his book for some bedtime reading. Before he made it to the armchair on the other side of the room, he stopped short. Outside the door there was an unmistakable whispery sound, like the soughing wind.

It only grew louder as he stood still and listened. The low whispering noise transformed into something rougher—

something borderline ragged—and then it dawned on him. The sound wasn't the wind but one of lungs, intaking a breath. Who those lungs belonged to, he hadn't the faintest clue.

Aiden's heart started racing and he straightened his shoulders. The sound was going nowhere, hovering outside the door. He had to check it out, investigate what was going on. In two of his long-legged strides, he crossed the room and pressed his eye to the peephole.

The hall was blanketed in darkness. Staring into the peephole was like staring at the inside of your lids. Yet, as Aiden held his eye against the hole, another strange premonition panged in his stomach. Whatever was on the other side of this door was staring back at him. It was peering into the same hole.

Gooseflesh pricked Aiden's skin and he backed away. The ragged breathing carried on for another few seconds, an ugly sound to Aiden's ears, before it faded. Farther and farther away it drifted until the sound died out and silence weighed in.

Aiden hurried over to his desk, grabbing the spirit box, the flashlight, and his copy of *War and Peace*. The spirit box and flashlight were to detect any unusual activity in the area. The thousand-plus page book was to use as a weapon if necessary. He threw a glance over his shoulder at the bed. Selene was still fast asleep, buried under the covers looking cozy and comfortable. He marched to the door and pulled it open.

Shadows ruled the hallway. Aiden stepped over the threshold, shuddering at the arctic cold in the air. He flicked on both the flashlight and spirit box, which crackled to life. Shining the flashlight down the hall, the shadows scuttled away. Nothing was out of the ordinary. The hallway looked as it always did, a stretch of oil portraits on the walls and doily-like area rugs sprinkled throughout.

The spirit box continued to crackle, its green lights weakly blinking. Aiden scanned the hall some more, his brow furrowed. If there wasn't anything amiss, then was he imagining the sound? Maybe he was more exhausted than he realized...

He was a second away from turning back and heading into the room. The lights on the spirit box flashed bright and the crackling noise intensified. His eyes snapped to what it had picked up on and his gooseflesh only spread across his skin in a cold wave.

Black ink dribbled from the vent in the hall. It trickled down the striped wallpaper in a slow descent. He walked over and shone his flashlight onto the vent. Selene had been right all along. Whatever it was they were dealing with wasn't human.

CHAPTER ELEVEN

"**Y**ou look well rested," said Mr. Mhoon the next morning.

Selene looked up from her bowl of oatmeal and gave a polite smile. "I've been sleeping well the last few nights."

"That's great to hear! That's what fine accommodations will do for you! It can't be too comfortable sleeping in some old van."

Aiden remained silent, but his face said enough. He glowered, spooning oatmeal into his mouth. He had bags under his eyes and hadn't bothered combing his hair. Apparently, he hadn't been able to sleep at all last night.

"That food at Chanler's Kitchen tipped you over the edge. Enjoy a large dinner at Chanler's and you're done for," said Mr. Mhoon, laughing gruffly. He moved on from their table without another word.

Selene scanned the dining room. The Jacksons were at their usual table, perusing the morning paper with coffee mugs. The guest in the room next to Selene's, a woman by the name Esther, slurped milk from her bowl of cereal. A few others passed by carrying danishes in napkins, heading back up to their rooms.

But no sign of Yvette.

Selene and Aiden left breakfast and went to her room to map out their plans for the day.

"Maybe we should check on Yvette," said Selene as they trooped down the hall. "She hasn't been getting too much rest."

Aiden gave a disinterested grunt. Selene unlocked her hotel room door and couldn't bite her tongue a second longer.

"You didn't sleep and you *always* sleep," she said. She gave a long sweep of her arm and the door closed shut. Her purse rose off the bed and floated alongside her phone. Both stopped in front of her and she plucked them out of the air. "Don't tell me you stayed up doing research."

"Selene, you really have no clue?" Aiden gaped at her like she was a madwoman.

She shook her head and her shiny curls bounced. She was wearing them down today, paired with a headband to keep them out of her face.

Aiden stepped closer to her, his eyes clouded with an emotion she couldn't place. Concern? Unease? Fear?

"I've never seen that look on your face before," she said quietly. Her insides turned to quivery mush. "Is this about your parents?"

"Last night," he said, inhaling a shuddering breath, "I saw *it*."

"It?"

"Outside our door. It was on the other side, breathing."

Over the next five minutes, Aiden told her everything that had happened last night. By the end, Selene's mouth had dropped open and her eyes had doubled in size. Shock paralyzed her, tingling its way through her body. Finally, she gulped and closed her mouth, blinking up at him.

"You think it disappeared into the vent?"

"I *know* it did. It was oozing from the slits. Whatever it is, Selene, it prowls the hotel at night."

"Why didn't you wake me up?"

"Are you kidding? You were out cold," he said with an incredulous look. "I've never seen you in such a deep sleep."

Selene bit her bottom lip and averted her gaze. She *had* slept well last night—maybe the best sleep of her life. Once again she'd fallen asleep quickly, jumping back into her last dream. Luna had been waiting in the living room of their family home at 1221 Gifford Lane. She smiled when Selene wandered back into the dream and joined her by the roaring fire. They sat and chatted, though in waking life Selene couldn't remember about what. She woke with a delightful warmth in her heart that told her it had been magical.

But could she share that with Aiden? He was so concerned about the creature in the hotel. Would he think her dreams about Luna had anything to do with the creature? He hadn't forgotten about her moon hallucination the night of their stakeout.

"Maybe we should close the vents," she said. She pointed at the vents in the ceiling. "If it's how this thing's traveling, we need to close them in every room."

"The Mhoons aren't going for that. It'll interrupt their cozy hotel atmosphere if the rooms are freezing."

Selene waved her hand, magicking the door open. "Then we'll have to convince them."

———

"Absolutely not. That's not reasonable," said Mr. Mhoon. He balanced his tall, mountainous build on a stepladder, hanging up string lights in the courtyard for Phoebe and Tom's wedding.

Aiden glanced at Selene. She frowned and stepped forward. "But it'd only be for a couple nights. If it's how the creature's traveling, we want to contain it."

"We also don't want it getting into any guests' rooms," Aiden added.

Mrs. Mhoon put her scissors down and wrung her hands, a wrinkle on her brow. She'd been focusing on making paper lanterns, cutting up sheets of card stock. "Willy, maybe we should consider it. We can give the guests space heaters."

"Since when do you recognize there's an evil presence here? You've spent years denying it," he snapped at his wife. "Now, Aiden and Selene, I've told you, you can film anywhere you want on the property. You have free rein, but one thing I can't allow is turning my hotel into Antartica. Not days before Phee's wedding. It's out of the question."

They launched into another explanation, but Mr. Mhoon barked at them he'd made up his mind. With no more room left to argue his points, they waved their imaginary white flags and gave in. Mrs. Mhoon returned to cutting up her paper lanterns and Mr. Mhoon hung up more string lights.

"I bet you're thinking Maresburg has been sunshine and rainbows, but you're wrong. We're at a loss for what we're dealing with here," said Aiden minutes later, holding his camcorder up as he filmed. They cut across the cobblestone pavement in front of the Mhoon Hotel and crossed the street. "Right now we're headed to the library for more research. This time we're looking into different paranormal creatures to gain a better idea of what we might be dealing with. As you can see, I'm a zombie today. Selene looks as amazing as ever."

Selene smiled and waved as he aimed his camcorder at her.

The librarian at the Maresburg library greeted them with a firm nod. Aiden captured some shots of them perusing the aisles and heaving large, dusty books into their arms. They spread them out at a study table and set to work, rifling through hundreds of pages.

"We might've overestimated what we're going to find," said Aiden, halfway through his first book.

Selene looked up from hers. "You mean it's not a wendigo haunting the Mhoon Hotel?"

"It could be. Stranger things have happened."

"We know we're not dealing with your standard spirit," said Selene. She nudged her glasses up her nose and stared off into space. "My mother never talked about the paranormal —or anything magical, really—but I do remember her mentioning an evil spirit that inhabits the body of a dead person."

"Did that spirit usually dribble a strange inky substance everywhere?"

"Not that I know of. That evil spirit sounded a little more considerate of people's carpets."

Aiden held in his laugh, throwing a cautious glance over his shoulder. The librarian had cast them a dark look for interrupting the serene silence. They flipped through a couple more books before giving up altogether. Aiden carried the stack to the return cart, wiping his hands of the pile of books.

Selene rolled her eyes, checked for any witnesses, and then gave a quick flick of her wrist. The books rose up from the cart and danced midair, returning themselves to their rightful spots on the shelves. This time Aiden didn't hold his laugh back. His hazel eyes twinkled as he shook his head.

"How do I still forget you can do that?"

"Old librarian trick," said Selene, winking. Her phone buzzed in her peacoat pocket and she glanced down at the screen. "It's Noelle. Should I answer?"

"If that librarian catches you, she'll kick you out. That'll make two libraries you've been banned from in one year," Aiden teased. "My girlfriend's such a rebel."

"Shh!" Selene shushed, fighting off a smirk as she pressed the green button. She dropped her tone another decibel and whispered, "Noe, I can't talk now. I'm at the library—"

"Dreamling! It's a Dreamling!"

"What's a Dreamling?"

"It's a creature that feeds off of people's dreams!" Noelle answered. She must've been outside, because the whoosh of wind and traffic sounded in the background. "Bibi and I were talking about what's going on over there. Of course Bibi dropped that pearl of knowledge like nothing, then nodded off in her chair. I googled, and apparently it's some old urban legend that must actually be true!"

"Did Google say anything about how this thing came about? How is it at the Mhoon Hotel?"

"There were a lot of origin stories. You know how the internet is. Everybody has their two cents. But I figured at least this might be a new lead for you and Fudgeboy to look into," said Noelle. More honks and tires screeching drowned her out.

"Thanks, Noe. Maybe we need to hire you on as a third host for the show." Selene and her best friend hung up as the librarian swooped into their aisle in full attack mode. She chased Aiden and Selene from the premises and slammed the doors shut behind them.

"Is it in poor taste to say 'I told you so'?" Aiden asked in another tease.

"Never mind that. Noelle might've just helped us solve this thing," said Selene excitedly. "Have you ever heard of a Dreamling?"

"No, but whatever it is, it sounds like it might be friends with the wendigo."

"Aiden, I'm serious! We need to look into this thing. It might've started out as an urban legend, but most stories have some level of truth to them."

"Let's say this Dreamling is the real deal. We might be working behind the Mhoons' backs."

"You mean after the vent debacle? Probably," admitted Selene.

"If we're honest, the whole Mhoon family is strange."

"I try not to judge strange families," said Selene with a thoughtful bend to her mouth. "If you knew my uncle Zee, you'd understand why. But you're right. They're all a little weird. We still haven't figured out what Omar's up to, have we?"

They started down the street again, the afternoon wind messing their hair. Around them other townspeople browsed shops and happily chatted with one another. Either they had no clue of how truly dangerous the creature at the Mhoon Hotel was or they simply didn't care.

Selene nudged Aiden when her gaze traveled to the opposite side of the street. A gasp caught in her throat and she questioned if she were seeing things. Detective Humbolt stumbled his way out of the town liquor and spirits shop, carrying a brown bag unmistakably full of liquor bottles. He looked the roughest they'd seen him yet, his sharp jawline covered by a patchy beard. His trench coat billowed in the wind, revealing his wrinkled and stained clothes underneath.

When they followed him from the other side of the street, studying him as he walked, they spotted dark rings around his eyes. He hadn't slept in days and judging by his pallid complexion, he wasn't feeling too great.

"And then there's Humbolt," said Selene at Aiden's side. "Something's definitely going on there."

"No kidding. The guy looks like he's been hit by a semi-truck. He makes my under eye bags look good."

Humbolt popped the trunk to his bronze Cadillac and stashed his brown bag inside. He moved to the driver's side, but then stopped, his cold gray gaze lifting and landing on them. Both Aiden and Selene took half a step back; they hadn't expected him to pick them out of others on the street. When neither of them said anything, he called out to them.

"You should know better than to follow a police detective." He crossed the street without looking, earning the honk of a horn from a truck passing by. As he stepped onto the sidewalk, the stench of malt whiskey permeated the air. "You'll be happy to know the case is done with."

"The investigation into Freddie Koffman?"

"That's right. Captain doesn't think it's a good idea for me to be around the Mhoons."

"You mean Phoebe," said Aiden.

Humbolt scowled. "It's for the best."

"What's all that booze for?" Aiden jutted his chin in the direction of Humbolt's bronze Cadillac.

"I missed the part where it was any of your business."

"I hope you weren't planning on driving," said Selene.

Aiden held out his hand. "Car keys, Detective. We'll drive you. You need to sleep off that whiskey."

Humbolt glared at them for another long moment before

he caved. He forked over his car keys. Selene pocketed them and Aiden told him to follow them. They were driving him home in Ghost. Humbolt remained silent for the duration of the drive, slumped in his seat, eyes on the window. When Aiden offered to help him inside his home, he waved them off and mumbled something about sleep.

"Your keys!" Selene said, tossing them.

The ring of keys hit him square in the chest, his reflexes too sluggish to react in time. They waited inside Ghost, idling along the curb, as he stumbled his way to the front door of his home. Once he was inside, Selene turned to Aiden with both brows raised.

"Still think he's some mastermind orchestrating the attacks at the hotel?"

"For what it's worth, I still think he's an asshole," Aiden replied bluntly.

"He has nothing to do with what's going on at the Mhoon Hotel. He's too sloppy, too preoccupied. That's not a man who has helped carry out years' worth of attacks on innocent guests," said Selene. She glanced out the van window at Humbolt's small colonial home, her mind racing with thoughts about what had happened today. "But it *is* looking like this monster—the Dreamling—isn't working alone."

CHAPTER TWELVE

Aiden inhaled a deep breath and pressed "Mom" on the contact list on his phone. It had taken him days to work up the nerve to call her. When it concerned matters of the heart, he wasn't the best communicator and neither was she. They sounded a lot more like two androids conversing than a mother and her son. But he couldn't avoid her forever; if Mom and Dad's marriage was imploding, he needed to speak with them about it.

Mom answered with the clang of what sounded like pots and pans. "Finnie, I wasn't expecting to hear from you. Where are you now?"

"I'm in Virginia filming another episode for the show."

She grunted. More pots and pans clanged in the background.

Aiden cleared his throat and said, "I spoke to Cara the other day. She told me what's going on."

"Did she also tell you there's no use talking about it? What's done is done."

"Actually, maybe talking about it would do us some good," he said cautiously. "Have you and Dad—"

"Your father and I haven't spoken in a week. I'm *very* happy." She banged some more pots as if to emphasize her point.

"You don't sound very happy."

"Finnie, if you pay no mind to your house plant for weeks, what d'you think is gonna happen to it? It dies!" she said crudely, traces of her Irish brogue audible. "The plants haven't been watered here for years."

"I realize it's a long shot, but in the hypothetical event Dad does start watering the house plants again, would you reconsider?"

"I've waited thirty years for a change. Am I supposed to wait thirty more?"

"Couldn't you give it another year or two? Here's a crazy idea for us O'Hares—how about marriage counseling?"

"Aiden Finnigan O'Hare!" she shrieked so loudly, he held his phone a bit farther from his ear. "Don't you think we've exhausted options? Don't you think I've held on for as long as I can?"

Guilt anchored in his stomach as he nodded to no one. "I'm sorry. That was insensitive. I…I guess I'm still shocked it's happening. I never thought it would. I thought you would always be together."

"Tell me what good's being together if it's misery?"

The call ended after a few more words edged in. Mom banged more pots and mentioned being busy in the kitchen. He sighed as he hung up, sliding his phone into his jeans pocket. He probably wouldn't have much more luck if he called Dad. That was if he answered.

With slumped shoulders and a heaviness in his stomach, Aiden went downstairs. He and Selene had agreed on another nightlong stakeout. Since Mr. Mhoon had refused to close the vents, they had little faith the creature could be contained.

Their only hope was that they would be ready when it made another appearance.

"What are you two up to tonight?" Mrs. Mhoon asked in her hair rollers and slippers. She had finished closing at the reception desk and dimmed the foyer lights. She shuffled into the parlor and delivered them two mugs of hot chocolate.

"We're staying up," said Selene. She smiled in thanks at the Mhoon matriarch as she accepted her warm mug.

"All night long?" Mrs. Mhoon frowned.

"We're filming and investigating," Aiden answered. He also accepted his mug of hot chocolate. They might have been serious about tonight's investigation, but there was no reason he couldn't sip on hot cocoa in the meantime.

"Well, so long as you don't disturb the guests, I suppose it should be fine." She clasped her hands in front of her and her hesitation spelled itself out on her face. Her eyes crinkled and she scraped her teeth over her bottom lip before she continued. "About Willy and the air vents—he takes this hotel as seriously as I do. We want the guests to be comfortable and we want Phee's wedding to be perfect."

"Of course," said Selene. "Mrs. Mhoon, can I ask you a question?"

"Go on."

"These incidents at the hotel have been happening on and off for decades. Do you know anything about the previous owners?"

"I'm sure you can read up on more than I can tell you," she balked. She padded over to the parlor door. "I know odd things first started happening way back when the Poes were the owners. It's why Mr. Poe thought his wife was unwell."

"Unwell? In what way? We haven't been able to find much on them," Aiden cut in.

"Oh, I wouldn't know. I'm sure you'll be able to find

out much more than I could ever tell you. Remember to keep it down. We don't want to disturb our guests, now do we?"

They wished Mrs. Mhoon a good night and waited several minutes until she was gone. Their thoughts were on the same wavelength as they passed the time sipping on the hot cocoa. Aiden glanced at the doorway of the parlor when certain the coast was clear.

"Every article I've found on the Poes doesn't mention anything about her being unwell," he said, brows connected.

Selene thought for a second. "She passed before he did, didn't she? I'm sure there has to be something."

"Let's hope it's public record." Aiden pulled out his laptop from his backpack of stakeout supplies and powered it on. They had the next eight hours to pass before sunrise. Why not spend some of it doing research?

Selene perched herself on the armrest of his chair and watched as he searched through marriage records online. He typed in "Samuel Poe" for the state of Virginia. The results populated on the screen and they both leaned in closer to read.

"Maya G. Poe," he read aloud. "They married in 1957 when she was twenty."

"How old was he?"

"Thirty."

"Bit of an age difference. Especially given the times. I'm sure the power balance was equal in that marriage."

Aiden's fingers blurred as he typed fast on the keyboard, looking up Maya G. Poe. "She passed away in 1960."

"That's a young age to go. Does it say the cause?"

"Undisclosed. No cause of death given."

Selene glanced around the parlor room with its antique-style mahogany furniture and oil paintings hanging on the walls. "It wouldn't surprise me if Mrs. Poe died right here at the hotel."

———

Over the course of the next few hours, Aiden and Selene performed property-wide surveillance checks. Aiden recorded their walk-throughs as they explored the dark hotel on yet another night, searching for abnormal activity.

"Checking in for another nightly stakeout. Things have been quiet so far," he explained as they roamed down a hallway on the third floor. He let the camcorder pan over the walls and path forward before turning it back on himself. "We're keeping an eye out for anything out of the ordinary. Remember, this inky substance we keep finding is our only tangible clue so far."

Selene moved ahead of him, fiddling with their EMF meter. The number on the screen fluctuated only minimally, rising by a digit and then dropping again. She reached the end of the hall and turned left, holding out the meter in hopes it would pick up on changes in the electromagnetic field.

When they explored the entire third floor and discovered nothing new, they headed downstairs for another break in the parlor. Selene withdrew a deck of cards from her leather book bag and started a game of solitaire. Aiden dropped onto the chair near hers and massaged his temple. His head was pounding in a dull headache. His lack of sleep combined with the dread over Mom and Dad's divorce exhausted him. He hated to even think it in the middle of an investigation, but he might need a break.

As if reading his mind, Selene asked, "Did you wind up calling your mom?"

"I did...but it didn't change much. She called herself a house plant and said she hadn't been watered for years."

Selene's face twisted with confusion. "Huh? Does that mean what I think it means?"

"If you have any clue, please feel free to share. Because I was lost," he said, sighing.

"It sounds like your mom's implying—how can I put this? Um, is your dad the romantic type?"

"Are you kidding? He's even less romantic than me."

"You're plenty romantic," Selene said with a vague smirk. She abandoned her game of solitaire and slid into his lap for a kiss. He welcomed the affection, his arm hooking around her hips. After a couple seconds indulging in soft kisses, she pulled back and continued. "But my point was, it sounds like your mom is saying she feels unappreciated. Maybe the romance has died in their marriage."

"I'm not sure there was any romance to begin with."

Selene raised a brow. "Oh, c'mon...I'm sure there was. There had to be a reason why they fell for each other. Have you spoken to your dad? Maybe if they spice things up a little—"

"Why does that conjure up the imagery of them getting it on to some Marvin Gaye?"

"Aiden!" Selene giggled. "But it's true, maybe they need to spend time together. It could help them remember why they fell in love in the first place."

"Selene, I know you mean well, but you don't know my family. It's always been dysfunction. Both are set in their ways."

"All I'm saying is, it can't hurt to try. Who knows? It could change things."

"I'm too cynical to believe that," he sighed. He rubbed both hands over his face. His fingers drifted up into the short auburn strands of his hair and he blocked out any more thoughts about Mom and Dad's divorce. Grabbing the notebook he kept his research in, he opened it up to the most recent page. "How about we take a look at what we've found out so far. I made a chart with all of our suspects. We agreed whatever it is we're dealing with—if it's the Dreamling like Noelle suggested—it's probably being aided by someone at the hotel. Why else would it be so selective about who it targets?"

"Looks like you included everyone at the hotel."

"Guilty until proven innocent," he remarked with an amused half grin. He gestured to the notes he had scribbled on Humbolt. "If we haven't ruled him out, he's been lead investigator on the Koffman case, and hasn't made any leeway. He's issued several thinly veiled threats. He's shown up at the hotel at the drop of a hat. He has a personal connection to the Mhoons through Phoebe. Taken off the case by his own police captain. Let's not forget him reeking of booze."

Selene shook her head. "I don't think Humbolt has anything to do with this. What would be his motive?"

"Good point. There's Omar Mhoon. We caught him snooping in his brother's office. They seem to have a frosty relationship. Could he be staging these attacks to get back at him?"

"I guess it's possible. But Mr. Mhoon did mention Omar was in town to get his life together. How would that explain the past attacks?"

Aiden's finger drifted down the suspect list and landed on Mr. Mhoon. "Okay, fine. Let's move onto the head honcho. He's profiting off of these attacks. He's eager to control the narrative, but also strict about odd aspects of the investigation."

"Like the vents."

"Exactly. He wouldn't want his access to his victims cut off."

Selene frowned. "I don't know I buy Mr. Mhoon as some paranormal monster."

"Who says he *is* the monster? He could have some type of control over it, like a master with a pet."

"Speaking of monsters, we need to look up the Dreamling for ourselves. Don't make that face! I know you hate giving credence to any paranormal creatures, but you said it yourself," Selene lectured him sternly. "Whatever we're dealing with isn't human. Now Google."

Aiden stared at Selene, half amused and half aroused by her bossy tone and how she turned up her nose. He obliged, grabbing his laptop and typing Dreamling into the search engine. More pages than he anticipated came up on the search results. He scrolled through with Selene leaning across the table for a better look.

"It's not the cutest creature, is it?" she asked, grimacing at the morbid artwork under the images tab.

"It's definitely not the sparkly vampires from *Twilight*."

The images people had drawn of the creature varied. From gigantic, spooky sketches of a shadow man with a jagged mouth and slits for eyes to a black cloud of what resembled fog. Even a doughy figure that vaguely reminded Aiden of the Pillsbury Doughboy.

He clicked on the first webpage, a detailed account by a guy with the username bmxrider92. He had posted his experience with the Dreamling while living in a rural town in Florida.

"He comes at night and the room gets really, really cold," Selene read aloud. Her frown had tipped even more downward. "Then you feel like you're hallucinating and don't know what's real and what's fake. He's a dark shadow, but can transform."

"Into what?"

"He doesn't say. It seems like he's implying anything."

"A shadow creature that can turn into whatever it wants?"

"If he's attacking people in their dreams, that would make sense, wouldn't it?" Selene asked.

Aiden didn't get a chance to answer. The faint click of what sounded like a lock interrupted their conversation. Both Aiden's and Selene's heads snapped to the doorway. They sat still and listened to the clicking and then footsteps followed by the thump of a door closing.

"It's coming from the foyer," whispered Selene. "Someone with a key."

"Mr. and Mrs. Mhoon are asleep upstairs. Was Phoebe already home?"

"I think so. I saw her after dinner."

Their eyes met again and they said in unison, "Omar."

The footsteps continued in the silent night, soft thuds across hardwood flooring. Aiden and Selene flicked off the lights in the parlor and crept over to their doorway, waiting for a chance to peek at the mysterious person. Whoever it was seemed familiar with the hotel at night; he maneuvered through the foyer and hall with ease.

The shadows kept him shrouded from view, but he looked tall and skinny. He stopped halfway down the hall, his keys jiggling as he unlocked another door and disappeared inside. Aiden glanced over his shoulder at Selene.

"Mr. Mhoon's office."

Another second later, the figure emerged clutching a box in his hands. He slowly climbed the stairs, one by one. Aiden and Selene were on his tail without hesitation. They left the parlor, cut down the hall, and tiptoed up the stairs in his wake.

He made it to the second floor, stopping outside none other than Selene's room. Aiden's posture tightened up as a rush of unexpected anger swept over him. It didn't matter if Selene was with him. The fact that whoever this was was creeping around at night and lingering outside her room felt threatening. Was this the same figure who had been breathing outside *his* room the other night?

Aiden refused to wait any longer to find out. Selene held on to his arm to stop him, but he strode forward anyway. He brandished his flashlight, flicking it on and shining it down the hall, bathing the mysterious figure in bright white light.

Omar Mhoon jumped, fumbling with the black box in his hands, almost dropping it. Behind his wire-framed glasses, his eyes filled with terror and his body shook with tremors.

"P-please d-don't attack me!"

Aiden and Selene looked at each other and then at him. "We're not going to attack you. The real question is, who are *you* going to attack?"

"No one," Omar said in his quivery, froggy voice. He clutched his black box to his chest and shoved his wire-framed glasses up his nose. "I...I was trying to protect the hotel."

"By creeping around in the middle of the night?" Aiden asked.

"Isn't that what you're doing?" Omar pointed out, bushy brows raised.

He had a point. Neither of them could deny that. They redirected the conversation.

Selene pointed at the box in his arms. "What's in the box?"

Omar laughed. It was a nervous, shaky laugh, but it came

out naturally, like he considered her question a joke. "It's not what's in the box, it's what the box *does*. I'd expect you to know that. This is a spirit box—one of the best there is, in fact."

"Wait a second…why do you have a spirit box?"

"Shh," he said as their voices rose. He glanced around the dark hall lined with doors. "Do you want to wake up guests in the middle of an investigation? I've been tracking this thing and it's inside your room."

Aiden's stomach flipped. "Inside her room?"

Omar nodded. "*Something* is inside of there."

Selene took an uncertain step forward, her key card in hand. "Should we check it out?"

The three of them huddled in front of her door. Selene swiped her card in the slot and Aiden pushed the door open. Omar yelped and held up his large spirit box like a shield. Aiden shone the flashlight into the pitch-black room and stepped inside.

Selene flicked on the light switch on the wall and the three stared around for anything insidious. The room itself was empty. No mysterious black ink was to be found, but Selene gasped at something else. She rushed forward and picked up a broken hand mirror sitting in the middle of her bed.

"Is that yours?" Aiden asked.

"I've never seen this hand mirror before in my life. I have no clue how it even got in my room."

Aiden stood over Selene's shoulder and peered at the broken mirror. It looked like an antique, plated in gold and embossed with a floral pattern. The glass was hazy and cracked down the middle.

"Why would someone leave this for you?" he pondered aloud.

"That's...that's bad news—get rid of it!" Omar screeched, jumping a wide step back.

"Weren't you just shushing us? Keep it down." Aiden eyed Omar with disbelief. "Actually, it's about time we get a full explanation from you. Who are you really and what are you doing lurking around the hotel after-hours?"

"I'm family. This is a family hotel. My brother—"

"Then why are you creeping around at night? Does he know what you're up to?" Aiden asked.

Selene piggybacked off him. "And why did we catch you rummaging through his office?"

"I knew that was you!"

"Answer the question."

"I'm investigating because something fishy is afoot! Isn't that why you're investigating?" Omar asked shakily, backing away, hugging his spirit box. "In case you didn't know, I'm *also* a paranormal investigator. I've spent the last twenty-five years of my life investigating some of the most dangerous creatures your imagination can't even begin to fathom."

"That doesn't make any sense. Why would Mr. Mhoon hire us if his own brother is a paranormal investigator?"

"B-because...I don't have a famous show, do I? I'm just some...some crackpot nutcase who believes in the paranormal and has dedicated his whole life to proving ghosts, ghouls, vampires, and the like are real!" Omar answered. His bottom lip was quivering, though he had taken on an indignant expression. "I'm the kooky, failure little brother, but I refuse to be silenced this time! I traveled across the country to be here and investigate and I'm going to prove something's up around here. The reason I was looking through his office is because there's proof in there. It's just difficult finding a time when my brother isn't around to sneak inside. You may not've figured it out, but his wife is hiding something. She's not who she says she is."

Neither Aiden nor Selene knew what to say in the seconds after. They stood and stared at the tall, scrawny, shaky man and his spirit box and tried to put the pieces together. Aiden still wasn't convinced, but before he could hurl his next questions, Omar started with his own set of accusations.

He pointed at Selene. "And you...*you're* trouble. There's something off about you."

Aiden could sense Selene's unease. At his side she sucked in a quiet breath and her brows knitted together. She had told him about how being singled out in the past had affected her; how she always felt like she was on the verge of being found out in Brimrock...

"This isn't about Selene," said Aiden coldly. "This is about you and this mirror we've found in her room. You were lurking outside her door. Do you realize how guilty you look?"

"You investigate me and you see how far you get on that postulation! I have nothing to hide, but plenty of people under this roof do," warned Omar ominously. He backed away some more until he reached the door and grabbed its brass handle. "You need to get rid of that mirror now. If you don't listen to anything else I say, listen to this. Get rid of it."

CHAPTER THIRTEEN

"I'm hoping you can help me," said Selene as she barged through the front door of Hidden Senses. She had walked from the Mhoon Hotel deeper into town to visit Phoebe in private. Aiden had stayed behind catching up on sleep after last night's stakeout. Sleep was what she was avoiding most at the moment.

Phoebe was behind the glass case filled with crystals and stones in another off-the-shoulder sweater and her beehive hairdo. She didn't look up when Selene approached. She was examining a selection of pebbly crystals, holding them under a telescopic light as she then sorted them into two piles.

"Errr...am I interrupting?" Selene cleared her throat when several seconds passed by.

"You are, but you knew that already," said Phoebe, cupping another crystal in the palm of her hand. She lifted it to the light, studying its texture and dimensions. "I'm sensing this is a sit-down-to-tea type of conversation. Please meet me in the back."

Selene hung around by the glass case for another awkward few seconds before realizing Phoebe was serious.

The seer still hadn't taken her eye off the crystals she was examining. Selene padded through the shop, parting the curtain of beads that led into the back. The little room with Phoebe's table and chairs was as she remembered it.

Sitting on the table was a piping-hot kettle and two teacups already waiting. Selene frowned as a chill coursed through her. Had Phoebe known ahead of time she was going to visit? Selene hadn't told anyone—not even Aiden.

"I hope you like oolong," said Phoebe when she entered. She floated over and slid into the seat across from Selene. Another second passed where they sipped their tea and stared at each other. "Your heart is very heavy. It's weighing on you, but you won't feel lighter 'til you receive reassurance. Unfortunately, I can't give that to you."

"Oh, no…I didn't want you to—I mean, I was hoping for a second opinion," stammered Selene. The floral notes from the tea were almost overwhelming, wisps of steam curling in front of her. "I've been experiencing insomnia these last few weeks and it's been hard on me."

"I recommend a good melatonin before bed. Lavender tea will help as well. Many find it very relaxing."

"No, see, the thing is…ever since we've come to Maresburg, I've started sleeping again. I've actually started *dreaming*," said Selene. "I never dream. My sleep is always dreamless, but now I'm having vivid dreams. I'm…I'm dreaming about a special loved one."

The corner of Phoebe's lip curled. "Dreaming about a loved one is far from unusual."

"It feels real. It feels like I'm really with her."

"Dreams are projections," answered Phoebe. She swallowed more oolong tea, the teacup itself clanging against the saucer. "They're manifestations of probable realities. When you dream, you are in another dimension. Your body itself remains, but your soul and energy transcend the physical. You are on another plane, experiencing a different form of existence."

None of it made sense. Selene gawked at Phoebe, her expression of confusion. She had no clue what Phoebe was talking about when she mentioned probable realities and different forms of existence. What could be a probable reality of chatting with Luna?

Grandma Luna was *gone*.

"Lost?" Phoebe asked when Selene said nothing. She released a soft laugh. "I expected you to have a better under-standing of the dream state, all things considered. You must not be very in tune with yourself. You have a long way to go."

"I already told you I don't dream."

"Have you considered why you are now?" Phoebe asked. Her eyes sparkled as if she knew the answer.

Selene sighed. She had been worrying about it since last night. When Omar Mhoon accused her of being trouble and they found the mysterious broken mirror on her bed. Before that she had thought her dreams about Luna were strange, but what if Omar was right? What if her presence was making the situation at the hotel worse?

"I'm worried maybe I'm involved somehow," she confessed quietly. "I'm worried me being in Maresburg is bringing out the creature."

"May I remind you Freddie Koffman passed *before* you arrived?"

"It's just…it seems like someone is sending me messages. I've noticed the moon goes dark sometimes—like it's been shut off with a remote control, but my boyfriend didn't see a thing. He says I've been falling into this deep sleep he can't wake me out of, and then there's this inky substance we keep finding. Then it disappears. Last night someone broke into my room and left me a cracked mirror."

For the first time since meeting her, surprise flickered on Phoebe's face. One of her penciled brows arched higher and she said, "What type of cracked mirror? Describe it."

"It's a handheld one with gold plating and some flowery design."

Phoebe's complexion dulled. She pushed away her teacup and rose from her chair. "Follow me."

They abandoned their teacups as Phoebe led her back onto the shop floor. She pivoted left and glided down an aisle stocked with different kinds of books. Some on dream interpretations. Others on divination and herbology. Selene stopped following Phoebe when a dusty, vintage book stood out among the rest. The leather was a carob brown with cracks all over, but even its wear and tear couldn't take away from the fine stitching and beautifully embossed crescent moons on the cover. In the center was a crystal which gleamed a soft purple in the light.

For more seconds than she realized, Selene couldn't stop looking at it. The book captivated her, called to her as though familiar. As though the book was hers—or in the very least, should've been. Her gaze was still stuck on it when Phoebe spoke to her from down the aisle, stirring her from her impromptu trance.

"I found it!" Phoebe exclaimed, clutching a torn yellow piece of paper. She thrust it into Selene's hands as soon as she walked over. "That mirror is nothing good. You need to return it to its rightful place. It belongs in Mrs. Poe's room."

Selene's eyes dropped to the frayed paper. It was a handwritten entry to what must've been a journal. She scanned the wrinkled page, her stomach dropping with each melancholic word.

. . .

April 24, 1960

I've lost all hope. The days are long and lonely. The nights even worse. Guests check in and check out and haven't the faintest clue of the cruelty happening under the same roof. Samuel says it's for the best. That he's only looking out for me. That I get confused or under the weather when I'm out and about without him. That I'm going insane.

But he's wrong. I'm no less sane than anyone. I'm not imagining what I do. I'm not making it up. He simply can't handle what it is. What I am. He thinks he can drug it out of me, stamp it out by keeping me locked away.

What he doesn't know is I've found an escape. A place I can go where I can do anything I've ever dreamed of. I can be who I was meant to become, and he can't stop me. I just want to breathe in fresh air. Feel the rain on my skin or look up at the night sky and the beautiful moon. I just want to be free.

Unfortunately, I don't know how long my secret will last. I'm not sure what the future holds. If I'll ever find a way out for good. If there's a happy ending to this nightmare.

—*Maya*

"Wait...did Mrs. Poe write this?"

"It's a page from her diary. The rest is missing."

"How did you get this?"

"I'm a collector of a lot of things," answered Phoebe with

another flash in her brown eyes. "What you must know is that you are to return that mirror to her room."

"And which room is that?"

"My father is who you need to ask. He has the key."

Phoebe escorted to the shop door. Selene asked if she could hold on to the torn page, but Phoebe insisted it stay. Instead Selene snapped a couple photos with her phone.

"I have one last question," said Selene. "That spell book with the crescent moons and lunar crystal on it. Where did you get that from?"

"Did I not just explain I'm a collector of all things? I have many books on many subjects. Many which mean nothing."

Selene didn't have the chance for another word. The shop door swung open and Tom Lester marched in looking muscled and macho. He maneuvered through the narrow aisles and found Phoebe at the case.

"There you are," he said in his loud voice. "It's been a busy day at the mine, but I needed to come and see you. We need to talk now about Humbolt."

Selene would've stayed and listened in, but Tom threw her a cold glare and she got the hint. She waved goodbye to Phoebe and then left the shop. The sinking sensation in her stomach had gone nowhere as she wandered down the blustery streets of Maresburg. Her mind hopped from topics, bouncing from her dreams to her investigation with Aiden and Mrs. Poe's diary to the ancient spell book on the shelf in Phoebe's store. She glanced around her surroundings only when the paranoid feeling of being watched gripped her.

Looking left and right, up and down the street, nothing was out of the ordinary. No watchful eyes stood out from the residents of the town, but she quickened her pace anyway. Strange things were happening. Whether the watchful presence was real or a figment of her imagination, she wasn't sure. She feared learning the truth.

———

Nights in Virginia were frigid and windy, but Selene braved the cold for her lunar ritual. She snuck away after dinner as the streetlights flashed on and the moon rose high, a silvery disc with a shimmering glow. She held out her hand and the garden hedges jumped apart at her will, letting her slip through to the other side.

The woodsy terrain behind the Mhoon Hotel sprawled on for miles. Selene meandered down the dirt path of an old hiking trail. After days of on and off downpour, muddy puddles riddled the ground. She hopped over them like a game of hopscotch in the dark. Even the air smelled of rain and wet earth, a musky scent carried by the night's wind.

When she was certain she had put enough distance between herself and the hotel, she stopped. She dropped her book bag on a large mossy rock and opened the flap. Her things rose into the air and then flew over to the clearing where she'd perform her ritual. The magic chalk began drawing its line and the candles lit themselves.

Selene closed her eyes, turned her face up to the sky, and felt her body rise. Lunar energy poured over her, bathing her with its magic, eliciting a firework of tingles through her body. She became weightless, soaring higher and higher as she synced with the moon.

Time was irrelevant, falling away like the rest of the world. She was flying fast through time and space. She was spinning in a black sea of twinkling stars, speeding toward the silver disc that was the moon. But the faster she streaked like a shooting star, a bundle of lunar energy in her own right, the farther the moon drifted. The darker it grew, its glowing light dimming into nothing. Just an ink blob among the stars and black void. Gone as though for good.

A deep sense of dread filled Selene up to the brim as she fought to keep going, keep soaring toward the spot where the moon once was. She stretched her hand out to touch the black ink blot, hoping to bring it light again. So close and yet so far—

"*SELENE*!"

She was being shaken awake by strong hands gripping her shoulders. She gasped as her eyes flicked open and the night sky hung as a ceiling over her. She was lying in the dirt, shivering from the chilly wind. Aiden's pale face hovered into her bleary view.

"Aiden…what…?" She couldn't think enough to form a sentence.

"Selene, you fell from the air—you were levitating and then you dropped to the ground and started convulsing," he said in a mixture of fright and shock. He was staring at her like she'd pass out any second. "I couldn't wake you up. You…your eyes were moving beneath your lids."

He helped ease her up into a sitting position. Selene squinted. "Where are my glasses?"

"They fell off. Here."

"I don't know what happened. I was doing a ritual and then the moon went dark. I was trying to reach for it, but it was out of reach."

"Sounds like a dream."

"I *have* been having some weird—" She cut herself off and swallowed. She hadn't told Aiden about her dreams. She brought a hand to her face. Her head was aching in a horrible migraine and she felt hot and cold at the same time. "Did you follow me?"

"I couldn't find you around the hotel. I was worried."

Selene rose on unsteady legs. Even her knees felt weak. Aiden hung his way too large jacket over her shoulders and grabbed her hand.

"We need to make our way back. It's freezing out here."

They trekked in silence. Selene was trying to process what had happened, but her brain felt too slow and sluggish to sort anything out. What had started as a normal lunar ritual had transformed into something else. It was like she was venturing into a realm beyond her comprehension.

Aiden suggested they spend the night together. One look at him and his concern was clear. Not only did he not want to risk the mysterious creature visiting her room again, he wanted to keep an eye on her after tonight's incident. Selene agreed, waiting for the Mhoons to turn in before she padded over to his room.

"We need to figure out what's going on," said Aiden as they readied for bed. "Whoever left that mirror on your bed seems to be sending a message."

Selene paused midtwist of her hair and stared at Aiden in the bathroom mirror. "You think it has to do with the attacks?"

"What else could be the reason? Don't you think it's strange you've been unable to sleep for weeks, and now we're investigating a case where people are dying in their sleep and you're sleeping like a baby? Then this mirror turns up in your room."

"Aiden, what are you saying?"

He sighed, rinsing his toothbrush. "What if you're next? What if the Dreamling—or whatever paranormal creature we're dealing with here—has marked you as his next victim?"

A coldness seized Selene and caused her to shudder. She

screwed on the cap of her leave-in conditioner and left the bathroom without a word. The monster targeting her as its next victim had occurred to her when she pondered why the cracked mirror had been left in her room and Omar had accused her of causing trouble. While it was undeniably a possibility, she refused to spend her time in fear.

After her lunar ritual gone wrong, a night spent relaxing was needed. They settled into bed with books in hand and only the bedside lamps on. One of her favorite things about their nights together was reading in bed. She opened the Nora Roberts novel she had selected from her modest travel collection, but first snuck Aiden a sidelong glance. He always looked so cute when he was engrossed in a good book. Cute enough to bombard with kisses.

His brows drew together, his hazel eyes focused, his lips occasionally mouthing a line or two. She smirked to herself and returned her gaze to the book in her hands. More than a half hour ticked by with only the quiet flip of pages and intakes of breath as sound in the room. Her lids started to drop lower and lower before she caught herself rereading the same sentence three times in a row.

Yawning, she clapped shut her book. "If I stay up any longer, I might start hallucinating again."

She meant it as a joke, but concern immediately filled Aiden's face. He shut his book and removed his glasses. Both he placed on his bedside table. He shifted closer to her, his familiar arms slipping around her like her coziest winter sweater. She met him halfway, snuggling into him, resting her head on his chest.

"I know I'm always the sarcastic quip guy, but I don't find that funny," he said finally. "This investigation is becoming even more of a race against the clock. I'm beginning to question if it's worth it."

She inclined her head for a brief look at him. "You're not suggesting what I think you are?"

"Maybe we're in over our heads. We've been here a week, and we're no closer to solving this thing. Other than our Dreamling theory and some suspects, what ground have we gained?" he asked.

Her mind jumped to the page from Mrs. Poe's journal. It was a significant discovery Aiden needed to know about, but the thought of telling him as they lay comfortably in bed elicited an ache of protest from her tired limbs. Tomorrow she'd bring it up. After a peaceful, uneventful night of sleep.

"No more thinking tonight," she muttered exhaustedly. She circled the plane of his chest with her finger, drawing lazy patterns onto his pectoral muscle.

Aiden let out a single surprised chuckle. "We *do* do a lot of thinking, don't we?"

She nodded, eyes closing. She squirmed into an even comfier position against him, entangling her leg with his. He laughed again and brought the comforter higher up their bodies. Next he used the long reach of his arm to twist off his bedside lamp.

"You win. No more thinking," said Aiden as darkness filled the room. "Night, Selene."

She smiled, asleep within seconds.

———

"Mr. Mhoon, we need access to Mrs. Poe's room," said Selene the next morning. "The one that hasn't been in use for years."

Mr. Mhoon was hauling foldable chairs into the courtyard behind the house. With Phoebe's wedding a couple days away, the first floor of the hotel had turned into a wedding hall. Selene dogged Mr. Mhoon's steps as he set down another armful of chairs.

"How in the world did you hear about that?"

"It doesn't matter," dismissed Selene. "Mrs. Poe used to have a bedroom here years ago—the one Mr. Poe kept her locked in. I'm guessing the room's on the third floor."

Mr. Mhoon let several seconds pass before he moved again. He rasped out a sigh and fished into the pocket of his trousers. Motioning for them to follow him, he said, "If you insist on taking a look."

He led them into the house, up two flights of stairs, and down the hall. They stopped at the end in front of an unmarked door. Dust had collected on the doorknob, a clear sign it hadn't been touched in ages.

"I'm told this was her room. It hasn't been in use for decades. We were advised to leave it be. I don't even know the last time someone was inside here."

"We'll take a look around," said Aiden with a nod.

"Make it fast. I mean it." Mr. Mhoon unlocked the door, giving them a warning look before striding off.

Aiden entered first. He poked his head inside the dark, dank, dusty room. Selene followed as he flicked on the light switch. The ceiling light winked on and off several times. Even once it stayed on, the light was feeble and lifeless. Aiden picked up an end table and hauled it over to the door, propping it open.

"In case there's any funny business," he said when Selene gave him a questioning glance.

A strange sense of calm filled her as she looked around. She drifted through the room like she was browsing an antiques shop—and Mrs. Poe's room *did* look like an antiques shop. Aside from the fact that everything was caked in dust, the decor in the room dated back decades with old brass lamps and an iron-framed bed. Even the ugly floral wallpaper screamed vintage.

It was clear no one had taken care of the room. Motes of dust floated in the air, tickling their noses, disturbing their sinuses. Aiden released a great sneeze.

"Bless you," said Selene in an absentminded tone. Mrs. Poe's room was a cornucopia of mystery, like a past life of its own, filled with many untold stories. She stopped in front of the vanity table and oval-shaped mirror worn with age. Perfume bottles lined the tabletop alongside other beauty staples like a bottle of dried red nail polish and a hairbrush that looked notedly familiar. She gasped, picking it up for a closer study of its gold plating and pretty floral detailing.

Aiden moved closer. "What is it?"

"See this hairbrush? It's exactly like the hand mirror!" Selene ran her fingers over the prickly bristles dried and split by time, pausing to think about their situation. "I don't think we should return the mirror."

"It *can't* be anything good."

"Neither is what's going on here at the hotel." She whipped around to face Aiden, the vintage brush limp in her hand. "We give up the mirror, we give up a clue."

Aiden's jaw tightened, his brows connected. He hesitated another second and then said, "Fine. We'll hold onto it, but it stays in my room. In my safe."

Selene nodded to that compromise, setting the brush onto the vanity counter. "Something is telling me Mrs. Poe wanted me to find the mirror."

"Maybe we can ask her," said Aiden with a sprinkle of his dark humor. He pulled out his iPhone as a substitute for his camcorder and pressed the red button to record video. "We're here in Mrs. Poe's room now—the deceased wife of Mr. Samuel Poe, who owned the hotel in the '60s. The mysterious mirror that's been left on Selene's bed belonged to her. We're going to try and reach out to her now."

He walked the length of the room, holding out his iPhone, allowing its camera to rake over every inch of the distressed furniture and dated decor. Selene hung back and watched, half in her head as she studied Mrs. Poe's room.

"Are you there?" Aiden called to no one. "We'd love a chat, Mrs. Poe. Maybe we can even head downstairs for some brunch. Mrs. Mhoon makes a killer eggs Benedict. Even whips up the Hollandaise sauce herself. Impressive, huh?"

Selene would've been amused if she wasn't so paranoid and contemplative. Though she stood in the room in the light of day, even aided by the ceiling's artificial light, with Aiden mere feet away and the door propped open, she couldn't shake the uneasy feeling plaguing her.

Every sound made was exaggerated, five times louder than it should've been. Every smell hanging in the room was acute, ranker and mustier than seemed reasonable. Every surface she touched was sensory overload, from the prick of the hairbrush's bristles to the spongy carpet beneath her feet. Everything felt heightened, more intense, like she'd tuned into something beyond basic human senses. She leaned against Mrs. Poe's iron bed frame and covered her face with her hand.

"*Or* how about a stroll in the courtyard? The weather's pretty nice out. The most sun we've had in days," Aiden told an imaginary Mrs. Poe. His iPhone was still on record. He circled the room again, immersed in his witty skeptic shtick he played up for the show until his gaze fell on her, and he stopped in his tracks. He pocketed his phone and rushed over. "Hey, what's wrong? You look like you're about to pass out."

"I'm fine," she said as his arm banded across her shoulders. "Just…just a little overwhelmed being in here. I don't know what it is."

"Then let's go." He moved to guide them toward the door, but Selene resisted.

"Wait, not yet. There's something I have to show you. I didn't want to bring it up last night after what happened with my lunar ritual, but now seems like the right time. Take a look at this." Selene fumbled for her phone and pushed it into his hands. "It's a page from Mrs. Poe's diary."

Aiden's eyes skimmed her phone screen.

"How did you get this?" he asked once done reading.

"Yesterday when you were catching up on sleep, I went to Phoebe's shop. She said it was written by Mrs. Poe. Which means the rest of the diary—"

"Is probably in this room," he finished for her.

Over the next ten minutes, they searched the room. They pulled open bedside table drawers and desk drawers. Selene even checked the vanity's two small drawers, but found only more brushes and hair accessories. They foraged through the contents of her closet, pushing aside the clothes hanging on the rack, and digging deeper into the boxes stacked in the back.

Aiden wiped his brow, sweaty and dusty minutes into the search. He pointed out the trunk in the far corner of the room. "We should probably take a look in there."

Selene knelt beside him as he popped the lid off the trunk and another plume of dust floated up. They coughed and waved their arms, batting the dust mites away. She reached inside and started pulling out the big pile of scarves. Aiden joined her, the two extracting items like a sewing machine and spools of thread until the trunk emptied and they reached the bottom.

Mrs. Poe's journal was nowhere to be found, but tucked

underneath another scarf was a frayed envelope. Selene turned it over onto the floor, emptying the black and white photographs inside. She and Aiden picked through the scattered selection.

"Most of these look like photographs of a family," said Aiden.

"Her family? Here's one of a man." Selene grabbed the wallet-sized photograph and held it up for closer study. "This is Mr. Poe. I recognize him from the search results online. Still nothing of Mrs. Poe, though."

"Well, this was probably her." Aiden grabbed the last photograph in the scattered pile.

It was a man and a woman side by side in what looked like the courtyard outside the hotel. Someone had scribbled over their faces in aggressively thick pen marks, blocking them out.

"Did she do this?"

"Probably. Maybe out of frustration."

"I would've been too. It must've been miserable," said Selene, her expression solemn. "He locked her up in here and claimed she was unwell. Do you think it was true what he said about her—she was insane?"

"She doesn't sound insane in her diary. She sounds perfectly reasonable."

"That's the scary part," Selene whispered and she shuddered. "Back then it was so easy to have someone committed. For a husband to claim his wife was unwell. I...I bet no one believed her."

Aiden glanced at Selene. He curled an arm around her and pulled her in for a hug. "Are you sure you're alright? It sounds like this is personal for you."

She shook her head. "It kinda is. More than I thought. I was just thinking about how my grandma Luna was treated.

She was prosecuted because of who she was. There were people in Brimrock who thought she was crazy. They wanted her locked up or…or worse."

"And they were wrong. They were nothing but cowards—afraid of someone different than they were. Someone they didn't bother understanding."

"You're right. I guess it's on my mind because…" She inhaled a deep breath as if debating on what to say, her recent dreams on her mind, but then decided against it at the last second. "Let's get out of here. We've found all we're going to find."

The rest of the morning was spent in Aiden's room. Aiden was on his laptop, searching for more info on Mrs. Poe. Selene was on the bed, sitting cross-legged, studying the photos they had found in Mrs. Poe's room, lost in thought.

"I've tried all my tricks," said Aiden from the desk. His fingers jetted across the keyboard as he speed-typed more keywords into the search engine. "There's no record of Mrs. Poe in the years between her marriage to Mr. Poe and her death in 1960."

"What about Mr. Poe?"

He clicked on a search result and a page loaded with new info. "There's a last known address for him. It's two towns over in Tinsley."

"That has to be outdated," said Selene. "He would be in his eighties if he were still alive today."

"Still worth a shot. He might be able to give us more info about what happened here with Mrs. Poe. What do you think?"

Selene wiped her glasses on the hem of her sweater and then slipped them back onto her face. Mrs. Poe's photographs still lay flush in her lap. "We don't have many other options. Maybe a visit can't hurt."

CHAPTER FOURTEEN

The early morning sky was pale and gray as Aiden and Selene snuck out of the Mhoon Hotel. Aiden loaded their day's worth of supplies—a mix of snacks and investigative equipment—into the back of the van and slid behind the wheel. Today the old but reliable caravan needed to take them seventy miles west into a town called Tinsley.

Aiden stifled a yawn and started the engine. They had stayed up most of the night researching the case. Eventually they both nodded off into a fitful sleep. Normally a sound sleeper, he woke every other hour, a nasty concoction of dread and fear swirling in his stomach.

Where to even begin? Cara had texted him and mentioned Mom had moved into her apartment until the divorce finalized and she left for Ireland. Dad hadn't answered any of his texts or calls. Even his voice mail box was full. Aiden no longer had his best friend, Eddie, to vent to, and every time he opened his mouth to share with Selene, a pang of guilt hit him. She was dealing with her own issues. How could he put his on her?

Something was amiss. It was what kept him up at night more than anything. The fear he would wake and Selene would be gone; she would have wandered outside in another hallucination about the moon, or a lunar ritual gone bad. Then there was the night she had been in a deep sleep she wouldn't wake from. The next morning she had been in a serene mood, but none of it sat right with him.

"Are we ready?" Selene asked.

The question drew him from his thoughts. He blinked as another puff of heat from the vents blew into his face. He had zoned out sitting in the driver's seat, waiting for the van to heat up. Selene was buckled in and staring at him. He cleared his throat and gave a nod.

"Right. I guess I'm more tired than I thought," he half fibbed, gripping the steering wheel and pulling away from the curb.

"The more I think about Mrs. Poe's journal entry, the less interested I am in meeting Mr. Poe," said Selene with an unenthused sigh.

"The entry was brutal."

"What do you think she meant when she said he couldn't accept what she was?"

Aiden's brow wrinkled in a deep line and he cut a darting glance her way. "You don't think she could've been the Dreamling, do you?"

"It's not outside the realm of possibility," said Selene. She rummaged through her leather book bag and pulled out her phone and the black and white photos. "Samuel was keeping her locked up in that room. He was giving her some kind of medication to keep her complicit. He seemed to know something was unusual about Mrs. Poe."

"I know we said she sounded perfectly reasonable, but could it be true what Mr. Poe said? That she was unwell?"

Selene stared at the photographs. The faces Mrs. Poe had scribbled out. "My gut is saying no. She was misunderstood."

The caravan sped down the wet highway as they fell into another silence. Aiden kept his gaze on the road, though his mind traveled elsewhere. He spent the next leg of the drive overanalyzing Mom and Dad's divorce, Selene's strange sleep experiences, and even his failures as a son and boyfriend. He needed to do more than stew in his head. He needed to be supportive, emotionally present…

Aiden glanced sideways at Selene. The urge to confide in her rose up his chest and then his throat, but as he opened his mouth, he chickened out. The words wouldn't come.

"You've been quiet again," said Selene suddenly. "Any more calls with your parents?"

"Uh, no. This case has been taking up enough time."

"Hopefully you'll get a chance. Maybe today."

"Maybe." He searched for a distraction and then remembered the snacks he had stashed. One hand on the wheel, he reached over with the other and popped open the glove compartment. "I know you get snacky when we're on the road. I made sure to bring your favorite."

She smiled and pulled open the aluminum bag. "Kettle chips—just what I wanted so early in the morning."

"They make for a *very* nutritious breakfast."

"Says the guy who eats donut burgers."

"That was one time!"

"One too many." She laughed between munches on her chips.

The next hour on the road was full of a lot more breezy conversation and a lot less overthinking private thoughts. They snacked on kettle chips, chatted about recent events at the hotel, and had a few more laughs at each other's expense. Aiden gestured to Tinsley's town sign on the side of the road as drizzle started up and their drive came to an end.

"We're here," he said.

"That was fast. Where does Mr. Poe live again?"

"It's not far. It's one of these homes on the outskirts of town."

From between the sparse trees, homes with stacked stone chimneys peeked out, their curls of smoke floating into the sky.

"This area's pretty secluded. He must have a caretaker."

Aiden shifted Ghost into park once they reached Mr. Poe's home on Pine Grove Drive. His home was a small single-story cabin-style house. The windows glowed with light from inside.

"Somebody's home," said Aiden. He pulled out the camcorder and filmed another short snippet. "We're here outside Mr. Poe's home. We've run into a wall in this investigation, but we're hoping he can point us in a new direction."

A harsh gust of wind blew as they walked up the front path. The cold air hit their skin, prompting Aiden to pull up the collar of his coat and Selene to tuck her chin into her scarf. They climbed the slippery stone steps holding on to each other in case either tripped. Aiden gripped the ring-shaped knocker and tapped it against the door.

The noise from the TV was muted and a woman's voice croaked, "Hang on, hang on. Gimme a sec to grab the cash. Don't you go anywhere!"

Aiden glanced at Selene. She stared back with a clueless expression on her face. The door flew open and a bespectacled woman with a lopsided top bun and flannel nightgown answered. Her excited face dimmed into a confused, frowning one.

"Who the hell are you?" she asked them. "You're not

Gwendolyn. She was supposed to stop by with my Thin Mints and Tagalongs."

"Err, sorry to disappoint. We're not Girl Scouts. We're paranormal investigators," said Aiden, holding out his hand to shake hers. "I'm Aiden O'Hare. This is Selene Blackstone. We were hoping Samuel Poe was available. We'd like to ask him some questions."

The woman stuffed her cash into the pocket of her night-gown and shook her head. "Pa's no longer with us. He left this place to me. Paranormal investigators, you say? This isn't about his hotel, is it?"

"Actually, it is," said Selene. "Do you have a moment? Maybe we can ask you a couple of questions."

"Only if you have a box of Thin Mints hidden in that coat of yours." She raised her brows at them expectantly.

A light bulb might as well have flicked on above Selene's head. She grabbed the van keys from him and hopped down the stacked stone steps. She returned a moment later with snacks bundled in her arms and a hopeful gleam in her eyes. Aiden smiled wide, on the verge of laughter as he looked from Selene to Mr. Poe's daughter.

"We don't have Girl Scout cookies," admitted Selene. She held up a bag. "But we *do* have kettle chips."

————

Amelia Poe was the daughter of Samuel and his second wife, Elizabeth. She welcomed them into the living room with a lengthy explanation about the Poe family and how she had been estranged from her father for much of her adult life. Selene dutifully listened, offering polite input where neces-sary. Aiden busied himself with glances around the home, studying the wood-paneled walls and the photos that hung on them.

The home was toasty thanks to the blazing flames in the fireplace. They sat down on the couch with a furry bearskin rug beneath their socks (Amelia insisted they take off their boots in the house), and Amelia poured them coffee.

"You were born after Mr. Poe sold the hotel?" Aiden asked.

Amelia nodded. "After what happened with the hotel, Pa packed up and moved to Tinsley. Maresburg had too many bad memories for him. He got a job working in the local mines and met my mom, Elizabeth. Things between them worked 'til it didn't. They got divorced when I was eight. Ma moved away. I spent the rest of my childhood living here with him."

"Did he ever talk about his time at the hotel—or maybe even his first wife, Maya?"

"I know enough. Some of it from Pa. Some of it things I've pieced together myself over time. You say you're paranormal investigators?" she asked, frowning over the rim of her coffee cup. "Then you must know all about the hotel situation. Lots of weird goings-on."

Selene leaned closer, her elbows on her thighs. "We know no record of Maya after she married your father in 1957 up until her death in1960."

"Oh, *that*. Maya had a few different names. She was an aspiring actress and tried out some stage names. Pa never liked talking about her. If I'm honest with you, part of the reason he and Ma never worked out is 'cause he was still not over her. He felt very guilty about the whole thing. He wasn't the best husband."

"How so?"

"I'm sure you've heard," said Amelia. "He kept Maya at

the hotel most days. She wasn't really allowed to go anywhere. He thought it was for the best 'cause she was...she wasn't well."

"She had an illness?" Aiden prompted. He hadn't touched his cup of coffee in minutes, his gaze trained on Amelia.

"No...not exactly. He thought she..." Amelia inhaled a breath, gathering courage, and then dropped her voice to a whisper. "There was always talk about Maya being into witchcraft."

A quizzical look fixed itself onto Aiden's face. He glanced at Selene as her eyes clouded with worry behind her bold-framed glasses. He inhaled a frustrated breath at his ineptitude in comforting her and refocused on Amelia. He had to keep his cool.

"That sounds like a big accusation to make about your own wife," he said.

"I'm told strange things happened around Maya. Things like her levitating and her eyes going black. He had his reasons." She shrugged and drained the last of her coffee. She reached for Aiden's untouched cup and swallowed a large mouthful.

"Oh, actually, I was going to drink—"

"You don't mind, do you? You've barely sipped from this," she interrupted before another mouthful.

Aiden's cheek twitched, but he let it go with a forced chuckle. "Uh, no. Drink up. I'll grab coffee on the road."

"It's just talking about this makes me anxious. You know, bad family history."

"Is it alright for us to proceed?" he asked. She drained the last of the cup, wiping her mouth on the sleeve of her night-gown with a nod. "How did Maya pass?"

"That...that I don't know. Pa said it happened in the night. He checked on her before lights out and she was alive and well. Then the next morning he found her in her bed. She was clutching some mirror."

Selene met Aiden's gaze. She was thinking what he was thinking. The gold-plated, floral-patterned hand mirror had been left on Selene's bed. She hadn't touched it since Aiden had locked it in the hotel safe in his room.

"He was devastated—sold the hotel not long after. That's when the Dunn family bought it and that girl died."

"You mean the first incident?"

"Rhonda Dunn," said Amelia, nodding. "She died in her sleep. They found her in her bed—she was even younger than Maya. You'd think the tragedy would stop there, but nope. Ever since it's like the hotel is cursed."

"What did Mr. Poe think about what happened to the Dunns' daughter?"

"Not sure. He never discussed it, but I started researching everything myself when I got old enough. You know who you should talk to is Rhonda's sister," Amelia told them somberly. "Cordelia Dunn. She still lives in Maresburg last I heard. Rhonda's other siblings have all passed, but Cordelia should be sixty-four or sixty-five and she's still alive. I spoke to her once, and I saw it."

"Saw what?" Selene asked.

Amelia's eyes enlarged as she spoke in her hushed tone, "Why, the creature, of course. She said it herself. She's seen it with her own two eyes."

————

Their return drive into Maresburg was a silent one. Selene leaned her head against the headrest and closed her eyes. Aiden mulled over what they had learned from Amelia. He had already tried looking into the Dunn family. Mr. and Mrs.

Dunn had passed almost twenty years ago. The same was true for their sons, Ernie and Dick, who passed in the last five years. Only Cordelia Dunn remained, but he hadn't been able to find any info on her.

"Someone has to know something," said Aiden, thinking aloud. "If Cordelia Dunn is still alive, she might be the missing piece to the puzzle."

"I'm stuck on Mrs. Poe being a witch." Selene was frowning as she turned over Mrs. Poe's photos in her hands. Her fingers traced the smooth surface of the decades-old photographs.

"That explains why she said Mr. Poe didn't accept her for who she was."

"I understand her now. It must've been so horrible for her."

Selene's voice dropped off, as though even another word caused too much of an ache in her throat. She turned her head to the van window and watched the gray scenery whiz by.

Aiden clenched the wheel, searching his brain for what to say. Nothing seemed like it would be enough. Anything he thought up felt hollow and inadequate when the fact of the matter was he didn't know what it was like to live as a witch. He couldn't understand what witches experienced, living lives of paranoia and fear. As a man without paranormal powers, he would never know firsthand.

But it was also why he could no longer cling to sarcasm in uncomfortable moments like these. He needed to evolve beyond the logic-based, emotionless Aiden O'Hare he had always been—closed off and selfish like Dad. Selene deserved a partner who provided unrelenting vocal support.

"You don't need to stop if you don't want," he said, stretching his arm across their seats. He found her hand in her lap, curling it inside his. "You can talk about it anytime you want. I'm listening."

Selene inhaled a shallow breath and tore her eyes off the glass. "It's hard thinking about what witches like Mrs. Poe had to go through—what witches like Grandma Luna had to go through. I keep thinking, that could easily be me. It *was* me in Brimrock. I guess I'm more afraid than I thought of being in that situation again."

"You won't be," he promised. "I'm not going to let it happen."

A half-hearted smile tipped one corner of her mouth upward. "I appreciate the dedication."

"At your service. Twenty-four seven. Rain or shine. Three hundred and sixty-five days of the—"

"I get it," Selene interrupted with a short laugh like a beautiful melody to his ears. "But we can't give up now. We need to solve this thing. For everyone at the Mhoon, but for Mrs. Poe too. And Rhonda Dunn. Even her sister, Cordelia."

"Wait a second," said Aiden as the thought occurred to him. "Amelia said Cordelia would be sixty-four or five."

"What about it?"

"Her parents bought the hotel, then sold it. But we know Cordelia still lives in Maresburg."

"Aiden, I don't know where you're going with—"

"Remember what Omar told us the night we found him outside your door?"

"That something's off about me?"

"No, about Mrs. Mhoon. She's not who she says she is," he said as the town edges of Maresburg quickly approached. "What if Cordelia Dunn is Mrs. Mhoon?"

CHAPTER FIFTEEN

Phoebe and Tom's wedding day arrived to mixed feelings. Mr. Mhoon seemed happy he'd no longer be tasked with menial wedding prep chores. Mrs. Mhoon whined about the unfinished decor and forecasted gloomy weather. Omar expressed disgruntlement the nuptials were carrying on regardless of the paranormal threat at the hotel. Phoebe was calmest of all, either indifferent to her surroundings or accepting of them.

Aiden and Selene didn't plan on attending, but on the morning of, Phoebe told them they would be. They were seated in the dining room nibbling through breakfast when she floated by their table.

"You should show early if you'd like seating," she warned. Her box dye beehive hair looked redder and taller than usual, as if in honor of the special day. "My mother invited many people in town. I expect only a handful should show, but if you've seen the courtyard arrangement, you'd know the seating situation is lacking."

They started to interject, stuttering in a search for the polite words to tell her they wouldn't be there, but she wandered off before they could. Aiden stared blankly at Selene from across the table.

"I don't have a tuxedo," he said flatly. "I don't even have a tie packed."

"Who are you telling? The nicest dress I have is a sweater dress I bought on sale for twenty bucks."

Interest flickered in Aiden's hazel eyes. "Is that the blue one? I like the blue one."

"You say that about every dress," she answered with an exasperated laugh. "Actually, you say that about just about everything I wear."

"It's not my fault you look good in—*and out of*—everything."

An involuntary heat left her cheeks flushed. "Real smooth, Casanova, but maybe we should figure out what we're going to do about today before we get carried away. Maybe attending the wedding is a good idea."

"That might be the worst sentence I've ever heard come out of your mouth, and that includes the time you said the film adaption of *The Hobbit* is better than the book."

"It definitely is, but that's beside the point. We can use the wedding as a chance to do some snooping," said Selene, sneaking a glance around the dining room. The other guests finished their breakfast and headed off one by one. "It'll give us a chance to keep an eye on the Mhoons. Then while they're distracted, we can sneak off and gather intel. Omar seemed so sure something was in their office. I'm assuming he was looking for info about Mrs. Mhoon and her identity."

Aiden's hazel gaze brightened into an amber as he grinned. "That's actually a pretty good plan."

Selene returned his grin and hopped to her feet. "At this point you shouldn't be surprised. Now c'mon, we should go get ready."

———

It had been a difficult few days with the discovery about Mrs. Poe and Selene's worry over her dreams. Their investigation seemed to only grow more complicated the deeper they dug into the case. They were no closer to learning the truth as the day they arrived; every time they thought they had taken a step forward, they were forced another two back.

As Selene returned to her hotel room and pulled open the closet door, she ignored the self-doubt plaguing her. It sought to sabotage her anytime she tried to put her investigative hat on and prove she was a capable member of the *Paranormal Hunters* team. Anytime she thought about her dreams or the mirror that had mysteriously turned up on her bed. Were her vivid dreams a result of the creature in the hotel? Who had broken into her room and left the mirror for her to find?

In the very least, Aiden deserved to know the full extent of her dreams. On their drive back from Tinsley, she'd almost told him. Every time she considered it, flashes of her dream replayed in her head. The warmth she felt when she woke after seeing Luna, finally spending time with her, was indescribable. It was like a real moment in time and she wasn't sure if she was ready to give that up so soon.

Selene picked her cable-knit sweater dress off the rack and laid it on the bed for when she emerged from her shower. Hopefully the Mhoons wouldn't mind. Fancy cocktail dresses hadn't been on her list of must-haves when she packed for her travels with Aiden.

She showered, styled her curls into a crown braid, and applied light makeup. The navy blue sweater dress she paired with knee-high boots. After a last full body mirror check, she stuffed her key card into her bra and moved for the door.

"You look snazzy," came Grace's voice from behind. "I take it you're attending the big event today."

"Kind of by force," said Selene with a small smile. "Are you headed down?"

Grace smoothed her hands down the front of her black scoop-neck dress, her nails shining with a fresh coat of cherry apple red. "I went downstairs for a cup of coffee and lost track of time. Now I'm behind schedule. You go on without me. I need to fix my hair."

"See you downstairs."

Aiden was already waiting on her. Selene descended the staircase to the surprising sight of a full foyer. Phoebe might've been right about Mrs. Mhoon inviting the town. Selene knew almost none of them by name, but as the sea of people trooped down the hall, it was obvious there'd be a seating issue. She joined Aiden's side.

"You look handsome," she said, kissing his cheek.

For as simple of a dresser as Aiden was, he pulled off a white dress shirt and black trousers well—too well as her stomach gave a funny flip and the room grew hotter in temperature. The wedding didn't have to only be reserved for work; maybe they could have some fun themselves.

Aiden touched his hand to the small of her back and the heat flushed deeper on her skin. He moved closer as they walked, his lips hovering by her ear so no one else could hear. "We're supposed to be investigating right now, but it's a little hard to concentrate with you in that dress."

Selene's cheeks burned hotter than fire by the time they reached the courtyard. The worst part was she had to keep her cool. Pretend she wasn't hot and bothered as dirty thoughts invaded her mind and Aiden's touch only made matters worse. She was half a second away from hauling him off to a dark corner of the courtyard when Mrs. Mhoon stopped them.

"Oh, good…you're here!" she said in a more chipper mood than the past few days. "Phee mentioned you were coming. Some of the hotel guests didn't feel comfortable. I think the Jacksons had some sightseeing to do, and Yvette Howell declined too. You could've worn something a little more…wedding appropriate, Selene."

The Mhoon matriarch left them on that note. Aiden held in a laugh and produced a snort instead. Selene's eyes bulged before she spun around and tracked Mrs. Mhoon's retreating form with a glare. How dare she have the nerve to comment on her outfit?

"As if we wanted to come!" Selene said indignantly. "She does realize we're living out of a suitcase, right?"

"Would it be a chat with her if she didn't nitpick?"

Aiden was right. Selene smirked at him, angling her body against his as she rested a hand on his chest. "How about we get this snooping for intel thing over with? I want to enjoy the afternoon."

He waggled his brows and said, "That's some great incentive."

The courtyard filled up over the course of the next hour. Aiden and Selene blended in with the others, mingling when necessary. They even filmed another short update for their episode. When the ceremonial music began and guests moved to take up their places, they drifted to the outskirts of the courtyard and waited for an opening.

The moment everyone's attention was on the parents of the bride and groom walking down the aisle, they slipped away. Selene fronted their escape attempt while Aiden came up the rear. The first floor of the hotel was like a ghost town as applause and music from the courtyard spilled inside. They stopped outside the Mhoons' back office and checked left and right.

"Coast is clear," Aiden mumbled. He stood guard outside the door like a muscly bouncer at a club.

Selene held her hand above the doorknob. Her signature silver sparks emitted from her palm and the magicked lock unclicked. Inside the office, Aiden once again stayed by the door. Selene flicked on a light and rushed to the desk.

"Sheds some light on why Omar was doing what he was," said Aiden, arms folded. "He did say she isn't who she says she is. It'd explain why no online record exists for Marie Mhoon."

"He might be right. Her name has to be on one of these documents."

Selene sorted through the stack on the desk, but resorted to the drawers after nothing consequential turned up. The drawers were more of the same. She yanked open each one and searched their contents. The filing cabinets were next.

"Is everything in Mr. Mhoon's name?" Selene pushed shut another drawer on the filing cabinet.

"Wait a second, what about over there with the awards?"

Aiden crossed the office, stopping in front of the credenza. Mr. Mhoon had displayed various hospitality awards he had won over the years. The plaques gleamed from where they hung on the wall, but it wasn't the awards Aiden was pointing out. He crouched in front of the credenza's cabinet doors and drew both open. Selene headed over to watch.

"We might have something here. Behind this box of cleaning products. It's a…it's a tote bag."

Selene knitted her brows. "What would be important about a tote bag?"

"It's what's inside. Take a look for yourself."

She gasped as Aiden stood up and turned over the tote bag on the credenza counter space. From inside the tote bag poured an assortment of items, like manila folders, crumpled papers and identification cards banded together. She picked up the stack of identification cards and removed the rubber band around them.

"These are all different states. Different names," said Selene. "All with Mrs. Mhoon's picture."

"If that's her real name."

"Apparently not. Kelly Rhodes. Patricia Sanders. Marie Mhoon!"

"Any Cordelia Dunns?"

Selene shook her head. "None that I see. But if these are all fake, then maybe the real one *does* say Cordelia Dunn."

"Well, I think it's safe to say Mrs. Mhoon moves up the suspects list."

"I'm confused why she would have so many aliases in the first place."

"She didn't want to be found. The Dunns abandoned the business and moved after what happened to their daughter. The Mhoons didn't buy the place until the '80s. What better way to return to town than with a new and improved identity? No one who knew her as a child would recognize her as an adult."

"What about the Dreamling? How does that fit in?"

Aiden paused to think, a studious expression settling onto his face. "If she encountered it as a kid the night Rhonda died, she's been aware this entire time the Dreamling is feeding off of guests. Maybe she's decided to just…let it do its thing."

"None of the Mhoons have been harmed."

"It could be some sort of deal. You leave my family alone, you have free reign on the guests."

"Mrs. Mhoon has a key to every room in the hotel. If she's working with the Dreamling, she could've easily snuck into my room and placed the mirror on my bed," theorized Selene as shock jolted her.

"The question is, how do we bring this up?" Aiden asked. He picked up the Wyoming driver's license for a Regina Rayne and then tossed it back onto the pile of other IDs. "We can't march out there and interrupt the wedding. Actually, we can, but it's probably not the most socially acceptable thing to do."

"We'll have to confront her, won't we? Just…just maybe not right now."

Aiden considered her suggestion and then nodded. "Then we should probably put everything the way we found it and get back to the wedding before anyone notices we're missing."

———

"I do," said Phoebe with a dreamy smile on her face.

The courtyard erupted in cheers as Tom leaned in and kissed her. Even Aiden clapped with enthusiasm as the newlywed couple joined hands and jumped the broom. Phoebe's foot caught on the ruffled skirt of her wedding dress and she staggered toward the ground. Everyone *ooh*ed and *aww*ed as Tom caught her a split second before it was too late. The two laughed and waved, signaling they were okay before they rushed down the aisle to a shower of rice sprinkling down.

The festivities moved inside for the reception as the afternoon died and the sky darkened to a shade the color of ash. Light drizzle followed suit within minutes. Mr. Mhoon had set up several rooms for the reception activities, with the formal dining room being the epicenter. When Aiden and

Selene attempted to sit in the second dining room, he put an arm around both of them and led them away.

"Nonsense! You'll be in the formal dining room with us," he said heartily. "You're both two of our most important guests. *I* invited *you* to my hotel—you're helping us out with your investigation—of course you sit with family."

Aiden shot Selene a furtive look she understood. In light of their discovery about Mrs. Mhoon, everything the Mhoons said and did felt suspicious. Their eagerness to have Aiden and Selene in their proximity. Their written request to the show runners of *Paranormal Hunters*, begging them to investigate the hotel. Even the fact that they had purchased a hotel where tragic past events had occurred in the first place. None of it cast them in the best light.

The toasts started with Mr. Mhoon. For the first couple of minutes, he spoke about how proud he was of Phoebe and how happy he was she and Tom had found each other. His speech circled back to himself the longer it went on. Soon he held the room hostage as he rambled on about being a good father and husband.

Finally, a man seated near the head of the table cleared his throat and stood up. Judging by his sandy hair and workman build, he was Tom's father and he wanted a word in edgewise. Mr. Mhoon relented, but only after another minute of closing remarks. The rest of the speakers giving toasts were a lot less self-aggrandizing and a lot more succinct.

Dinner was served and the room broke out in a dozen different conversations. Aiden and Selene remained observant, keeping an eye on those around them, listening in for any discussions of interest. One of the servers Mr. Mhoon had hired approached and offered them wine.

Selene almost turned him down, but on second thought,

she raised her empty glass for him to pour. Aiden eyed her with the beginnings of a teasing smirk.

"Aren't we on the job?"

"One glass of wine doesn't hurt," she said, partially to convince him. *Also* partially to convince herself. "A little fun can't hurt anyway, can it?"

"We have been working hard on this case."

That was all Aiden needed to be convinced. He thanked the server with a nod for pouring him a glass. In a room full of a dozen different voices speaking at once and silverware clanging and clinking, they held their own toast. Their glasses clinked as they swallowed their first taste of wine.

Selene looked around the room. Mr. Mhoon and Mr. Lester were engrossed in a boisterous conversation, the two manly men like bears in a room full of deer. Phoebe and Tom were chatting with Mrs. Mhoon and another woman from town Selene didn't recognize, but she caught a word about the honeymoon.

It was then that the last of Selene's defenses lowered. Everyone deserved a day off sometimes. Besides, Mrs. Mhoon wouldn't ruin her daughter's wedding. It was safe to say no paranormal activity would be going down tonight.

Tonight was a night of celebration.

She turned back to Aiden, a pleasant smile curling her mouth, and said, "I'm actually glad we came. It feels nice to just sit and have dinner and not think about anything."

"Yeah, it does," said Aiden. He grabbed her hand, the brightness in his gaze turning his irises a green as verdant as spring. "How about no more case talk for the rest of the night?"

"So we can talk about how you tried to call me out today for saying *The Hobbit* film adaption was better than the book?" She exploded into a fit of laughter as horror washed over Aiden's face.

Dinner continued until everyone wiped their plates clean and guzzled down several glasses of their drink of choice. Phoebe and Tom cut the cake, which was a four-tier fondant-iced creation baked by Mrs. Mhoon herself.

"I might need to undo the button on my pants," said Aiden as he eyed his slice of cake.

"That's one perk of this sweater dress. No judgmental waistband leaving teeth marks on my skin," she boasted, sitting up straighter.

The party portion of the reception began with Phoebe and Tom's first dance. The drizzle had let up, at least momentarily, as music played and guests soon joined them on the impromptu dance floor known as the courtyard. Aiden chugged the last of his wine and then offered Selene his arm. Her brows jumped as she stared back at him.

Was he really suggesting they dance? What had this alien life-form done with the real Aiden?

"You're not drunk, are you?" she asked in a tone that struck a perfect balance between amusement and suspicion.

He pulled her into him, his ears burning red. "The wine might've lowered an inhibition or two."

"Mmm, sounds promising."

Time ran away from them as the night wore on and the reception continued. The music was a constant, a diverse playlist of slow songs and party songs demanding even the most self-conscious guests start dancing. For that moment the paranormal activity at the Mhoon Hotel didn't matter. It was the furthest thing on anyone's mind.

Selene's stomach hurt from laughing. She and Aiden were a disaster on the dance floor, but that was half the fun. They bungled their way through line dances like the Cupid's

Shuffle and invented their own steps to slower numbers, spinning in their own orbit in a corner of the dance floor.

Aiden held her close for another slow song, his smile small and mysterious. The twinkling string lights reflected in his eyes as they swayed. Another reminder Aiden might not have been the most vocal man, but he expressed himself in other ways—like his studious stares that never failed to conjure warm fuzziness in her chest.

She almost asked him what he was thinking, then stopped herself. It didn't matter what he was thinking. Or what she was thinking. It was a rare carefree moment to bask in before the reality of tomorrow set in. Tonight was theirs.

Mr. Mhoon called for everyone's attention by tapping a fork to his glass. The crowd in the courtyard gathered around as Phoebe and Tom gave another speech. Phoebe mostly offered spiritual platitudes while Tom took a page from Mr. Mhoon's book and boasted about himself and their relationship.

"They prove opposites do attract," Aiden mumbled for Selene's ears only. "They couldn't be more different."

Selene bit back a smile. Aiden had a point. Phoebe Mhoon and Tom Lester had wildly different personalities and outlooks on life. They seemed to exist on different planes. But that must have been what worked for them.

Phoebe announced it was time to toss the bouquet. A gaggle of female guests pushed their way to the front of the crowd, eager for the chance to snag the bouquet before anyone else. Mr. Mhoon counted her down and she threw it into the air from over her shoulder.

Selene looked up when it was already too late. She'd stayed at the back of the crowd beside Aiden with thoughts already on grabbing another slice of wedding cake. She hadn't expected to glance up and spot an airborne bouquet flying toward her. Before she could react, the bundle of flowers bopped her across the head and then dropped to a pitiful stop at her feet. The gaggle of women rushed toward the fallen bouquet in renewed competition.

Aiden grabbed her hand and pulled them out of the line of fire. They escaped inside as shrieks filled the air. One of the women must've wrangled the bouquet from the others. Selene was still in shock when they stopped in the hallway.

"I definitely didn't plan on catching the bouquet," she said, shocked.

"You didn't really catch it, did you? It more so…kind of…ricocheted off your head."

Selene snort-laughed, clapping a hand to her mouth as more threatened to follow. Aiden joined her, his own laugh throaty. She straightened her glasses and leaned against the wall as her laugh died down. Aiden saw the opening and snatched it up. He bent forward and kissed her softly on the mouth. She leaned upward into his kiss, banding her arms around his neck.

It was the private, intimate alone time she'd secretly craved all day. The chance for them to bask in each other's affection without prying eyes. Time to themselves where they could be as flirty and playful and mischievous as they wanted.

The sounds from the reception party echoed from outside. The beats from the music and din of voices sounded both a world away and second away as they hid out in their dark, secluded corner. Nobody was around. Nobody was the wiser.

Selene's feet left the ground as Aiden lifted her up and kissed her harder, more insistently. She gripped his hair with her fingers, drowning in his hot and passionate kiss, dizzied by the lightheadedness it evoked. Her legs found his waist and he began walking them toward the nearest door.

"Some privacy," he grunted, blindly palming for the brass doorknob.

They slipped inside, the door snicking shut behind them. For another stretch in time they stood in the unknown dark space, mixed up in each other's fervent kisses. Selene dragged her mouth along his jawline, fingers still in his hair, kissing her way down his neck. Aiden groaned in throaty approval and carried them deeper into the dark space until what felt like soft fabric brushed her spine.

Finally drawing back for a dizzied, lip-swollen glance around, it dawned on Selene they were in the coat closet. An unfettered giggle escaped her before she bit down hard on her tongue. The shadows fell heavily in the cramped space, but Aiden was grinning, more felt than seen. He brought them up against the blank wall next to the hanging coats, his lips grazing hers.

"We can always run up to one of our rooms," he whispered. His hands traveled lower, skimming the supple underside of her thighs. Her sweater dress rode up, exposing more intimate skin. His body heat emanated off him in thick waves, making her already damp panties that much wetter.

She kissed him to distract herself. With her core throbbing in hunger, she was a goner. The overwhelming need for him to fill her up consumed her like a flame, setting her skin on fire. Light beads of perspiration broke out as she gripped the back of Aiden's neck and parted her lips. He was no different, slipping his tongue into her mouth, the skin beneath her fingers burning.

Their chests pressed together as their kisses grew fiercer and impatient. She was breathless in the most wonderful way, the speed at which her heart raced proof enough. Aiden's heartbeat was as fast, thunderous with no signs of slowing down.

"Tell me, Selene," he groaned, kissing up her throat. "What do you want?"

"I want to untangle my foot from this coat sleeve."

"Huh? Oh. *Oh*! Let me—"

Quiet snickers filled the closet as they fought off the coat sleeve wound around Selene's foot. At one point, Aiden almost fell backward into the rack of coats, but saved himself and Selene at the last second. Once her foot was freed, Selene kissed him, encouraging him to pick her up again.

"This moment wouldn't be us if there wasn't a mishap," she muttered breathily. "And to answer your question, doing it in the coat closet has just been added to my bucket list."

He puffed out a laugh and resumed his kisses on her throat. His hands were fast. One held onto her, keeping them against the wall. The other fished for a condom in his back pocket. She provided the assist with his pants, unbuckling his belt like a pro. It took some maneuvering to slip on the condom, slip off her panties, and slip comfortably back into position, but within seconds, they pulled it off.

Selene gasped as he fitted the length of himself inside her. Even after so many times together, it was still a shock to the system—taking him in was no short order. She wrapped her arms tighter around him and reveled in the electric current rippling through her body down to her toes.

As Aiden began pumping into her, she pressed her lips to his neck. At first in kisses then in love bites, staving off the moans which begged for escape. She bounced with him, sliding her hips back and then forth in sync with his. For each deeper thrust, she squeezed him harder. Her mouth met his and he filled his hands with the cheeks of her curvy backside.

They were on the fast track to exploding. Their movements frantic and their bodies sweaty, they stopped caring about making noise. A primal grunt tore from Aiden's throat as he planted one hand against the wall, bracing himself. Selene's mouth fell open for a moan, the electric shockwaves intensifying whenever his length tapped the right spot.

Then a third voice joined them. Out of nowhere, drowning out their pants and moans, was a spine-chilling scream piercing the night.

The horrifying sound caught them so off guard, Aiden almost dropped her, and Selene pulled a little too tightly on his hair. He managed to set her safely down on her feet as they fought to catch their breaths. They rushed to right themselves, buttoning and zipping. In Selene's case, stuffing her discarded panties in Aiden's pants pocket.

Just like that, their lust-fueled haze dissipated. Gone without a real finish.

Aiden popped his head into the hall and then stepped out with Selene closely behind him. The others were starting to file in from outside. Mrs. Mhoon appeared at the top of the staircase, looking more frazzled than they'd ever expected to see a prim and proper woman like her.

"It's Yvette Howell!" she screeched. "S-she's dead!"

CHAPTER SIXTEEN

Yvette Howell's death mirrored Freddie Koffman's. She was found lying in bed, eyes wide open. No injuries or other bodily harm. Just a stopped heart.

Emergency responders flooded the hotel minutes after Aiden phoned 911. The wedding guests were ordered to go home. Any hotel guests like the Jacksons and Esther from room four were told to wait in the parlor downstairs. Aiden and Selene were relegated to the first floor too, despite their best efforts to sneak upstairs for a look at the scene.

Humbolt showed up, much to their surprise, looking like a new man—at least in terms of wardrobe. His shirt was no longer untucked and his pants were ironed. His gold badge was pinned proudly to his chest, and if Aiden didn't know any better, he had chucked his old, drab trench coat and purchased a new one. He cast them a gloomy look from afar before he disappeared upstairs.

"We should be up there," said Selene, arms crossed. "The Dreamling got Yvette. We should've seen this coming."

Aiden couldn't disagree. Though he had hardly said a word to his fellow hotel guest, Selene had kept him in the loop about Yvette's difficulties sleeping. She had appeared more and more distressed, more exhausted over the past few days. Even tonight, she had turned down the Mhoons' wedding invitation and had shut herself off alone in her room.

He sighed. "We could've done more. We could've...we could've kept a better eye on her."

The troubled expression on Selene's face said enough. She dropped her face into her hands. Her own exhaustion became apparent as she lost her straight posture and her shoulders caved inward. He put his arm around her, fighting the feeling of dread pitted in his stomach.

Detective Humbolt descended halfway down the staircase. His gaze landed on them in the foyer and he beckoned them up. They accepted his wordless invitation, following him upstairs. He brought them to the icebox that was room nine.

Aiden glanced at the thermostat on the wall. Thirty-three degrees. "How did it get this cold in here?"

"That remains to be determined," said Detective Humbolt. He was eying them closely. "You've been working this case the past few days, haven't you?"

"Yes, but you haven't," said Aiden. "I thought you were pulled off the case and that it was closed."

"It's been reopened as of an hour ago." Humbolt motioned for the last uniformed police officer in the room to leave and then shut the door after him. He cut across the room, letting his gaze travel from the bed where Yvette's body had been to the other furniture nearby. "Look, I don't have time for bullshit. Something is up at this hotel. With a second death in weeks, I'm now convinced the explanation might be less than...rational."

"Is that your way of saying you think it is a paranormal entity, Detective?" Selene asked boldly.

He glared at her. "It's my way of saying I know you two are as suspicious as they come. I wouldn't be surprised if you're hiding pertinent info from the case."

Aiden and Selene shared a glance. Neither uttered a word aloud, but their look was enough; their telepathic communication was unmatched. Selene didn't think it was a good idea to share what they had learned in recent days. Aiden couldn't argue with her; not only was Humbolt untrustworthy, he was still an asshole.

"We're stumped," said Aiden flatly. He shrugged. "Sorry, Detective."

Humbolt sneered, baring his teeth like a dog on the attack. "Yeah, I bet you're sorry. I'm sorry too. Sorry this hotel is closed 'til further notice. Let's head downstairs and let the Mhoons know. I'm sure they'll be pleased their trusted paranormal investigators have failed to help them."

Aiden and Selene hesitated as Humbolt held open the door and waited for them to pass through. With reluctant sighs, they had no choice but to play along. Before Aiden followed Selene out the door, he glanced at Yvette's empty bed, still with the grooves of her body in the sheets, and his stomach flipped spotting the small glob of ink on the carpet. When he looked back at the door, Humbolt was surveying him with a heavy brow. Aiden walked past him with his shoulders square and gaze equally as cold, but one thing was clear. This wasn't going to be pretty.

———

Mr. Mhoon was furious. He waited until Humbolt and the authorities had left before he exploded in the parlor room. The guests had gone upstairs to pack their things; they had to leave the next morning. That left Aiden and Selene alone with the rest of the Mhoons.

"What is the point of having you two here?" he demanded in his booming voice. "I've got a second death on my hands. The guests are hysterical. Now my business is shut down!"

"Mr. Mhoon, we're going to do our best—"

"The situation has gone from a quirky haunting to a dangerous and deadly one. Two bodies in two weeks means this is out of control," he ranted. "You were supposed to bring me some notoriety with your show. You weren't supposed to bring *more* death."

Omar spoke for what seemed to be the first time that evening. For the duration of the wedding, he had sulked in the background. "Willy, you can't possibly think this situation was ever a positive one?"

"Shut up, Omar! I've already told you, this isn't one of your crackpot investigations!"

Aiden and Selene stood in shock as the brothers quarreled. Omar glared at his older and bigger brother with umbrage before he listened. He fell silent, blending into the background once again. Mr. Mhoon rounded on them.

"You have less than forty-eight hours to solve this thing!" he growled. Mrs. Mhoon and the others watched in stunned silence. They didn't dare utter a peep. "If you fail to do so, guess what? You're fired! And I won't be paying your stupid show for wasting my time! You've done nothing but make the situation worse!"

Aiden had had enough. He wasn't going to stand around letting Mr. Mhoon berate him and Selene. A coolness washed over him as he stuck his hands in his pockets and held Mr. Mhoon's contemptuous gaze.

"Selene and I have been hired to solve the paranormal mystery at this hotel," explained Aiden, his face deadpan and his tone matter-of-fact. "That's exactly what we've been doing, which explains our confusion when we found out the truth about your wife."

Mr. Mhoon sputtered, his cheeks bulging as he filled with angry, hot air. "What. Are. You. On. About?"

Selene stiffened at his side, but Aiden continued. "We know about the aliases. We also know that your wife has been hiding the fact that her family—*the Dunn family*—used to own this place. She has access to every room in the hotel. She left Mrs. Poe's hand mirror in Selene's room. Tonight she happened to come across Yvette Howell's dead body. If I didn't know any better, I'd think she possibly has something to do with the creature that's been on the prowl here."

"I…what?" Mrs. Mhoon gasped for more air, a hand clutched to her chest.

"So you aren't who you say you are!" Omar blurted out from his corner of the room. "I've long suspected. I've been trying to dig up your past for a long while now."

Offense flashed in Mr. Mhoon's eyes as he growled, "Why would you feel the need to look into my wife's background, Omar?"

"You married and met out of nowhere, Willy. The whole family was curious."

"Bull! Mama never said a bad word about Marie—"

"To your face!" Omar snapped. "Then she fell ill and was too sick to express concern."

Mrs. Mhoon's mouth fell open and then she shook her head side to side. Tears filled her eyes, though they did not fall. She used a doily off the nearby table to dab them away.

"I suppose it's like Juliet says in *Romeo and Juliet*," said Aiden calmly. His focus was on Mrs. Mhoon. "What's in a name? That which we call a rose by any other name would smell as sweet—except in this case, it smells rotten."

Mr. Mhoon and Omar fell silent. Mrs. Mhoon gasped. Selene's brows had jumped high on her forehead as she watched the confrontation unfold. Aiden pressed harder.

"I don't mean to be presumptuous, Mrs. Mhoon, but is there a reason why you've changed your name six times? Well, at least six. There could've been more counterfeit IDs, but we lost count."

The Mhoon matriarch gawked at him as if a bucket of freezing cold water had been dumped on her. Mouth agape, eyes bulging, she couldn't speak, offering sharp intakes of air. Mr. Mhoon jumped in with the save for his wife.

"How dare you?" he bellowed. "What've you been doing, snooping around our private possessions? You have no right! I ought to call the police. Humbolt'll be back here in a flash!"

"Oh, give it up, Marie. Come clean with what's going on," said Omar.

Mrs. Mhoon broke down into loud sobs. She covered her face with shaky hands. Still in her reception dress, Phoebe shot up from her seat on the sofa and rushed over to console her mother. Mrs. Mhoon shrugged her off as she released a deep, wailing cry.

Selene frowned, looking sideways at Aiden. He knew that look; she was feeling guilty. Maybe he had gone a little too hard, but he didn't regret it. The hotel was closing and the mysterious creature was still afoot. The innocent who had died deserved justice in some fashion. As did their families.

"Look what you've done!" Mr. Mhoon said over his wife's cries. "If I'd've known you'd do nothing but cause trouble, I never would've hired you."

"They're not causing trouble. They're solving a mystery you've profited off of!" Omar exclaimed.

"Don't you mouth off!"

"Mrs. Mhoon," said Selene gently, "if you could just tell

us what's going on. We need to know if we're going to solve the case. Why did you change your name? Is it because you didn't want any association with what happened to your sister?"

"My sister? What on earth are you on about?" Mrs. Mhoon shrieked. "My sister never passed and my family never owned this hotel!"

"Of course they did. The Dunns purchased this place from Mr. Poe."

"I'm *not* a Dunn!"

"We found your IDs in your—"

"The fake IDs have nothing to do with the creature and everything to do with me!"

Aiden stared. "I don't understand."

Mrs. Mhoon lowered her hands from her face. "My life hasn't always been so…so put together. I haven't always been perfect! I have a past I'm not proud of."

"Marie…" Mr. Mhoon warned.

"No, Willy, it's time to come clean." She sniffled. Her bottom lip trembled as she looked at Phoebe. "My only daughter deserves to know her mother was a criminal."

"Criminal! What type of criminal?" Tom asked with judgment imbued in his tone. "What kind of family have I married into?"

Everyone ignored him. Phoebe took a step closer to her mother. "I always suspected something was amiss. Your natal chart has always hinted at a big, dark secret in your past."

"Mrs. Mhoon, I'm not following. If you have no relation to the Dunn family, then why do you have the fake IDs?"

"B-because I used to commit identity fraud. I used to create fake identities and rack up large bills under those names," she explained between gasps of air. Her feathery gray hair wilted the harder she cried. "I created over ten different personas and racked up thousands in credit fraud. I was sentenced to five years, but was released after two on... on good behavior. We've been paying the money back ever since."

Selene directed her attention to Mr. Mhoon. "That's why you've been so eager to profit off of the paranormal activity! You've been making mugs and T-shirts and conducting interviews about owning the most haunted hotel in the country to pay off the debt!"

Mr. Mhoon folded his bulky arms and muttered, "It's none of your concern what my wife and I do with our profit."

"Willy and I met when I was in prison. He was participating in a pen pal program and we fell in love over our letters," said Mrs. Mhoon. "He promised I could have a fresh start when I was released and we did...we started over with this hotel! It was all very romantic."

Aiden and Selene exchanged dubious glances.

Phoebe slowly lowered herself onto the sofa. "I didn't foresee our family history being so sordid."

"So you have nothing to do with the Dunn family," repeated Aiden as frustration set in. He brought his hand to his forehead and massaged his temples. He had been sure this was the lead they had been searching for. How could they have gotten it completely wrong?

Selene sighed, sharing his sentiment. "I'm so sorry we accused you of being involved, Mrs. Mhoon. Your past is none of our business. We were only trying to solve the case."

"It doesn't matter. Pack your bags!" snarled Mr. Mhoon. "You've outed my wife's past and caused her distress. You failed to do your job and catch the creature. Now my hotel is shutting down because of your incompetence. It's time for you to go!"

"We can go if that's what you want," Aiden said coldly.

He refused to let Mr. Mhoon raise his voice at Selene. "But it's not our fault we've struggled with this case. If it was easy you, or even the Maresburg Police Department, would've solved it decades ago. Yet here we are."

"He has a point. You've never wanted it solved, have you?" Omar asked his older brother. "You've enjoyed the notoriety, the cash flowing in!"

"Shut up, Omar!"

"NO!" Mrs. Mhoon screamed. Her shrill voice was loudest of all. When everyone fell silent again, she cast a stern and motherly glare. Her tears had dried up and she was no longer crying. "We can't go on like this anymore. It's…it's time for this to be resolved. What have we become that we're willing to give up our business because of some evil being in our home? Willy, we can't fire Aiden and Selene. They have to solve this."

Mr. Mhoon gave a begrudging nod. "You have two days. Then I'm putting this place on the market."

He didn't wait for an agreement. He stormed out of the room. Aiden and Selene remained where they were as the others slowly left one by one. Omar was last, shooting them a curious glance before shuffling off. Once alone, Aiden turned to Selene. She stared back, nibbling on her bottom lip.

"What now?"

Aiden exhaled a low breath, a glum feeling roiling in his stomach. "Back to square one."

CHAPTER SEVENTEEN

The house was cozy and warm as Selene descended the staircase. The once-dusty chain-link chandeliers were lit up, illuminating the area. With the shadows gone, the family portraits no longer peered down at her with scowls. Instead their lips stretched into small, amused smiles, their gazes seemingly following her.

There was a slight blur to everything inside the gothic home, like it had been bathed with a dreamy filter. The curtains were no longer drawn over the windows. Outside snow fell and neighbors caroled, their cheery voices faint but pleasant. Selene padded down the first-floor hall, glancing at the festive decorations they'd put up. Evergreen wreaths and tiny sprigs of holly hung and the fresh scent of cinnamon was in the air.

Yukie trotted over with her tongue out. Selene bent down and scooped up the furry little terrier, walking into the living room. She stopped as she set her sights on the others. Everything was just as it was supposed to be.

Mom and Uncle Zee were by the large stained glass window with cups of cider. Noelle and Aunt BiBi were seated on the sofa, chatting away. Aiden was by the fireplace; he winked when he saw her. Luna was in the middle of the room, arms wide open, eyes twinkling. The long black dress she wore swept the floor as she welcomed Selene.

"We've been waiting for you, Selly," Luna said softly.

Selene wandered deeper into the room, sitting down in the armchair. Her gaze fell on the book on the coffee table. The cover was familiar, but the title was fuzzy. She picked it up and opened to the first page. Those words were a blur too. She took off her glasses and wiped them on the hem of her sweater.

"Have some cider, Selene," said Mom. She smiled and raised her glass. She looked exactly as she always had, tight jet-black curls and an apron hanging over her front from her meticulous cleaning.

Selene forgot about the book and smiled back. "I didn't know you all would be here. Is today Christmas?"

Luna only simpered. She stepped forward and brandished a neatly wrapped gift for Selene to take. "We got you something special."

"Open it!" urged Noelle. The others nodded enthusiastically and leaned closer.

Selene's smile widened and her fingers tugged on the red ribbon tied across the top. The ribbon fell away and she gently tore apart the wrapping paper. The box itself was plain and white. She opened its flaps and peered inside.

Empty except for a coil of braided rope.

She stared at the rope in puzzlement, wondering if it were possibly a gag gift of some kind. Her eyes flicked upward and she gasped. The box tumbled from her grasp and to the floor. The others in the room had changed. Noelle and Aunt Bibi were gone. Mom and Uncle Zee had disappeared from their place by the large window. Aiden was no longer by the fireplace, winking at her. Even Luna was nowhere to be found.

Replacing them were faces she never thought she'd see again. Miriam from the library fixed her horn-rimmed glasses and sneered. Mayor Grisby was by the window, eviscerating her with a faraway glare. Other faceless townspeople flanked him, like vultures. Directly across from her was none other than Priscilla Myers and her sickly sweet smile—her eyes ringed with dark circles and her gray gums exposed.

"Stupid girl," she cackled in her bloodcurdling, witchy tone. "I see you've learned nothing."

The others in the room began to creep closer, caging her in. The rope from the box flew up on its own accord and curled around her body, winding tightly like a snake with its prey. Strapped down to the armchair, no matter how hard she fought against the binding, she couldn't break free. Panic set in with a rapid heartbeat as she squirmed and squirmed. Priscilla stopped in front of her and raised her wizened, claw-like hands. Two orbs of crimson red light hovered above her palms as she prepared to set fire to the armchair.

"Did you really think it was over?" she asked Selene. "Did you really think you'd gotten away?"

Selene opened her mouth and screamed.

Her body rolled to the left and smacked hard into the floor. She was sweaty and shaking, still screaming. She was back in her room at the Mhoon Hotel, bathed in morning light. She jumped to her feet despite the aches coursing through her body from the fall and dashed for the door. Her heart thudded painfully in her chest as alarm bells rang in her ear.

If she knew nothing else in that moment, she knew of the need to run.

Selene almost collided with Grace out in the hall. The

graceful woman was already dressed for the day, her pin curl hair and red-lacquered nails both shining. She gasped and held out her hands as if prepared to catch Selene should she fall.

"Selene, what's going on? Are you alright? You look like you've seen a ghost."

"AIDEN!" Selene screamed. "Where's Aiden?"

She hurried down the hall and stopped outside his door. She pounded her fist, her chest erratically rising and falling. She couldn't calm herself down no matter how hard she tried, failing to inhale a good breath of air.

Her dream had felt so real. It had been real as far as she could tell. Right down to the voices and the scents. Even the scratchy feel of the rope as it burned into her skin.

"Selene, what's wrong?" Aiden asked from behind. He had come up the stairs and spotted her outside his door. Using his long legs, he closed the gap between them in a single stride. His arms wrapped around her as she buried her face into his chest. "You're trembling and soaked in sweat. Let's get you inside."

He unlocked the door with his key card and guided her inside his room. He eased her into the chair by the window and brought her a cup of water. The concern was written on his face, his reddish-brown brows pushed together. As she sipped the water, he knelt before her and gently brushed sweat-damp curls from her face. The lightest graze of his palm was an immediate comfort and she closed her eyes, using it as incentive to calm her erratic heartbeat.

"Tell me what happened," he said calmly.

It was time to come clean about her dreams. Selene sucked in a breath and then started at the beginning. She told him about how exhausted she had been when they arrived at the Mhoon Hotel. She went into detail about the first time she'd enjoyed a night of uninterrupted sleep and how she'd dreamed of Grandma Luna.

Though he kept his expression neutral, a range of emotions flickered in his eyes. First, relief when she described her night of sleep and then confusion when she told him about how real the dreams felt. She finished with confessing why she had hesitated telling him about them.

"I knew you'd think it had to do with the case," she said tiredly. "It was stupid of me, but…I don't regret it. I've never known Luna and these dreams made me feel like I did."

"Selene, you could've told me."

She couldn't look him in the eye. She stared at an arbitrary spot on the hardwood flooring instead. "I wanted to. I guess you're not the only one keeping things to yourself."

"We should probably stop doing that." He leaned closer and pressed his lips to her brow. His left hand smoothed back more moist curls while his right fell in her lap and gripped her thigh. "We're a lot better when we work as a team. Both in our relationship and our investigations."

"It's called a learning curve," she teased with the scantest smirk.

Her heartbeat had settled and she was no longer shaking. The fear had receded at least for the moment. Aiden's words helped, but also his presence and touch. They *were* on the same team and it was important to never forget that. So long as they stuck together, they'd figure out a way forward.

"I need a shower. I'm a sweaty mess." Selene pulled off her glasses and dug her fingers into her limp curls.

Aiden grinned slowly. "It's a weird coincidence, but I happen to have one in my room."

She bit her bottom lip and said, "I walked right into that one, didn't I?"

———

By late morning, Selene was feeling like herself again. She dressed in a V-neck shirt, some jeans, and her favorite patch-work cardigan, stuffing her curls underneath a knitted beanie. Aiden drove them into town for some coffee and breakfast at Ms. Coco's, but first, she suggested a pitstop at Hidden Senses.

"I need answers from Phoebe about my dreams," said Selene.

"Aren't she and Tom supposed to be leaving for their honeymoon?"

"I think that's delayed with everything that's going on. She wasn't at the hotel so that must mean she's at her shop. The last time I visited, she seemed to know more than she was letting on about my dreams."

"Why would she keep that from you?" Aiden asked as he switched the turn signal on. He hooked a left at the intersection and searched for parking on the street.

"Everything Phoebe says is cloaked in mystery. She double-talks a lot."

"Do you believe she's really a seer?"

Selene hesitated for a second. "I'm not sure. I believe in the paranormal and the mystical—how can I not being who I am—but there's a good chance Phoebe follows in her parents' footsteps."

"You mean as a fraud?" He cut her a sideways grin as he pulled Ghost into the first open spot he found.

"I was trying to be a little more tactful."

"Good thing I'm not big on social niceties. They're a family of frauds," Aiden said bluntly. "You have Mr. Mhoon capitalizing off of his haunted hotel and Mrs. Mhoon assuming a new identity every other day. It makes sense their daughter would scam people with fortune-tellings and palm readings."

Selene couldn't argue Aiden's point. He wasn't lying. His honesty was often too much for many people, but it was one of the things she loved most about him. He rarely minced words and it was refreshing.

The beads jiggled as Selene walked into the shop followed by Aiden. Her gaze shot to the counter, expecting to see Phoebe with her beehive hairdo and velvety, off-the-shoulder sweater. Instead Tom was standing there, donning a windbreaker jacket that covered his muscly arms and clutching a hot coffee.

Selene tilted her head sideways and asked, "Where's Phoebe?"

"Is that what passes as a good morning around here?" he grunted. "We've got more manners at the coal mine."

"Speaking of the mine, why are you here and not there?" Aiden asked in a clipped tone, coming up on Selene's side.

"I'm opening up the shop for Phee."

"She wasn't at the hotel," said Selene. They had checked, knocking on her door to no answer.

Tom's stony face sharpened. "She's with her folks. You might've not realized this, but the family is under a lotta duress right now. Their hotel is shutting down and our honeymoon is postponed 'cuz you two nitwits couldn't solve what's going on."

"Insulting us certainly doesn't help the situation," said Aiden. "It would be a little easier to investigate if the Mhoon family was more forthcoming, including Phoebe."

"Don't you badmouth Phee!" Tom argued.

"We're not badmouthing Phoebe. We were just hoping to talk to her," said Selene coolly. "When you see her, please tell her to call me or find me at the hotel."

Tom grunted as he slurped more coffee. It was the best answer they were going to receive from the coal miner. They shook their heads, turned around, and left the new age specialty shop smelling of coffee and sage.

"That was a bust," she said, sighing.

Aiden put his arm around her as they walked down the wintry sidewalk. "On the bright side, Ms. Coco's is half a block away."

The morning crowd had dispersed, which meant the small coffeeshop was almost empty by the time Aiden and Selene turned up. They stole the table by the heating lamps and the front window. Aiden went up to the counter to place their order while Selene hung her coat on the back of her chair and processed what had happened in recent hours.

Her dream had been scarily vivid. The good and the bad. All of her loved ones had gathered at her home for what was a cozy, festive celebration. Even the thought of such a reality created a somber ache in Selene's heart. It was a dream that would never come true, and deep down, she knew it.

But then it transformed into her worst nightmare. The people who hated her materialized before her eyes. Priscilla Myers was in front of her for the first time since their magical duel at the library. The evil witch and succubus had looked even more frightening in dream form.

Selene shook her head, forcing the echoes of Priscilla's witchy cackle to quiet down. Aiden returned unsuspecting and in good spirits, carrying their coffees and cracking a joke about Ms. Coco. She breathed in relief, grateful for the distraction, and thanked him for the coffee.

"She should be bringing over your favorite any second now," he said.

"Snickerdoodles?"

"*Freshly* baked." Aiden winked.

The friendly coffeeshop owner appeared no less than a minute later. She set down a plate loaded with snickerdoodle cookies and then smiled at the couple.

"Heard you're having a rough morning," said Ms. Coco. "I told Aiden I'd give you a batch right out the oven. Now you can dunk 'em in your coffee all you like."

"You're the best. How can I ever repay you?"

"You remember what we talked about for my sixty-fourth birthday. I want *him* jumping outta cake," Ms. Coco joked, gesturing to Aiden with her thumb.

Aiden's face reddened and Selene laughed. The woman walked off to tend to the rest of the coffeeshop and they dove into their coffee and cookies. Aiden was pondering how serious Ms. Coco was about her birthday request as Selene listened with a mixture of sympathy and amusement. She dunked her first snickerdoodle in her coffee and bit off a large chunk.

"She has to know I was kidding, doesn't she?" he asked, his brow creased. "Maybe my sarcasm was a little too undetectable. Hopefully a birthday card will suffice."

Selene giggled and then it hit her. The half-eaten snickerdoodle tumbled out of her hand and flopped onto the table, crumbling into pieces. Her brown eyes had doubled to twice their size from behind her glasses. Aiden noticed with a tilt of his head.

"What is it?" he asked.

It was so obvious she didn't know how she hadn't figured it out sooner. She looked from Aiden to the opposite end of the coffeeshop, where Ms. Coco was arranging pastries in a glass case, oblivious.

"Cordelia Dunn," said Selene in a shocked tone. "She's Ms. Coco."

CHAPTER EIGHTEEN

A moment passed before Selene's theory sunk in. Aiden tore his gaze from his brilliant girlfriend and glanced over his shoulder at Ms. Coco. The older woman was humming as she used tongs to place pastries in the glass case. She looked as unsuspecting as she had since the moment they had first met her. Could she really be Cordelia Dunn?

"Think about it," said Selene. "If you do the math, Ms. Coco's the same age as Cordelia."

"We said the same thing about Mrs. Mhoon. I'm sure there's several sixty-four-year-old women in Maresburg."

"Who happen to go by a nickname that could easily be taken from Cordelia?"

"It's not outside the realm of possibility."

"Ms. Coco knows a lot about town," she went on with a pensive frown. "She's the one who told us about Mrs. Poe, remember?"

Aiden considered her point. "She did give an ominous warning about the hotel."

"She said she doesn't step foot anywhere near the hotel anymore. What's the reason?"

Before Aiden could ponder aloud, Ms. Coco returned to their table to check on them. Her smile was cheerful as she gestured to their cooling coffee cups and said, "The coffee wasn't too strong this morning, was it, babies? Mr. Rogers mentioned it was a little too caffeinated today."

Selene inhaled a deep, audible breath and said, "Ms. Coco, did your family own the town hotel before the Mhoons?"

Her question was met with a choked yelp from Ms. Coco. She dropped the tray in her hand, but didn't bend to pick it up. Instead she stared googly-eyed from Selene to Aiden.

"I don't mean to catch you off guard," said Selene softly. She gathered the fallen tray for her. "It's just…we've been investigating for over a week now, and we're running out of options. We really need to speak with someone who has experienced this creature firsthand."

The reddish undertone drained from Ms. Coco's complexion, giving her brown skin an uncharacteristic dullness. She swallowed with a gulp and pulled up a chair from a different table. She didn't ask as she grabbed Aiden's mug and downed his coffee. The second time that had happened to him in a couple of days.

"I really need to drink my coffee faster," he muttered under his breath.

"What was that?" Ms. Coco asked.

"Errr, nothing. Please continue." Aiden lined his shoulders into a straighter sitting position, motioning for Ms. Coco to go on.

"Well, I haven't talked about it in decades. I hoped going by Coco and staying away from the property would help me forget. It'd help me shut out thoughts about it."

"We don't want to push you, but I think it might help the investigation," said Selene.

Ms. Coco shook her head, eyes clenched shut. "I figured there'd come a day—matter of fact, as soon as you two came to town, I just knew it'd come to this. But you should know, I'm still not sure what I saw."

"Any info helps," said Aiden.

"It was Halloween night. Our father had just purchased the hotel from Mr. Poe and was gonna do a whole reopening of the place. Mr. Poe himself was a strange fellow. Even as a girl, I thought so. He was the dark and brooding type—spoke very few words. Anyway, our mother said he was in mourning over his wife," said Ms. Coco with a belaboring sigh. "I was a very nosy girl bored that night. My older sister, Rhonda, had kicked me out of her room. I needed something to do."

"And that's how you stumbled across Mrs. Poe's old room," supplied Selene gently.

"There was a chill in the room. Something very unsettling in the air. I felt it as soon as I walked in, but instead of doing the smart thing and turning back, I snooped around. I poked my nose in places I shouldn't have. I was spellbound by Mrs. Poe's things. She had luxurious tastes much like Rhonda. I suppose it makes sense. Rhonda dreamed of being a singer. Mrs. Poe dreamed of being an actress. Anyhow, I came across that awful hand mirror."

Aiden shot a glance at Selene, checking for her reaction. Her brows had pushed together and she leaned closer as if she didn't want to miss a single word Ms. Coco said. He couldn't help his instant concern; Selene had convinced herself the mirror had been left on her bed because she was a witch. Was she blaming herself for what was happening at the hotel?

"Things went dark," said Ms. Coco, shuddering even under the heating lamp.

"Dark?" Aiden asked. "What do you mean?"

"The moon. It…it blacked out. So did the lights. I dropped the mirror and it shattered. I knew it was bad then. I just knew we were in trouble. I hid under the bed and there was this shadow overtaking everything. I ran for it eventually, but it was like something bad had been set loose. Rhonda went to bed that night and never woke up."

Silence followed that somber revelation. Tears glistened in Ms. Coco's eyes. Selene offered her a napkin from the dispenser. Aiden sat and pieced together everything she had told them about that fateful Halloween night. If the Dreamling emerged from the broken mirror then that meant it was loose in the hotel. The mysterious inky substance left at the scene of every incident came to mind…

They thanked Ms. Coco for sharing her story and apologized if it triggered any grief. She waved a hand, still using the other to wipe tears with the crumpled napkin. "It's for the best I told you. Now maybe you can do something to stop it. My family was never the same after Rhonda passed. Maybe you can save whoever's targeted next."

Cold dread invaded Aiden's stomach. He looked at Selene as the bad premonition rocked him. Though they were determined to solve the case, he couldn't shake the feeling the worst was yet to come.

———

Phoebe was at the hotel when they returned. She explained she had spent the morning helping her parents find a place to stay. With the hotel shutting down, the last of their guests checked out, and the Dreamling still on the prowl, they no longer wanted anything to do with the premises.

"And where are you staying?" Selene asked, tugging off her cardigan and draping it over her forearm.

"I'll be with Tom. It's a tall order navigating the future," said Phoebe in her airy lilt. She emerged from behind the reception desk and spread her arms out, gesturing to the foyer around them. "The clock is ticking and you're running out of time to save the day. Then my parents' business goes up in smoke. Tell me how I can assist your investigation."

The offer was unexpected. Aiden crossed his arms over his chest and said, "You can start by telling us what you know about the dreams Selene is having. Are they connected to this creature?"

"I'm afraid I can't tell you. I wish I knew, but from what Selene describes, she's crossing into another realm with these dreams."

"What other realm?" Selene asked.

"Some sort of dream world," said Phoebe. "Your consciousness is leaving your body and crossing over."

"But wouldn't everyone's when they dream?"

"Not necessarily. Not if they're surface-level dreams. It seems like you're tapping into something else entirely— somewhere this creature is also existing and in control. The others were targeted by the Dreamling and didn't live to tell the tale. You've tapped in and out several times with no harm done."

Aiden didn't like the sound of what Phoebe described. He stuck his hands in his trouser pockets and searched for an argument to refute what she was saying. Unfortunately, nothing rose to mind. More cold dread slithered inside of him and he tried to keep his composure. On the outside, he might have looked his usual calm, cool, casual self, but his insides told a different story. The sick feeling was unlike anything he had ever felt. He couldn't tell Selene and alarm her...

"I think Mrs. Poe was able to do the same," said Selene with shock on her face. "She was able to travel into whatever dream world this is."

"Until she wasn't," Aiden pointed out. "From what we know, she ended up *dying* from entering this dream world one too many times."

"Still quite unusual," said Phoebe, looking between them. She had quirked a penciled brow, hands on her svelte hips. "It poses the question, how have Mrs. Poe and Selene managed such a mystical feat?"

Neither answered the seer. Aiden had a sneaking suspicion Phoebe Mhoon knew why both Mrs. Poe and Selene had entered the dream world. She was merely poking around, testing the waters to see if they would divulge Selene's secret identity.

Luckily, Omar clambered down the staircase and interrupted their conversation. His wire-framed glasses almost slipped off his face, but he impatiently nudged them back up the bridge of his nose. He bustled over to Aiden with clumsy, heavy-footed steps.

"I just received a phone call from an old paranormal buddy. He has the solution to all of our problems," he panted. "The EMBM 2400."

"The *what*?"

"The Electromagnetic Brain Monitor 2400!" Omar said impatiently. He was sweating. "It monitors brain waves by using electromagnetic fields, and can even alter brain activity! It's normally used during scientific research, but has also been used for paranormal activities such as demonic possessions!"

Aiden had lost his point along his rambling, eying Omar

with more agitation than usual. "I'm not following what this has to do with our investigation."

"Don't you see? Whatever this...this thing is, it's occupying the dream space of people in this hotel," explained Omar fanatically. "If we connect someone to this machine as they dream, we might be able to manipulate their dream state!"

The others looked around at each other. Even though Aiden didn't want to admit it, what Omar proposed made sense if the Dreamling worked as he claimed it did. But then that led them to deciding who would be the person subjected to the dream experience. He had a sinking feeling who.

"Where is this machine? Do you have one?" Selene asked.

"No," Omar admitted, "but that's where my paranormal buddy comes in. Bono owns an antiques shop in Quinton, the next town over—he collects all sorts of fun paranormal gadgets. He's willing to lend us his. If we pick it up this afternoon, we can get started tonight."

All eyes fell on Aiden. The van keys to Ghost suddenly weighed down his pocket as he stared back at them. He exhaled a reluctant sigh and said, "If we leave now, we'll be able to make it there and back by sunset."

"Excellent. Let's get a move on!" Omar exclaimed.

"I'll set up a seance room. If we're going to be dabbling in alternate realms, speaking to this dream spirit, we need the scene to be as conducive as possible," said Phoebe. She gestured to Selene. "You should be relaxed. We need your mind as open as it can be if we're to tap into this dream world."

"Hang on," said Aiden. "Why is Selene going to do it?"

Phoebe scoffed as if it were as obvious as two plus two being four. "She's the only one with the connection to this dream realm. It's very important she's able to free her mind and relax completely before we attempt this."

"Can I speak to you for a second?" Aiden grabbed Selene's hand and pulled her down the hall, outside of earshot from the other two. He rounded on her and said, "It should be me."

Selene's brows wrinkled in confusion. "Mrs. Poe was a lunar witch. There's no other explanation for it. It's how she was able to enter the dream world like she was. It's how I'm able to do it. That's why it needs to be me."

"We still don't know that about Mrs. Poe. It's too dangerous."

"Then why are you volunteering to do it?"

Aiden's jaw tightened as he fumbled for an excuse. "Because...because I haven't been affected at all by the Dreamling's powers. If one of us is going to be used as an avatar into this world, why not someone who hasn't been targeted?"

"You're trying to protect me," she said with a tender note to her voice. "I'm going to be okay. You heard Omar. The EMBM 2400 will be able to monitor everything that happens. You can wake me up as soon as something goes wrong."

Aiden studied her face, unable to shake the terrible premonition in his gut. She offered him comfort in the form of an adoring smile and he couldn't resist kissing her, clutching her face in his hands. Her lips touched his, softer than the clouds in the sky, spurring an all-too-familiar palpitation in his heart. The window to tell her how he was feeling—how much she meant to him—opened, but the words just lingered on his tongue. Mom and Dad's divorce bubbled to the surface in his mind, sabotaging him with thoughts of how horribly they had crashed and burned. He tightened his arm around her, holding her in a snugger embrace, and settled for the feel of her, the sweet smell of her hair as it brushed against his chin.

"This…this isn't what I had in mind when I asked you to be my investigative partner," he said in a strained whisper.

"Go," she urged in a murmur just as quiet. "I'll be here. You heard Phoebe. I need to relax and free my mind if we're going to do this. You pick up the machine with Omar and then we can end this case once and for all."

He nodded warily. "And never do this again."

"*Go*," she repeated with an amused tone. "You're wasting time."

Aiden gave her one last look before he inhaled another breath, pulled his keys out of his pocket, and turned down the hall. Omar was still waiting in the foyer. The two headed for the door, promising to be back soon with the EMBM 2400. So why did it feel like such a permanent goodbye?

CHAPTER NINETEEN

"Your boyfriend cares deeply for you," said Phoebe minutes into their awkward silence. The two were in the parlor setting up for the experiment.

Selene pushed one of the lounge chairs against the wall, wiping the flecks of dust from her hands. Her skin was warming over thinking about Aiden and their relationship. It was only minutes ago the two had snuck off down the hall for whispered words and passionate kisses. The tight grip of his arms around her was impossible to forget.

"Hmmm?" She feigned difficulty hearing, dragging another lounge chair across the room, its legs scraping on the floor and making noise.

"No need to be uncomfortable," said Phoebe sagely. "It's in the way he looks at you. Communication is more than words—oftentimes, if you pay enough mind to someone, you can learn all you need to even before they utter a word. Body language is a powerful tool."

"I'm sorry, but I'm not following where you're going with this. What does this have to do with the investigation?"

"Maybe nothing," answered Phoebe with an innocuous shrug. "Or possibly everything."

Selene stared at the self-proclaimed seer. "Speaking of relationships, do you speak in riddles with Tom too or is it only for show?"

"I'm exactly myself at all times. In case you haven't grasped the situation, you need to be in a relaxed state. Your mind needs to be clear. Your heart needs to be open. You'll never transcend realms otherwise. What brings you happiness?"

Aiden. Selene understood as soon as the reflexive smile curved her lips. Lots of other things brought her happiness, such as good books and freshly baked sweets. Snowy weather and her best friend, Noelle. Even her dog Yukie's little yips that once echoed through her home in Brimrock.

But Aiden was who first sprang to mind. His face was the one that floated into view when she thought of recent happy memories. She cherished their good times together and wouldn't trade them for gold. If she needed to be relaxed and at ease, thinking about him and their relationship would help.

"Do you think this is going to work?" Selene asked.

"It doesn't matter what I think. My opinion has no bearing on the outcome," replied Phoebe, walking up to the table by the window. She gave it a pull, but the mahogany was too heavy.

"You know a lot about the dream world. More than any of us. You have to have some kind of idea if it will."

"It's more conducive for me to create the right environment than worry about opinion. What's in my control is the atmosphere, is my assistance in guiding you. That's what I'm focusing on."

Selene sighed and plucked her glasses off her face. Specs

of dust had floated onto the lenses. She wiped them off on her T-shirt. "I guess you can say I'm a little nervous. What if I can't tap into the dream world like I've been doing the past few nights? My dream last night turned into a nightmare."

"Different theories exist on our agency in the dream state. Some philosophers believe if we retain some semblance of consciousness, we are able to exert control in our dreams…to a degree. Others believe the opposite, we are merely vessels when dreaming," said Phoebe. "You'll discover the truth during this experiment. You may be surprised to discover you have a lot of untapped power that'll likely come in handy tonight."

Phoebe glided across the room with an airiness that was almost magical. She admired their handiwork in the room, rearranging the furniture, and then moved to draw the drapes. Selene watched the seer with a new question rising to mind. Hopefully one Phoebe would answer.

"Are you a witch?"

Phoebe smirked. "What do you think?"

"I know you know a lot about the paranormal. You seem to believe in different types of mystical powers. I'm assuming that includes magic?"

"I've told you what I am," said Phoebe, walking over to face Selene. She still wore her smirk, like she harbored a fun secret she'd never tell. "But that doesn't mean I don't know the truth."

"The…the truth about what?" Selene asked, feeling fidgety.

"The truth about you, Selene. You shouldn't fret over it, though—not now. You need to center yourself. Relax. Think happy thoughts."

Selene nodded and moved for the parlor door. If she was

going to relax, she needed a hot shower. She needed to change into loose, comfy clothing and maybe a snack. It was a shame Ms. Coco wasn't there or else she could've baked her more snickerdoodle cookies. If she was going to have to face the Dreamling, the *least* the universe could do was let her enjoy a plate of the warm, chewy, cinnamon-sprinkled treat one last time.

Selene climbed the staircase and muttered to herself, "And a glass of milk too."

———

The shower heated up fast. Steam rolled through the bathroom as Selene untied her robe and stepped into the tub. She had her shower cap on, protecting her curls, and her sugar body scrub in hand. She'd dimmed the lights and put on some ambient instrumental music. The blazing hot water cascaded over her body and she closed her eyes, basking in the heat's soothing effects.

Aiden and Omar would be back any minute. They would start the experiment with the EMBM 2400. Selene would fall asleep and do her best to enter the dream world. In recent nights it'd been a cakewalk. She hadn't intentionally pulled off the feat; it happened as soon as she closed her eyes. Best case scenario she'd have similar luck tonight.

After exfoliating and bathing in lightly scented lavender body wash, Selene twisted off the shower and grabbed her towel. Thick clouds of steam still wandered the bathroom, but even the shower's heat seemed no match for the sudden cold. She walked out of the bathroom in her thigh-length cotton robe and discovered the rest of the hotel room was now dark and chilled over.

She shuddered, the comforting heat on her skin quickly

dispersing. Instead goose pimples sprang up as tiny bumps along her arms and legs. She hugged her robe tighter against her body, flicked on a light, and stopped in front of the thermostat. Her jaw dropped.

Thirty-seven degrees.

When she had come upstairs and gone into the bathroom, it had read seventy. The shower itself should've warmed up the room even further. How had the temperature decreased so drastically so quickly? It made no sense unless the central heating happened to go out. The coincidence seemed a little too unlikely.

Selene's eyes darted to the window. The sky had darkened in record time. The streetlights were only just coming on. She rushed over for a better look, searching for the moon. Clouds gathered in a thick, silvery formation, a haze similar to the steam in the bathroom. The moon itself was gone, faded into the blackening sky.

She backed away from the window and returned to the thermostat. Punching different buttons to turn on the heat and increase the temperature didn't help.

It was broken.

Selene grabbed the T-shirt and pair of sweats she was going to wear for the experiment and slipped both on. She wrenched open the hotel door and rushed into the hall. The cold hadn't spread to other parts of the hotel. In the hall, the blast of heat from the vents could still be felt. She marched down the hall when someone called out to her.

"Are we feeling better than earlier?"

She whipped around and discovered Grace. The hotel guest wore a sleek scoop-neck midi-length dress. Her jet-black pin curls were pulled into an updo, showing off the graceful length of her neck and the arch of her cheekbones.

She held her clutch purse and walked as though on a Hollywood red carpet.

"You were so frazzled earlier," said Grace in her softly delicate voice. "Don't tell me you're still feeling unwell."

"No…I was looking for someone. The thermostat's gone out in my room." Selene led her inside to show her the broken thermostat. In the minute since she'd dashed from her room the temperature had decreased to thirty-four degrees.

Grace stared at the digital fixture on the wall. "That really is odd. It looks like it's frozen."

Selene was hardly paying attention to what Grace said. She had turned around and glanced at the mirror perched atop the dresser. Her reflection stared back at her, bold-framed glasses, messy curls, baggy sweats and all. However, the space next to her was empty. Nothing—and *no one*—was beside her but the broken thermostat on the wall.

Chills danced across her skin as she looked to her left, where Grace was standing, and at once, everything clicked into place. In a hushed tone, Selene said, "Grace, why are you still here?"

"I'm sorry, why am I still what, Selene?"

"All of the guests have already checked out this morning," said Selene. She took a wide step back. "It's only me, Aiden, and some of the Mhoons left. How are you still here in the hotel?"

"Oh," said Grace. She folded her hands and eyed Selene with a steadily sharpening expression. "I'm checking out tomorrow. The Mhoons made an exception for me."

"You're not real, are you?" Selene asked. She took another step back.

Grace scoffed as if the accusation was preposterous. "I have no clue what you're talking about, Selene. Maybe it's time for you to lie down."

"You're a ghost."

"I promise you I'm no ghost."

"But you're…you're Mrs. Poe."

A dark smile crossed the woman's face and she shrugged with an air of graceful indifference. "So what if I am?"

CHAPTER TWENTY

O mar Mhoon stole glances at Aiden whenever he thought he wasn't looking. The scrawny, meekly mannered paranormal investigator with his wire-framed glasses and touch-and-go of gray hairs sat in the front passenger seat of Ghost and clasped his hands in his lap. He said nothing, but in the van's silence, it became apparent he was a mouth breather.

Aiden ignored what was Omar's fifth or sixth furtive glance and reached for the volume dial on the dash. He turned up the NPR station, drowning out Omar's next Hoover-like suction of air.

To be honest, Omar still wasn't trustworthy. He might have volunteered to help with the investigation, but that didn't mean Aiden had forgotten their tepid beginning. On his and Selene's first night, Omar hadn't so much as made eye contact, tuning out dinner conversation and eating his meal with fewer words to utter than a mute. Shortly after they had stumbled upon him sneaking around the hotel at night.

Aiden had looked up Omar Mhoon online, digging for whatever info he could find on the failed paranormal investigator. His search hadn't turned up much beyond an amateur blog Omar abandoned in 2013, detailing his hunt for various paranormal creatures, and a couple news articles about his arrest for trespassing. Apparently the youngest Mhoon brother had a penchant for sneaking around in places he wasn't supposed to be…

But if he was correct about the EMBM 2400, how could Aiden turn down his offer to work together? The clock was running out and they needed to solve this case. If not for the sake of the Mhoon Hotel itself, for those who had lost their lives to the creature haunting their dreams. For *Selene*.

He didn't know how he hadn't picked up on it sooner. Selene had been plagued with sleep trouble for weeks. Those issues seeped away within days of their arrival in Maresburg. His mind jumped back to their date night, where she had fallen into a frighteningly deep sleep in the van. He had tried everything to wake her.

His stomach clenched as he thought about the possibility it would happen again tonight.

"Your girlfriend's going to be fine," said Omar as if reading his mind. His beady gaze flicked to Aiden and then swept away again. "The EMBM 2400 is some of the finest brain wave technology out there. If she's stuck in a sleep cycle, we'll be able to use its electric pulse technology to jolt her awake, kind of like a defibrillator for the brain."

Aiden gave a restrained nod. "There's something I'm confused about, though. Your brother's hotel has been haunted by the Dreamling for decades. Why are you just now taking an interest?"

The muscles in Omar's face pulled tight, his chin pointier than usual. "If you're implying I've intentionally not helped—"

"I didn't say that. I'm asking a simple question. Your

brother has owned this hotel since I was a boy playing Legos and reading comic books. There have been how many attacks over the years? *Why now*?"

"You know our history. Willy and I haven't been on the best of terms," said Omar indignantly. He glared at Aiden, making no attempt to hide his staring this time. "We used to be thick as thieves before he met his con artist wife. Then our mother fell ill, and our relationship was never the same. When I did try and offer my paranormal services, he balked. He acted like I'm some...some nutjob. But soon I'll prove it to him. I've been right all along!"

Aiden let Omar's rant go on without interruption. He launched into a series of complaints about how Mr. Mhoon had belittled his career as a paranormal investigator for many years; how he had left Omar to suffer in a jail cell one of the times he was arrested rather than bail him out. He even went far back to their childhood and grumbled over Mr. Mhoon's bully ways.

"Explain what you meant about Selene," Aiden said finally. He had had his fill of Omar's therapy-like venting about the time he was picked last for basketball. "The night we caught you snooping around the hotel, you told her she's trouble."

"Have you not been listening? I've been a paranormal investigator for years and years!"

"I hate to break it to you, Omar, but that doesn't carry the gravitas you think it does. I say this as a fellow investigator of all things paranormal."

"Your girlfriend throws off my EMF detector," hissed Omar without hesitation. "You might not realize this, but when you first arrived, I investigated you both! As soon as I saw her read on my detector, I knew something was up about her. Something…something was off. Then I saw her one night."

Aiden almost forgot he was driving. He turned his head for a long, severe look at Omar. "When did you see her at night?"

"She was outside wandering off. She disappeared into the wooded area behind the hotel. Who goes for a walk at midnight?"

"I wasn't aware when someone goes for a walk was any of your business."

"Anything suspicious is my business during an investigation. I tried to follow her, but she just…disappeared. Almost like it was magic."

"*Or* almost like you were half asleep and imagining things."

"Oh, come off it! If this were anyone but *your* girlfriend, you'd be suspicious."

Though Omar was right, Aiden didn't want to admit it. If he had caught anyone else wandering into the woods in the middle of the night, he would've slipped into investigator mode. But Selene's identity as a witch was a secret he was willing to take to the grave. It was none of Omar's business if she snuck off for a lunar ritual.

"We're here," said Aiden, steering Ghost into the bumpy parking lot of a small strip mall. He braked in front of the antiques shop. "Are you sure it's still in business?"

The antiques shop looked abandoned. The front window was marred with dust and grime so thick it was near-impossible to peer inside the shop. Cobwebs hung above the door in intricate patterns, undisturbed by human presence in what must've been some time. Lettering had long ago fallen off from the shop sign on the building, but no one cared enough to replace it.

Aiden's brows touched as Omar strode up to the door and tapped his knuckles. "Bono wouldn't let me down. He's in there. You can trust me on that."

"There's no cars in this parking lot. In fact, I don't think any of the shops in this strip mall are open," said Aiden. He folded his arms over his chest and glanced around the cratered asphalt and barren shops. "Something tells me your pal Bono was lying."

"Nonsense. We just have to wait for him to open."

Omar curled his spidery fingers into a fist and banged on the door some more. He dragged on his knocking for the next five minutes. The muscles in Aiden's jaw pulled tight as minute by minute his patience thinned. The distinct feeling Omar was stalling washed over him.

He must've sensed Aiden's mood souring, because he threw a glance over his shoulder. "Um, maybe I should call him."

"That might be smart," said Aiden curtly.

Omar groped for his phone in his shirt pocket and then searched his contacts list. His call to the elusive Bono went as well as his knocking. No one answered. Omar flashed a placating smile to Aiden and said, "Maybe if I try again—"

"Is Bono real, Omar?" Aiden interrupted. His last shred of patience evaporated into the evening air. He scooped his van keys from his pants pocket and turned around. "We don't have time to waste playing games. This was a dead end."

"Hang on a minute! Where are you going?"

"Back to Maresburg! Back to the hotel to figure something out with Selene." Aiden popped open the driver side door and cast Omar a severe look, his mouth a straight line. "If you're coming, you have five seconds to hop in the van."

Omar scampered over like an uncoordinated foal. "Driver's rules. Back to Maresburg it is."

Aiden glanced up at the sky through Ghost's windshield. The day had withered away, the miserable pewter gray purpling before his eyes. Where had time gone? Theirs was running out...

Omar waited until they were on the road before he spoke again. "Bono's not usually this irresponsible. He's a reliable sleuth in the paranormal investigation community."

"Paranormal investigation community?"

"You really need to educate yourself on the paranormal. We are all over the world investigating the paranormal. It's easier to have a network to track these sort of things. One day we'll reveal the truth about paranormal dangers to the world with irrefutable proof. That moment might just be tonight."

"Uh, sure. Right." Aiden humored his ramblings as he applied pressure to the gas pedal. Ghost dutifully shot forward down the highway, carrying them toward Maresburg and away from Quinton. The roads were empty save for the occasional semi-truck, but a car parked on the shoulder of the highway was unmistakable. Bronze and wide and long as a boat, the Cadillac could only belong to one person.

Humbolt.

Aiden sped up, the needle on the odometer tipping ten over the speed limit. Omar was still prattling away about the worldwide network of paranormal investigators. Aiden debated between flat out telling Omar he didn't give a damn about what random paranormal investigators in Montreal were up to, and blatantly ignoring him by dialing up NPR.

He settled on a compromise. "Are any of these anecdotes supposed to mean something to me?"

Omar scowled. "How do you call yourself a PI, but you don't care about what's going on in the community?"

"I care about what's going on here in Maresburg, at *your* brother's hotel."

"The only reason you care is because it's your girlfriend on the line."

"What did you say?" Aiden snapped. His eyes darted from the road and onto Omar.

The whir of a siren cut off anything Omar was about to say. Blue and red lights bounced in the rearview mirror as the siren spun and the Cadillac in back of them trailed behind. Aiden swore under his breath and pressed the brake, pulling over onto the side of the road.

Just what he needed—another run in with Humbolt.

As Humbolt got out his car and strode over, gravel rolling underneath his shoes and his trench coat billowing in the wind, Aiden flicked his eyes up to the sky. Thick clouds floated across the now rich purple canvas, disguising the moon and any stars from view.

His heart started racing. Selene had mentioned the moon disappearing before. His chest heaved as he sighed and turned off the van engine.

Humbolt stopped feet from the van and commanded, "Step out of the vehicle. Both of you."

CHAPTER TWENTY-ONE

"Maya Grace Poe. Nice to meet you," said Mrs. Poe with a polite smile.

Selene touched a hand to her stomach, trying to calm the queasiness churning inside. "You've been a ghost all this time? You've…you've been pretending to be a guest at the hotel when you're really *dead*?"

"I'm not a ghost," said Mrs. Poe, offended. "And I'm not dead."

Selene knitted her brows and blurted, "You're buried at the local cemetery. Gravestone and all."

"My body might be gone, but I'll have you know, I'm still very much alive. I have thoughts and experience feelings. I'm still the same Maya Grace Walker born and raised in Kibbens, Tennessee, who unfortunately was a silly girl when she ran away and married a man a decade older. The worst mistake of my life was the day I fell for Samuel's tricks."

"Mr. Poe," said Selene, enshrouded in a wave of shock she couldn't shake off. "You married him when you were twenty and moved to Maresburg?"

"Maresburg wasn't the first place we tried to start over

in," answered Mrs. Poe. "But for me, I guess you can say it was the last."

"He kept you locked up here, didn't he? He told everyone you were going mad."

"I'm perfectly sane. Thank you." Mrs. Poe sailed past Selene and stopped at the window, peeking through the part in the curtains. "Samuel didn't understand me. I was too much for him. So he labeled me as an unstable young woman who didn't know left from right. Up from down. Coming from going. I was evaluated. Put on medications. They were meant to keep me dazed, but most importantly, compliant."

"Couldn't you leave him? Couldn't you tell the doctors—"

"I was a young, penniless black woman in the 1950s," interrupted Mrs. Poe. Her tone had chilled, her classically beautiful face cold. "Believe me when I say nobody was listening to a word I had to say. I answered to Samuel and Samuel answered for me."

A hard lump formed in Selene's throat, blocking her efforts when she tried to swallow. "I'm...I'm sorry. I can't imagine what that was like."

"I had big dreams," mused Mrs. Poe, still gazing out the window. A sense of longing had washed over her as her eyes flicked up to the dark sky. "I wanted to be a big Hollywood actress, like Dorothy Dandridge. She was my idol. You know I met her once?"

"It doesn't sound like Samuel was too supportive," said Selene. She couldn't begin to process what was going on. Her brain felt like scrambled eggs and the persistent chill in the room wasn't helping. Still, if she could keep Mrs. Poe talking, she could stumble her way into solving the case. She moved closer, bridging the gap between them.

"Of course, he wasn't supportive. He was a cruel man. I didn't know to what extent until it was too late."

"Until he locked you up?"

Her nod was slight. "Until I discovered it was by design. Samuel was a witch hunter."

"A witch hunter?" Selene's jaw dropped open as she wondered if her ears deceived her.

"That's right. He tracked down my family. He tricked me into falling in love with him. Then he tried to destroy me," she explained, face darkened by the bad memories. "He kept me locked up in this hotel and never let me out—in that little room with no exposure to the sun, and even worse, the moon. He would've lit the fire that burned me at the stake if given the chance."

Selene reached out to touch Mrs. Poe's shoulder, but her hand passed through her, an icy sensation trickling across her skin. She pulled back and folded her arms across her chest. "So that's it. You're a lunar witch like me?"

Mrs. Poe turned away from the window, pacing the room. "Why else do you think you're the only one who can see me? You never wondered why no one else was around whenever we spoke?"

"I never really thought about it. You seemed so real."

"I *am* real."

"Then I'm confused," admitted Selene, twisting her mouth into a frown. "If you're not alive in the sense of having a body, but you're not dead, then what are you?"

Mrs. Poe sighed, her hands falling to her slim hips. "I'm trapped, which, if you can believe it, is terribly worse. When Samuel locked me away, I lost my lunar powers. It forced me to begin experimenting with other types of magic. I had a chest filled with heirlooms that had been in my family for generations. Green magic and solar magic, even divination.

Some of the objects in the chest helped me, like my grand-mother's old cauldron and spell books. He eventually found out about those and took them away, but there was one—an item harmless to the nonwitch eye—that he didn't know about."

"The hand mirror. *You* left it for me. You left it on my bed."

"I did. I've known about your dreams. You've been projecting your consciousness into the dream world. Quite impressive for such an inexperienced witch," said Mrs. Poe. "I first learned to cross over with the mirror. I discovered its powers as a portal to other realms."

"There's more than the dream realm?"

Mrs. Poe clucked her tongue, making a ticking noise. "Estelle didn't teach you a thing, did she?"

"How do you know my mom's name? She was born *after* you died."

"You sure have a lot of questions. I have all of eternity to answer them, but I'm afraid I simply don't want to," she said bluntly. She admired the shine on her manicured nails as if bored. "The mirror is a magical portal to other realms—the underworld, the dream world, the astral planes, the realm of time, among many others. Then of course there's here, waking life. It's some of the most complex magic there is. I started using the mirror to travel to the dream world, where I could live the life I deserved. Samuel was none the wiser."

"But the mirror broke and trapped you," said Selene. It finally felt like the puzzle pieces were fitting together.

"Not exactly. Do you know what it's like to experience your dreams? Your biggest wishes in life, granted just like that," said Mrs. Poe, snapping her fingers. "The ability to create a reality with your imagination is a very powerful thing. Lunar witches have a natural inclination for manipulating the dream world. Your average person may stumble into the dream realm here and there, but they have no control, no power to bend what happens. I discovered I did. I could control everything that happened in my dreams, or so I thought."

Selene held off on asking her next question, though a new thought floated to mind. In her recent dreams, everything had been perfect. She had been back home at 1221 Gifford Lane and was surrounded by friends and family. Luna was there, the bright twinkle in her eyes the same from any photo Selene had seen of her. It had been what she'd always wanted, but was that her own doing? Had she unknowingly curated her own dreams?

"See, the dream realm isn't as innocent as it sounds," said Mrs. Poe, interrupting Selene's thoughts. A bitter smile crossed Mrs. Poe's face. "Just like with every realm, it's not without its evils. I didn't understand that the Dreamling was feeding off of me. Every time I escaped to his realm, dreamed up the perfect scenario, he was feeding."

"*Feeding*? That can't be good," Selene mumbled.

"On my hopes, my fears. It makes him stronger and you weaker. That's what he wants. Then, the dreams turn into nightmares. You can't escape him. He consumes you," Mrs. Poe explained grimly. "But I managed to get away, if you can believe it. I escaped through the portal before he could take my consciousness."

"I don't understand. If you got away, then how did you die? How are you a ghost?"

"For the last time, I'm not a ghost and I'm not dead! I'm a consciousness, a soul without a body. I was robbed of mine many years ago, and if you're not careful, you'll end up just like me," Mrs. Poe snapped. She squeezed shut her eyes as if to urge herself to calm down. "When I escaped, I was never able to sync with my body. It looked like I died in my sleep, but I've still very much been around. Samuel found me the next morning lying in my bed."

Mrs. Poe covered her forehead with a hand, a pained expression shaping her features. She looked past Selene at the window. Selene followed her gaze, twisting around, spying how dark the sky had gotten. The stars were gone and so was the moon, like it had never existed.

Selene shuddered and wrapped her arms around herself. She didn't have a good feeling about tonight.

"The worst part, Selene," said Mrs. Poe on a sad note. "He followed me when I escaped. He followed me through the portal."

"He's *here*? In the hotel? Right now?" Selene whipped her head left and right, glancing around the quiet room. Nothing had changed, but a new eeriness lurked in the air. Who was he? What was he? She couldn't stand around chatting for another second. She rushed to the door and said, "I'm going to find the others!"

The door was locked. She jiggled on the brass handle to no avail. Her eyes narrowed in hardened determination and she waved her hand, aiming to blast the lock off with her magic. Instead her tiny silver sparks bounced off the brass and then faded into the air, like nothing. She tried again, mustering an even more powerful blast of her lunar energy, but it was no good. The door remained unscathed, locked into place.

She didn't turn around, speaking through gritted teeth. "Let me go. You've...you've done something to the door."

"I haven't, Selene," said Mrs. Poe.

"Then why won't it open? I need to go find the others!"

"The others aren't here."

Selene shot an angry glare over her shoulder. "You're

lying! Phoebe's downstairs waiting for me. Aiden will be back any second—"

"No, he won't, because Aiden's not here. He's *not* coming," said Mrs. Poe with a calmness that produced goose-bumps on Selene's skin. "Selene, you're *already* asleep."

"That...what do you...I'm not..." Selene stuttered, losing her breath. Her hand flew up to her chest as she tried to breathe and realized no air came. She rushed across the room to her collection of books at her bedside table, picking them up and rifling through the pages, but the words would not come.

The words were a blur no matter how hard she tried to read them. The book slipped from her grasp and crashed to the floor. She didn't bother trying to pick it up as the terri-fying revelation sunk in and she racked her brain for how she could've fallen asleep and not realized it. What was real? What was a dream?

Mrs. Poe had walked over and stopped in front of her. Her once warm brown eyes were now somber, her red lips dipped into a frown. "I'm sorry, Selene. But I have to do this. He says it's the only way. Goodbye."

CHAPTER TWENTY-TWO

"I don't have time for this," growled Aiden. "This is an emergency. I have to make it back to the hotel."

"I don't care," said Humbolt. He motioned at the door. "Get out of the vehicle. Now."

Anger burned in Aiden's chest as he struggled to breathe in and then out. His nostrils flared and he bit down hard, forcing himself to keep cool. He let go of the steering wheel and pulled on the door handle. The driver side door sprang open as the passenger one did the same on Omar's end. For a moment, the only sound was the crunch of asphalt as the men got out the van and faced Humbolt.

The corners of Humbolt's mouth tipped up, a pleased look on his face. "Are you aware of the speed limit on this road, Mr. O'Hare?"

The asshole was stalling. Purposely dragging out the time in order to hold him up. And he was deriving a great sense of pleasure from doing so. The tension clenched Aiden's jaw even more as he glared at him, making no attempt at civility.

"Well? Do you?" Humbolt asked when he didn't answer.

"It's fifty," he choked out.

"And how fast do you believe you were driving?"

"Just give me the fucking ticket," spat Aiden. He rarely cussed out loud, but he also rarely lost his temper. Few could bring him to such a point. Humbolt, he now discovered, was one of those select few. "That's where this is going, isn't it? I was speeding and you decided it was the perfect chance to mess with me. So do it—give me the ticket and let me go about my night!"

Humbolt sneered, plunging his hands into his trench coat pockets. For the first time since pulling them over, he directed his attention onto Omar. "I expected you to do better, Omar. You only managed an hour."

Puzzlement curled Aiden's features as he glanced between the men. What was going on?

"He was a lot more impatient than I thought," answered Omar. "He didn't want to wait for Bono."

"That's because Bono wasn't real, was he? Neither was this EMBM 2400!" Aiden rounded on Omar as he fired off his accusation.

Omar's eyes narrowed behind his wire-framed glasses. "The EMBM 2400 is very real. Once again, this shows how inept you are as a paranormal investigator. I have to say, I'm quite disgusted you call yourself one. To think, you're even sleeping with the enemy."

"What are you talking about?" Aiden asked, his insides twisting.

"Where is she? If we want this over with tonight, we have to get a move on." Humbolt pulled a hand out of his trench coat pocket and unclipped the pair of handcuffs attached to his belt. "Aiden O'Hare, you're coming with me."

"I'm not going anywhere! I don't know what the hell is going on, but I'm out of here—"

"Don't you get it? Aren't you supposed to be an intellectual?" Omar blurted before he could stop himself. He rushed closer, a crazed gleam in his eyes. "I've already told you all you need to know! I've been investigating you and your girlfriend since the moment you got here! I know all about the strange occurrences that seem to follow her around wherever she goes! Didn't I tell you on our drive just now? I'm going to prove to the world I'm no nutcase. Did you forget I'm a seasoned pro at this? Have you underestimated me like my brother?"

"Omar," said Humbolt, his tone bored. "Enough."

"Dangerous paranormal creatures are real. Your girlfriend happens to be one of them. She's a *witch*!" Omar shrieked. "I know one when I see one. You can't fool me. I've come across dozens in my life—and they've always slipped through my grasp. But not this one. She's not going to get away. You've been too stupid to learn the Dreamling is feeding off of her. She's next on the list. Her time is *up*."

"I said enough, Omar," interjected Humbolt.

"And when the Dreamling gets her, she'll be done with," Omar went on as if Humbolt had said nothing. He took another step closer to Aiden. "Do you know how many millions she can go for? How much study will be done to figure out the magical components in her veins? I'll be rich *and* famous, world renown as the first paranormal investigator—the first witch hunter—to capture a *real* witch!"

"You take another step toward me and I'll break your nose," warned Aiden. He shot a razing glare at Humbolt. "I take it you're one too? Some kind of witch-hunting paranormal investigator?"

"Not originally. Omar came to me about you two. You can call us impromptu partners. My job tonight was to help keep you from making it back to town. Which I intend to do." Humbolt shook the handcuffs, the metal clink resounding in the late evening air. "Put your hands up and move them slowly onto your head."

"You can take those cuffs and shove them up your ass. I'm out of here."

Aiden didn't wait for a word from either. He spun around and rushed for the van, using his long legs in quick strides. Omar came at him first. The clumsy, bespectacled paranormal investigator was clearly not much of a fighter. Neither was Aiden, but he had been in a grapple or two growing up. As Omar lunged toward him, Aiden threw out his hand, the base of his palm colliding with Omar's nose. He howled from the brunt impact, clutching his nose, teetering to the asphalt.

Closing in on the van, the cock of a hammer sounded from behind. Humbolt's voice was even-keeled but dangerous, carrying a note of warning. "You move another inch and be prepared to get well-acquainted with a bullet or two. Hands up now."

Aiden grit his teeth as he did as told. He held his hands up midair but didn't turn around. A knot formed in his throat, his brain scrambling for a way out. He could take his chances and hop into the van, pray Humbolt was a bad shot, and slam on the gas pedal, fleeing down the road. He could try the more reasonable approach and talk Humbolt out of this. Though something told him there was no reasoning with the hardboiled detective. Neither were great options. Both were likely to fail.

"Get up, Omar," said Humbolt, exasperated. The gravel crunched under his shoes as he approached Aiden. "It's just a little blood."

"My nose is broken!" Omar cried, his words muffled by gushing blood.

Humbolt ignored him, stopping directly behind Aiden, holstering his firearm. He grabbed both of Aiden's arms and twisted them behind his back. Aiden sucked in a breath. If he was going to escape and make it back to Selene, he had to act.

Now or never.

So he did the very uncharacteristically Aiden O'Hare thing to do, and resorted to violence a second time. He bucked his head backward, colliding his skull with Humbolt's as hard as he could manage. Humbolt stammered and swore, fumbling for his firearm. The handcuffs tumbled to the ground with another clank. Aiden vaulted for the van, diving inside, starting the engine.

"GET BACK HERE!" Humbolt shouted, fumbling for his gun.

But he was too late. Aiden was already flying down the highway road.

———

For the rest of the drive into Maresburg, Aiden's heartbeat raced as fast as Ghost down the highway. The knot in his throat had gone nowhere, still a blockage whenever he tried to swallow. With each passing minute, the situation seemed grimmer.

Selene was almost certainly in trouble. Omar had said it himself. The Dreamling was after her. She was his next victim. Worse yet, no one had ever escaped his clutches. No one had been targeted by the sleep creature and made it out alive.

Cold sweat beaded on Aiden's skin as he twisted the steering wheel and Ghost whirled around a sharp street corner. The few town residents who were still occupying the streets gaped at him as he sped by, outrage on their faces. People weren't used to seeing someone barrel down the quaint streets of Maresburg—and after dark, no less.

His gaze flitted up to the sky. Any trace of day was gone. The sky was dark and the moon darker. That couldn't be a good sign. Had it gone black because the Dreamling was coming?

Aiden slammed on the brakes. Ghost's tires screeched as the old caravan lurched into a sudden stop. He flew from the van, barely bothering to shut the driver side door. His long strides carried him down the path leading up to the hotel in half the steps of someone shorter. The double doors were within arm's reach when they burst open for him.

Phoebe stood in the doorway looking spooked. Her beehive hair was disheveled, coming undone.

His heart dropped before she even uttered the words. "It's…it's Selene."

Aiden raced past her without a word, launching himself up the wide staircase. She trailed in his wake calling up at him in a pant. She caught him only as he reached the door that was Selene's hotel room.

"I…I found her passed out on the floor. The Dreamling must've gotten to her," said Phoebe shakily.

Aiden pushed the door open and hurried into the eerily quiet room. A rush of cold air hit and forced a quiver out of him. Only the table lamp was on, the rest of the room engulfed in shadows. Even with the feeble light, he spotted Selene at once. She was on the floor by the thermostat, her normally luminous brown skin tinged faintly blue. She wore her bathrobe, her feet bare and her hair still pinned up, as though she had recently showered and then collapsed.

The theater of his mind still empty, he acted out of pure, frightened instinct. He darted over and checked her pulse. Weak but alive. He sputtered out a strangled breath of relief, a wave of dizziness capturing him as he faintly realized he hadn't been breathing after all.

Aiden scooped her up and carried her over to the bed, wrapping her in the weighty comforter to warm her skin. Her lips were chapped and blue. Her face a blank slate, devoid of the usual bright effervescence he loved about her. Pain shot to his heart, piercing it like a sharp arrow.

He choked out another breath and tried to think. Nothing came to him and he clenched his jaw, biting down hard as he urged his brain to work. Selene lay clinging to life and he had no game plan. He had no idea how to fix anything. He was powerless and running out of time.

"Selene, wake up. *Please*," he muttered. He touched her shoulder and gave her a shake. His hand snaked up the side of her throat, then up to her cheek. Her skin was ice cold. She was dying.

He pressed the base of his palms into his eyes, failing to keep the tears at bay. If anything he felt worse. As soon as his eyes closed, the earlier image of her flashed into his mind. The two of them in the hall downstairs, entangled in each other's arms, her soulful eyes on him, her mouth shaped into a soft smile. He had kissed her goodbye, already with plans for when he returned.

But there had been a premonition lurking inside of him. A bad feeling he hadn't been able to shake even then. Why had he left her at the hotel? How could he not have seen this coming? It had become apparent she was a target. The Dreamling was after her.

This was his fault. He had brought her here. He had begged her to come with him on his travels. He had insisted they solve the case, even when he knew she was experiencing strange dreams. If she never woke up, it was on him. His selfishness. Like his father.

A sick feeling flooded his stomach and he held in the urge to vomit. He forced an inhale, exhale for some air and racked his brain for a way forward. That was when it hit him. There was only one thing left to try.

Aiden flung the door open, hurtling down the hallway toward his hotel room. Phoebe called after him, "Where are you going?"

He ignored her. His breathing was ragged and out of control as he stuck the key card into his door's lock. The door banged against the wall and he sped inside. The mirror was his last hope. He switched on the light near the safe in his room and punched in the code. Each correct number clicked until the metal door swung open and he reached inside for the broken mirror.

Aiden carried it over to Selene's room, peering into the shattered glass. Now to figure out a way to get it to work.

"C'mon," he muttered under his breath. His heart was still racing, his hand shaking. "C'mon, open up. Take me to this dream world. Let me save her."

As if understanding him, as if alive, black ink began to stain the glass. It unfurled into puffs, rising into the air. Aiden held his breath and felt the ground beneath his feet drop. His mind floated away from his body like a balloon escaping into the sky.

CHAPTER TWENTY-THREE

"**B**oo!" Noelle exclaimed, jumping out from behind a bookcase.

Selene flinched. Her armful of books fell from her grasp and splayed open across the library floor. "Noe, how many times do I have to tell you? *Don't* sneak up on me! And shh....or Miriam will happily have my head."

"Nope. Ol' girl is busy fixing the copier. She's covered in ink! A cartridge exploded in her face." Noelle released an unapologetic laugh, leaning against a bookcase with arms crossed. Today's quirky fashion was a pleated skirt with an oversized T-shirt she half tucked in. Somehow Noelle made it look good, her legs long and lean, her cropped hair showing off the modelesque bone structure in her face.

Noelle was fearless and bold. Selene loved that about her best friend. She smirked at the green witch and then knelt to pick up her collection of fallen books. She had been in the middle of sorting the *R*'s through *T*'s. A slow frown took shape on Selene's lips as she grabbed a book and turned it over in her hands.

No matter how many times she rotated the book, she

couldn't find the front. She couldn't find the title, or even the author.

"Hey," said Noelle suddenly. "Come with me. Let's take a break."

"But Miriam—"

"I told you," lectured Noelle with a spark of rebellion in her gaze, "stop worrying about her. Trust me, you won't get in trouble."

Noelle grabbed Selene's hand and pulled her along through the maze that was Brimrock's library. The aisles were longer and taller than Selene remembered, stocked to the brim with so many books, it was surely impossible to read them all in a lifetime.

In the background were visitors seated at tables or wandering past with books tucked under their arms, but they were always a touch too far to truly see them—just far enough away that they were faceless blurs. Before Selene could glance for a second look, Noelle had already dragged her outside into what was an abnormally bright, sunshiny afternoon.

The sky was cartoonishly blue. The clouds were white, fluffy, and floating. The fresh grass in the courtyard crunched beneath their feet as they dashed over to a bench. Selene was about to ask what was going on when Yukie crawled out from under the bench, one of her soggy chew toys in her mouth.

"Yukie!" Selene scooped up her furry terrier and scratched her behind the ears. "What's she doing here?"

"I took her out for a walk. The weather was too good today."

"It is, isn't it?" Selene glanced around her familiar neighborhood. Brimrock had never been a town fizzing with happy-go-lucky warmth and good feelings. Though home, it had always been a place of rigid tradition and formality, an uptightness lingering in the air.

Today was different. The vibe was mellower, almost fun.

Selene collapsed into the grass with Yukie. Noelle laughed watching them roll around and play. Selene sat up, legs crisscrossed, and tossed Yukie's soggy chew toy across the courtyard. The Yorkshire terrier scampered off to go collect the runaway toy.

"Too bad we can't have a picnic," mused Selene aloud.

"Funny you say that," said Noelle cheerily. She revealed a wicker basket from behind her back. "That was my other surprise! I packed everything we'd need."

Selene's mouth dropped open. "Noe, that's awesome. What's the occasion anyway?"

"Occasion? What occasion?" Noelle laid out a red-and-white-checkered blanket for them to sit on and then set up an array of goodies. She had packed everything from lemonade, sandwiches (she even cut the crusts off like Selene preferred), kettle chips, and snickerdoodles. "Freshly baked," Noelle boasted, holding up the plate for Selene to catch a whiff.

"I love these! But…wait a second, where are they from?"

"Who cares? Time to pig out and stuff our faces." Noelle dug into her turkey and Swiss sandwich.

Selene picked up a cookie and stared at the treat liberally dusted with cinnamon. She hadn't eaten snickerdoodles in Brimrock. As far as she could remember at least. They weren't even an item on the menu at Aunt Bibi's coffeeshop, the Magic Bean. She couldn't bring herself to shrug off that piece of knowledge, take a bite, and pretend it wasn't strange.

Instead she thought more about the moment. Her work at the library. Noelle's surprise appearance and Yukie's too. Now the picnic.

"Noe," she said slowly. "Why am I here?"

Noelle snorted between bites of her sandwich. "Selly, I love you, but I'm not gonna give you the birds and the bees talk. That's on your mom."

Typical Noelle, cracking a joke. Selene shook her head and pressed more. "You know what I mean. *Why* am I in Brimrock?"

A second passed in which Noelle quirked a brow. "What do you mean why are you here? Does it matter? YUKIE!"

Selene's head snapped in the direction Noelle shouted. Yukie had dashed from the courtyard, trotting down a path leading onto the street. Selene dropped her snickerdoodle, popped to her feet, and sprinted off after her dog. She didn't think to check if Noelle followed. Catching Yukie was a bigger concern.

"Yukie!" Selene whistled, vying for the terrier's attention. She cursed under her breath for the flats she had worn today. They weren't the easiest to run in.

The library shrunk into the background as Selene chased Yukie down the street. No matter how fast Selene ran, Yukie remained several paces ahead of her. Always within view but not within reach. Yukie shot around a corner and Selene trailed behind her, expecting a turn onto another street.

She was in front of 1221 Gifford Lane. She stumbled to a clumsy halt and stared up at the three-story gothic home with her brow creased. How had she run two or three blocks and ended up here?

It made no sense. Yukie had climbed the porch steps and ran inside the ajar door. Selene started down the path into the house. The cartoonish blue sky darkened around her, turning day into night in the blink of an eye.

The wind kicked up a notch, cool on Selene's skin. The curls framing her face jiggled from the strength of its gust.

Selene hated when the weather messed up her hair, but apparently she was already home…

The doorway loomed above her as she stopped at the bottom of the porch stairs. She never left the door unlocked, let alone open when she wasn't home; how the door had gotten that way, she had no clue.

"Selene, is that you?" a voice echoed from inside.

Selene's eyes widened behind her glasses as she recognized the familiar call. "Mom?"

In a couple of quick movements, Selene jumped up the porch steps and hurried inside. The house was dark, the lights in the hall off. She had the place memorized and wandered down the hall with her hand out. It landed on the light switch on the wall and she flicked it up.

The ceiling light didn't turn on. She tried again, turning it off and then on, repeating the motion. Still the ceiling light remained off. The bulbs must've gone out. She frowned and wondered why Mom hadn't replaced them.

"Selene! We're out back."

She followed Mom's voice, moving in the darkness. Yukie had disappeared. The rest of the light switches she came across had also stopped working. There was nothing but the dark and quiet as Selene stumbled into the kitchen and listened to the chaotic rhythm of her own heartbeat.

"Mom?" Selene stumbled out onto what couldn't have been further from her backyard.

Instead she was on the sandy shores of a beach. The waves crashing in the distance, the distinct smell of salt water in the night air, she shook her head to rid herself of the hallucination. How had she been inside 1221 Gifford seconds ago and now on the beach? One that didn't exist in Brimrock…

It made no sense.

The quiet hum of female voices pulled her gaze to the

right. A group of women stood gathered in a large circle, their flowy black dresses billowing in the beachy wind. In the center was a bonfire, the tall and vivid flames licking up at the boundless sky. What was going on?

"You're late," said Mom, breaking ranks in the circle. She didn't say it in her usual stern tone, but rather gently, coupled with an understanding smile. "We were worried sick about you. The ritual's begun."

Selene's gaze roved from Mom's sweet face to the others in the circle. The women were deep in concentration, their eyes closed and heads turned up to the night sky. None of their faces were familiar, though there was a mystifying sense of camaraderie in the air, carried by the wind, setting the scene at ease. Who were these women and why were they waiting on her?

She tried to process answers for these questions, but her brain was in too much of a fog, making it difficult to think clearly.

Then Selene spotted her. Standing in the circle, appearing out of nowhere, was Priscilla Myers. Her gaze was already on Selene. Her lips curled upward and she bared her gray gums and decayed teeth in a hideous witchy cackle. When the others looked over, their faces changed. Their serene, calm features morphed into sharper, uglier ones of anger. They transformed into the familiar and dreaded faces of Brimrock residents. Selene flailed backward, arms and legs spinning like a windmill before she lost her balance and dropped to the sand.

"What are you doing here?" she shouted as memories dumped into her head all at once.

She had been traveling with Aiden. They had started their first case together, investigating a sleep monster at the Mhoon Hotel in Maresburg, Virginia. Time was running out and she was supposed to infiltrate the dream realm to destroy the Dreamling, but first she had gone upstairs. She had showered, felt the steamy hot water on her skin.

Everything after that was fuzzy. The room had been freezing cold. She'd gone to investigate before—

"I'm dreaming," she whispered aloud. She scrambled to her feet only to bump into someone else in a long, rippling black dress.

It was Luna. The twinkle was gone from her eyes.

Selene hitched a breath, panic washing over her, and muttered, "Not you too."

The crowd had turned away from the fire and had started in her direction. They were coming for her. She looked beyond them to the bonfire, spying the chopped wood stacked at the base. It was no bonfire; they wanted to burn her at the stake.

Luna stepped between Selene and the approaching crowd, a graveness to her features. "Run."

Selene took off. The sandy ground fell away at a pace that was only a step behind her. She darted into the dark house with fast footsteps and a ringing in her ear. When she glanced over her shoulder, she shrieked as the kitchen crumbled, the cabinets and appliances breaking off into tiny pieces. The hallway met the same fate, the portraits and light fixtures crumbling to ash . It wasn't until she leapt down the porch steps and sprinted into the empty road that she spared another quick glimpse at 1221 Gifford, looking over in time to see the house collapse like it were made of playing cards.

Somehow, in what could only be the magic of a dream— or more so, a nightmare—a crowd of townspeople emerged from all corners of the street. They poured out from between hedges and raced down driveways to catch her. She held out her hands and flicked her wrists, attempting to magic the objects around her.

It didn't work. Her magic failed her.

Panic knotted in her chest and poured out of her in a breathless whine. She urged her legs to go faster, but they wouldn't listen. The crowd of Brimrock residents gathered ground, closing the gap between them. She rounded another street corner and racked her brain for what to do. Another minute and she was a goner.

And then it hit her.

Everything was up in the air in a dream—alterable at the drop of a hat. If only she tried hard enough. She puffed out ragged breaths running as she squeezed shut her eyes and tapped into her imagination. In her mind's eye, she visualized herself using magic. Her hands stretched out and produced tiny silver sparks. She blasted everything on the street from mailboxes to trashcans, sending them spinning at the crowd chasing after her.

When she opened her eyes, she gasped. Silver sparks traveled down the faint network of the veins on her arms, erupting from the tips of her fingers. She didn't give it a second thought, twisting around and firing off at the crowd. Like in her imagination, she magicked a trashcan, directing it to whiz through the air and knock down people like bowling pins.

She kept it up, shooting more and more objects at them, even using her imagination to dream up a wall of hedges that blocked them out. Though drenched in sweat while on the move, she counted it as a small victory and pumped her legs faster.

"Wake up, wake up!" she panted. Her cheeks were damp, cold from either sweat or tears, she wasn't sure. She didn't have a chance to decipher the difference as she pushed herself harder.

Soon the mob chasing her down vanished. The streets of Brimrock were empty and eerily lifeless. The chainlink swings on the playground creaked in the wind and the errant leaves scuttled across the road. She sprinted under streetlamps, scanning the area for the slightest sign of something amiss. Where had everyone gone?

Finally, she slowed up and inclined her head to the sky. Only the moon followed her, its presence comforting even when she was dreaming. If there was one thing that comforted her, it was the moon. It was herself and her magic. She simply had to find a way out, find the Dreamling himself.

Mrs. Poe's words reverberated in her head.

He followed me when I escaped. He followed me through the portal.

If "he" had followed Mrs. Poe between waking life and the dream realm, was he lurking now? Was he the architect of this nightmare?

It made sense. He lured unsuspecting dreamers into the fold by presenting them with the most perfect dreams. Perfection that slowly transformed into horrifying nightmares. He must've finished them off when he'd taken what he wanted.

On my hopes, my fears. It makes him stronger and you weaker.

Selene let out a gasp of a cry. She had been foolish, reveling in her recent dreams. It had been nothing but fiction. She had allowed herself to become easy prey, exposed her own hopes and fears for him to feed on. She should've pieced it together sooner, but she had been caught up in the wonder of bonding with Luna for the first time in her life.

The only way out seemed to be her imagination. She had to think about waking up. When she tried, forcing her thoughts to transform into pleasant ones rising from a long sleep, nothing happened. She gave it another shot. Visualized herself in her room at the Mhoon hotel. Focused on the steam rolling out the bathroom and the feel of hot water on her skin.

None of it worked. No matter how hard she tried.

Selene wandered over to a bench near some trees and shrubs with her hands covering her face. Plopping down and puffing out a breath through her fingers, she considered her options. Even if she had minimal use of her magic, she couldn't will herself awake. She was stuck, possibly forever.

The bushes rustled and Selene jumped off the bench. She expected the reemergence of the crowd. Maybe worse, Priscilla Myers herself. Instead she received a pleasant jolt of surprise that seemed too good to be true, more dream than nightmare.

Aiden emerged from the bushes as she remembered him. His tall frame stopped in front of her. His face lit up, his handsome features like his hazel eyes and his straight, pronounced nose so familiar with its faint smatter of freckles, she wanted to throw herself into his arms and kiss him.

But she held back. She was still asleep and this wasn't Aiden. This was some strange dream version of him.

"Selene," he said in his deep tone, "I'm so glad I've found you."

"Stay away from me!" She held up her hands, readying herself to magic the trash can to knock it into him.

He frowned. "I'm here to save you. You're asleep right now and won't wake up."

"*Aiden*?" she said, shocked. "The real you?"

He grabbed her hand. "The one and only. We don't have any time. We have to get out of here!"

CHAPTER TWENTY-FOUR

"I don't understand how you're here!" Selene shrieked as they ran. They cut through more bushes and darted across what was the Brimrock park grounds.

"I used the mirror," Aiden panted. "I pulled it out of the safe and asked it to take me to the dream realm."

"And it worked? Just like that?"

"Next thing I know, I'm here. I came in through the library."

"That's where I first was too!" Selene huffed, slowing down, but Aiden pulled her along with him. "Is that where we're going? You think there's some kind of portal in the library?"

"It makes sense, doesn't it?"

"But the Dreamling—"

They stumbled up the stone steps of the town library, which looked larger and creepier in the lone night, the building a large brick mass with dark windows. Aiden grabbed both handles and pulled, rumbling out a growl when the doors didn't open. Selene came up to his side, still wheezing from their long run.

"Stand back. I can sort of do magic here."

She blew the locks off the handle and the door flew open of its own accord. Aiden gave her a curious look.

"It seems to be an imagination thing," she said, shrugging. "Imagine yourself doing it."

"I'm imagining myself waking up now and nothing's happening!"

As though in answer, a thunderous, primal growl pierced the air. Aiden and Selene turned their gazes to the lawn and the flushed heat drained from their faces. Barreling toward them with canine teeth as sharp as any razor, was a pack of mammoth-sized wolves. At least a dozen on the attack.

Aiden could only gawk in horror as one proceeded to spit some sort of venom that burned through trees and left scorch marks in its place. Forget the shock he had felt the first time he witnessed Selene's silver sparked magic. This was on a whole new level of perturbing and unbelievable.

A second giant, carnivorous wolf opened its foul mouth and released another rumbling growl. Aiden caught on at the last possible second and grabbed Selene.

"GET DOWN!" he yelled as another blast of venom was spewed. This time in their direction as they dived out of the way. A hole was burned into the spot they had been standing in.

Aiden and Selene were already gone before the first sizzle, escaping inside the library. They sprinted down book aisle after book aisle until they reached the farthest corner of the library and paused for a breather.

Selene let go of Aiden's hand and stumbled to one of the bookcases, resting against its shelves and pulling off her glasses to wipe sweat from her face. "There's no way they can get inside of here, is there?"

"I don't think so," Aiden answered. He was trying to calm

down, but his legs felt weak. He hadn't expected to be confronted with one of his worst fears—anything that reminded him of the horrid husky attack from his childhood. Only this was so much worse. This was actual wolves. He swallowed down some air and ignored the muffled growls through the library walls. "I came in from over there when I used the mirror."

"Wait," said Selene, clasping her hand on to his arm. "We can't go yet."

His brow wrinkled. "If this is a joke, I'm missing the punchline."

"The Dreamling! He's still out there. He'll keep preying on innocent guests if we don't stop him!"

Aiden stared. "Selene, we have to go. Get the hell out of here. That's it."

"Then what'll we do when we get back? Leave Maresburg and forget we ever took on this case?"

He had to admit she was a good saleswoman. The imploring gleam in her warm brown eyes entranced him. Her soft fingers wrapped around his forearm sent tiny shocks through his veins. He stared at her, the determination written on her face, and he couldn't bring himself to turn her down.

She was right. They had started investigating this case and needed to solve it. But when he tried to reconcile that with his concern for their safety, he failed. If they chose to stay in the dream world and fight the Dreamling, they were putting themselves at risk. Selene was in danger, targeted by this sleep monster.

"Mrs. Poe mentioned something interesting," said Selene, oblivious to his troubled thoughts. "She told me the Dreamling feeds off of our hopes and fears. He uses it to present himself as anything—what we desire and fear most."

"Backpedal a second. When did you speak to Mrs. Poe?"

Selene filled him in on her final moments in her hotel room. She couldn't tell where reality ended and her dreams began, but after showering, the temperature in her room plunged near subzero digits. It was then she ran into Mrs. Poe and realized she shouldn't have been there.

"And she had no reflection," said Selene with a shudder. "I glanced in the mirror and there was no one standing next to me."

"Let me get this straight. The Grace you've been mentioning is the real Mrs. Poe and she's in cahoots with the Dreamling?"

"That's right, and Aiden, I think you were onto something when you brought up the victims having unfinished business. That's part of what draws the Dreamling. All of the victims had big dreams and aspirations, didn't they?"

"All the more for him to feed off of," Aiden said slowly.

"Exactly! Yvette said it herself—she was headed to LA to audition for an R&B group."

"Koffman was on his way to a science symposium to accept an award."

"The same for Yancy and Kerford. Even Mrs. Poe."

"And you?" he asked, a grim look to his face.

Selene rattled out a breath. "I'm experiencing life for the first time, aren't I? Me being free from Brimrock? That's always been what I've wished for. Me being a witch only makes him want me that much more."

The wolves answered Selene with a forceful thunk against the library windows. Aiden and Selene backed away from the window on their left as the wolves rammed into it and cracked the glass. They alternated among themselves, darting forward to attack the window one after the other until the jagged crack split the pane top to bottom.

Then it shattered completely. Glass shards sized big and

chunky to sharp and small were blown asunder, pouring down like torrential rain. Aiden and Selene scrambled from the blast zone, gaining as much ground as possible before the wolves dived through the broken windows.

Halfway across the study section, with its long tables and straight-backed chairs, Selene stopped altogether. Aiden made it only a few more steps without noticing. Once he realized she wasn't at his side, he called out to her, but she wasn't listening.

Selene was standing her ground. She faced the wolf pack rushing inside the library with her arms raised up. Aiden was half a second away from grabbing her and hauling her off himself when a flurry of thousands of books streaked through the air, like a hailstorm. Some missed the aggressive, predatory wolves. Many more slammed into them with such force it knocked them off course.

They whimpered and spurted venom at the barrage of flying books. Aiden hesitated for only a millisecond, swept up in a moment of paralyzing fear and wonder, as Selene possessed what must've been every book in the library, flexing a level of raw magic he had never seen of her before. She added to the bookish storm attacking the wolves, levitating tables and chairs and sending them flying. How could he stand back and do nothing? He had to face his fear.

Aiden joined her side. He might not have had amazing magical powers, but he was second-string pitcher on his high school baseball team. He grabbed fallen books off the floor and began hurling them at the mammoth-sized wolves. He nailed one center in his hideous face, eliciting a pained shriek from the creature.

With his brawn and Selene's magic, they cleared the pack in no time. But as the wolves with their giant paws and pointed muzzles dropped motionless to the ground, they soon evaporated into nothing. Aiden and Selene backed up, breathlessly glancing around the now quiet library for another sign of what was to come.

"Where'd they go?" Aiden asked.

"*He's* doing it. The Dreamling. I…I can feel something in the air."

Aiden looked at Selene. Her brow was wrinkled and she worried at her bottom lip. She scanned the high ceilings as though she sensed something bad was on its way. He didn't want to wait and find out what that was.

"We have to keep going!" He grabbed her hand and headed for the section where he had first appeared. If they could figure out how to use the portal again and leave the dream realm, they could regroup safely in the *real* world. "There it is!" he shouted in a burst of excitement. "It's right over there—"

The ground dropped out from under them. The library walls melted and its ceiling broke off into thousands of tiny blocks. They were two runaway people floating in sudden nothingness, surrounded by an ever-increasing black fog. The faster Aiden pumped his legs, the less it seemed like he was moving.

He gave up his efforts and let himself drift among the curling black clouds. Selene did the same, sucking in an audible breath. The fog was cold and wet, misting their skin with the most minuscule of droplets until they passed. Cloud by cloud their surroundings cleared, the fog rolling away as mystifyingly as it had come.

They were underneath a canopy of trees in what was a swampy forest. The ground beneath Aiden's feet was pliable sunken earth, pulling his boot in further for every step taken. His eyes locked with Selene's and they put into practice their well-developed silent communication.

They had no clue where they were and why, but their mission was the same: get the hell out of there.

Their fingers entwined as they waded across the swampy terrain, eyes peeled and ears perked up. More fog remained in the distance and their nervous thumping hearts were drowned out by insects clicking and animals scuttling out of sight.

Aiden urged himself to keep his cool. He couldn't panic or else they were doomed. Selene had mentioned if they used their imagination they could manipulate the dream. He focused on their swampy surroundings and imagined they transformed into the hotel. He envisioned him and Selene waking up from their nightmarish sleep, safe and sound.

Nothing happened. He had never been an imaginative sort of guy—quite the opposite with his more left-brained leaning. He was the facts and figures guy, not the guy who daydreamed the unreal.

But Selene was. He turned to her. "You can use your powers here. You can manipulate this realm. You need to imagine us waking up."

"What do you think I'm trying to do?" she asked, a tremor of frustration in her voice. She shook her head. "It's not working. I don't understand the rules of this place."

"The rules are, there are no rules. Except the ones *I* make."

Aiden and Selene looked up at the sound of the cold, sterile voice echoing across the land. It didn't seem to have an origin point until Aiden peered into the foggy distance and spotted the outline of a man walking toward them.

Selene held out her hands, readying herself to conjure more lunar magic. Aiden snatched a broken branch off the earthy floor for use as a weapon. Neither preemptive defensive action fazed the mysterious man. He kept walking toward them, breaking through the black fog and coming into view.

He was both regular and irregular at the same time. At a first glance, he looked like a man off the street, average height and average build with tapered brown hair and an unremarkable face. Upon a second look, he was unlike any other man Aiden had met in his lifetime. His skin was waxy and translucent. His eyes were cold and inhuman. His movements were too fast, too animatronic.

"Who are you?" Selene whispered.

He laughed, the sound bottomless and hair-raising. "Selene, you already know who—what I am. You've been visiting me for how many nights now?"

She took in a sharp breath. "So it's true. You're the Dreamling. What do you want with me? What do you want with any of us?"

"I want your hopes. And your fears. And everything in between," he answered without thought. He was smiling, a sparkling white smile that was sinister as it was perfect. "The more you give me, the stronger I get. The stronger I get, the more I want."

"But…but why?"

His laugh rang through the swampy air. His facial expression never changed, remaining the same as though permanently plastered on. "You silly humans and your whys. Why me? Why you? Why, why, why! There is no why! There is no other way!"

The last part he bellowed, his tone evolving into a deafening, monstrous growl, sending chills down their spines. Aiden stepped forward, holding his branch as though it were a baseball bat.

"Enough. Let us wake up now."

"Or else…what? You're going to hit me?"

"That sounds like a pretty fair ultimatum to me."

"How?" the Dreamling asked. His left brow ticked upward. "Do you comprehend where you are? Do you understand the extent of my power? Go ahead. Hit me."

Aiden's threshold for bullshit had long ago reached its maximum. He swung his branch at the man, using all of the strength he could muster. The swing was swift and powerful, but he struck air. The man vanished from where he stood and popped up behind them.

"How did that work out for you?" he asked. He snapped his fingers and the branch in Aiden's hand disintegrated into ash. "You really don't seem to get it. I can be anything I want to be. Anything you don't want me to be."

His smile stretched unnaturally and he morphed before their eyes. His form was no longer a man. He was an elderly woman with a hunched back. Then he was a venomous rattlesnake and after that a predatory lion circling them. He transformed for every passing second, turning into a terrifying tarantula and a squat toad. Even inanimate objects like a monster pickup truck with a roaring, revved up engine. Lastly, he morphed into Aiden, wearing his same vicious smile, staring at them with the same inhuman gleam in his eyes.

Aiden took half a step back in alarm, his heart racing at lightning speed. It wasn't real. He wasn't real. None of it was. Inhaling an unsteady breath, Aiden said, "Are we supposed to be scared? I was more terrified when I investigated the Goatman's Bridge. It was rumored he was inhabiting the surrounding woodland. Spoiler alert: it was some deer wandering through."

"Not scared? How about now?"

The ground beneath him and Selene caved in upon itself. They fell waist-deep into a pool of gunky ink. Aiden recognized its ropey texture. It was the ink from the hotel; the kind he had found at the scene of the crime. He tried to move his legs in the ink, but it was no use.

The ink was too thick, too gelatinous. *Too alive.*

It roped them in, sinking them further. The panic Aiden had long since been holding off erupted in his chest, tightening his rib cage without mercy. All of a sudden, he couldn't breathe. He couldn't think. He couldn't even move as the ink pulled him and Selene beyond their waists.

"Stop it!" Selene yelled. The desperation in her tone only made Aiden's chest clench that much harder.

"Why would I stop it now?" the Dreamling asked. He had returned to his natural state, an inky shadow, a menacing jagged smile cut into his blank slate of a face. "I have you right where I want you. I've gotten your hopes. I've gotten your fears. I don't need you anymore."

Selene released a strangled gasp as she tried in vain to shift in the hungry ink. They had sunk to their chests, lowering still. She freed one hand, narrowing her eyes in concentration, producing silver sparks that danced through the air. The ropy vines on the surrounding trees sprang to life, unfurling from the bark and extending out to them.

It wrapped its tentacle-like vines around them and heaved against the ink's pull. Aiden and Selene were torn from the pool as the ink touched their necks and lifted into the air by the vines. The magicked vine plopped Selene down on the ground. Aiden's moved to do the same, but the Dreamling had seen enough.

"Did you really think that would work?" he asked.

With a snipping sound, the ropes banded around Aiden were cut in half. He fell in what felt like weightless slow motion, dropping from midair as his stomach bottomed out.

He had barely registered what was happening, that he was falling backward, when he touched the inky pool's surface.

Selene's face was the last thing he saw. The tears shining in her eyes as she rushed forward and cried in raw heartbreak, "*AIDEN*!"

But it was too late. He sank into the pool, the ink swallowing him up whole.

CHAPTER TWENTY-FIVE

I n the span of a second, the sentient ink latched on to Aiden and pulled him under. He disappeared from existence. Selene tumbled to the outer banks of the pool, knees dropping onto the sunken earth. Her next breath ripped from her lungs. When she screamed her throat dried up, producing a hoarse sound.

The vines that had sought to save him plunged deep into the ink in another rescue attempt, but it was futile. The ink resisted and the tension from the push-pull became too much for the vines. They snapped into pieces and the rest recoiled to safety, banding themselves back around tree trunks.

Selene hadn't taken her watery gaze off the spot where Aiden had last been. A fat tear rolled to freedom, sliding sideways down her nose, then clinging to her chin. She didn't wipe it away, immobilized by the shock taking root inside of her.

"He's gone now," taunted the Dreamling, like Aiden's loss was of no consequence. "You must realize by now what happens in this realm correlates with waking life? He never should've come."

Selene could barely blink let alone speak. Let alone breathe. A thousand-pound weight had been pressed against her chest. And yet her heart soldiered on with its frantic pounding, thudding faster by the second. She bent forward on her knees and her hands caught her, weak arms holding herself up.

The fight drained from her. She didn't have the energy or the willpower. She couldn't go on and pretend like nothing had happened. Not right now. Not minutes after losing Aiden. If she could just curl up and close her eyes. Reminisce on those wonderful times they shared weeks ago, tourists traveling city to city.

The ring of Aiden's warm laughter reached her ears and more tears spilled from under her shut lids. He had come to the dream realm to save her, but she hadn't been able to save him...

"You're an interesting one, Selene," said the Dreamling. The unnerving weight of his inhuman stare was felt, even with her back turned. "Every soul I've claimed, I've sought them out. I've gone to them, slinking into their room, pouring myself into them, taking over their subconscious. You may not realize this, but *you* came to *me* first. From the moment you laid your head on a pillow, you were already tapping into my world—whether you realized it or not. You can imagine how pleased I was. You did my job for me."

Selene wasn't listening, closing her eyes to keep more tears from falling.

"And I must say, most people fear quite stupid things," he went on dryly. "Heights. Spiders. Wolves, like your boyfriend. But you fear being persecuted. Being abandoned and left alone. I can't say I blame you. Your life has been filled with being hated for who you are. It's been full of loved ones abandoning you. You'll have to add your boyfriend to that list."

She clamped hands over her ears, tuning him out. She busied herself creating her own reality in her head. One outside waking life. One away from the horrid dream realm she was now trapped in. The one where Aiden was still alive and well. The muddy earth beneath her knees disappeared. The acrid stench from the inky lake faded. The current of cold air surrounding her was no more, replaced by a fuzzy warmth.

When she next opened her eyes it was to the familiar view of her room at the Mhoon Hotel. She was on the floor in her cotton bathrobe. Fresh steam rolled through the open bathroom doorway. She pushed herself onto unsteady feet. Had she manipulated her dream or was she finally awake?

Selene glanced at the thermostat. The numbers on the dial were blurry. She rubbed her eyes and looked again. Still blurry.

The door blew open with the power of gale force winds. Mrs. Poe strode into the room wearing the same belted dress with cuffed sleeves and not a single curl of her bouffant updo out of place. Selene had backed away from the door and prepared for the worst.

Mrs. Poe faced her and said, "You're still not out of the woods yet, Selene. You need to try harder. You're almost awake."

"Save it. You'll excuse me if I don't trust a word you say. I'm in this mess because of you! You did something to me when I came out of my shower."

"I helped put you to sleep, but...I'm warning you now. You have to focus if you want to wake up. You're halfway there."

"Why should I believe you? Stay over there!" said Selene as she leapt backward, putting space between them.

"I saw what happened with you and your boyfriend—how the Dreamling took him—and I can't help him anymore. I can't be a part of it," said Mrs. Poe grimly. She wrung her hands, her cherry-apple red lacquered nails shining. "He's never going to set me free. He was never going to let me trade my soul for yours. He lied to me. His plan was always to take us both."

Selene gave a cold laugh. "Is that why you've done what you've done? He told you all you had to do was trick me so you can be free?"

"You have no idea what it's like. I've been trapped like this for almost sixty years. Just a soul caught between life and death. I only want to be set free," she said with a tragic note in her voice. "You're the first one to come by in decades. It was finally my chance."

"First what?" Selene demanded impatiently.

"Lunar witch. That was the deal. A lunar witch for a lunar witch."

Selene exhaled a shallow breath. "And what's so special about us? Why would he want us?"

"It's simple. He feeds off everyone, but lunar witches provide more power. It's the magic in our veins. It makes him infinitely stronger. You've been marked from the moment you walked through the door. He's been desperate to get his hands on you," she explained. "If he does, I'm afraid I don't see how we can beat him. He won't even be contained to the hotel anymore. He'll be unstoppable."

"So let me get this straight," said Selene slowly. "This Dreamling, who has terrorized this hotel for how many years, is now almost strong enough to break free of the hotel? To terrorize the whole town?"

"Possibly more," Mrs. Poe replied.

"And *you* decided it was a good idea to help him feed off of me?"

Selene's question went unanswered. The roof above their heads was snatched away by a monstrous hand. Rubble fell from the detached ceiling, plunking down into the room. Selene covered her head and dodged the falling pieces.

The monstrosity peering down into their room like a doll-house was possibly the ugliest creature Selene had ever seen. Its skin was gray and rubbery, stretching over his gargantuan frame as if it'd been pulled too tight. When he opened his mouth and bared yellow, pointed teeth, a putrid stench filled the air that made Selene retch. His one filmy eye was on her, a vertical pupil that was as dark as coal. He lifted his monstrous claw-shaped hand and snatched for her.

She leapt out of the way, landing hard on her stomach. She didn't have a chance to regain her senses. He swiped his hand again in another attempt to scoop her up. She rolled to the left, narrowly avoiding his sharp fingertips. On her back, she focused, aiming her hands at some of the furniture in the room.

The dresser rose into the air and then jetted toward the trollish creature. He grunted and smacked it away as though it were an irksome fruit fly. Selene promptly followed up, demonstrating a power she hadn't fully experimented with. She harnessed the lunar energy coursing through her veins and blasted it in the monster's direction. It traveled as fast as a jolt of lightning, comprised of thousands of tiny silver sparks, and stung him in the chest.

He howled, blowing more of his foul breath into the air. Selene used the free second he was distracted to rise up on her knees for another shot. She fired off a storm of lunar sparks, releasing a long-held scream. As the sparks left her body, it was like the anger and sorrow from losing Aiden was too. The dark emotions were expelled from her heart, the weight on her chest lifting, even if only for the moment.

She was fighting back. She was going to keep fighting 'til the bitter end. No matter the outcome.

The gargantuan monster stumbled backward, dizzied and encircled by a barrage of electric lunar sparks, before he crashed. The ground quaked as his thousand-plus-pound body dropped into the street outside the hotel. Selene hurried over to the window and peered at his fallen body.

"It's not over," said Mrs. Poe from behind. In her corporeal state she hadn't been affected by the falling rubble or the monster's clawing hands reaching into the room. "You have to wake up, Selene. Now or he'll be back."

"Sorry if it's a little hard to focus after everything I've been through tonight!" Selene snapped, breathing raggedly. She closed her eyes and formed thoughts about waking up, visualizing herself waking once more, but this time for good.

It didn't work. Instead of opening her eyes to waking life, she opened them to the rubble and debris surrounding her. Only the monstrous creature was gone. She looked over at Mrs. Poe, a sense of dread slithering inside of her.

"You're more powerful than I thought, Selene," said the Dreamling. He wandered into the room in his human form, his average build, fair skin, and lifeless eyes back. So was his smirk. "But if you think you're in control, you're wrong. I'm still the master of the dream realm."

"We're not in the dream realm!" Mrs. Poe exclaimed, working up nerve. "She's in her non-REM cycle and there's not a thing you can do about it. How else is she able to override you? She's waking up!"

"I won't let that happen. If you insist on going down with

a fight, it'll be worse for you. You might even end up trapped like this one," said the Dreamling.

Mrs. Poe lowered her gaze to the floor and fell silent. Selene refused to be intimidated. She stepped forward and lifted her arms, producing a small orb of silver sparks above each hand.

"You took my boyfriend away from me," she said in a quiet rage. "I won't let you get away with it."

"The problem is, I can do whatever I want. I can even mimic your powers. See?" He waved his hand and produced a spurt of silver sparks. "We've been over this, Selene. You can't beat me at my own game."

Selene glared at him, weighing her options. Then an idea came to her. She didn't move as she settled her thoughts onto the portal. The gold-plated hand mirror they had found on her bed nights ago and that Aiden had locked away in the safe in his room. The image of the heavy-duty steel box materialized in her mind's eye. Its sleek, cool surface was a pewter gray with a keypad on the front. The clicking noise it made when it opened resounded in her ears.

The safe door swung open and the mirror floated from deep inside. The crack down its center was as jagged of a line as ever. What had it looked like when it was whole?

The glass repaired itself. The broken pieces glued themselves together, even glinting in the light.

Selene expelled a calming breath and then opened her eyes. It had felt real enough to reach her hand out and touch; real enough that it existed somewhere in this plane between waking life and the dream realm. She only had to find it.

"I've had enough of this back and forth," barked the Dreamling. "What's it going to be, Selene? Are you coming quietly or am I going to have to take you by force like the others?"

"You'll have to deal with me first!" Mrs. Poe shouted, rushing in front of Selene. "I've made my mistakes, but I'm done doing your bidding. I won't let you do to her what you've done to me. Tonight we break the cycle!"

"Maya, move out of the way. You're not a witch anymore. You're not even a real spirit. I don't even know what to call you but a pathetic, miserable soul of a woman."

"I said it to Samuel, and I'll say it to you! I'm not going to let you talk to me like that anymore." Mrs. Poe's corporeal form began to flicker in and out. Her human features diminished, blurring and losing their shape until she was nothing but a sphere of bright light. She streaked across the room faster than any bullet, crashing into him, knocking him off his feet.

Selene seized her chance. She bolted for the door, fleeing from her hotel room and down the hall. Mrs. Poe colliding with the Dreamling had slowed him down, but it hadn't stopped him. He was on Selene before she could even reach the door to Aiden's room. Now an ever-growing, ever-heightening inky shadow, he sought to eclipse her, darkening everything around her.

She magicked the lock to untwist itself and the door to fly open. Diving inside, she pivoted a hard left for Aiden's safe. The numbers on the keypad were even clearer than in her mind's eye, only slightly fuzzy as she punched in the code. The Dreamling darkened the room with his expanding presence, boxing her in with a canopy of darkness.

"Take the Dreamling home where he belongs—to the dream world!" Selene screamed, the gold-plated mirror clenched in her hands. She gritted her teeth and held it up as the menacing shadow reached its peak height and then crashed over her in a tsunami-like wave of darkness. She urged the mirror to listen with every fiber of her being, letting her imagination take the lead, envisioning the mirror trapping him inside its depths once more.

The dark was everywhere, eating up every inch of the room. Her grip only tightened on the mirror handle. Her body shook, droplets of sweat beading on the crown of her curly head and gluing her cotton robe to her skin. A whoosh like the wind filled her ears and her feet left the ground.

She was spinning in a blur of color. She opened one eye and gasped. The mirror was sucking up the inky shadow like a gravitational force to be reckoned with. The Dreamling fought off the mirror's power, refusing to go easily. He resisted the gravitational pull, his inky form drawing back until unable, retreating into the corners of the room. There was nowhere else to go.

Drop by drop, the mirror sucked in the black gunk like a vacuum, forcing the substance to break with himself. He was no match for the portal to his dream world. He released a monstrous growl of protest as it seemed to dawn on him his efforts were fruitless. Whether he wanted to or not, he was headed back.

The mirror siphoned every last dark bit of him, its glass gleaming afterward. Selene hadn't let go of it, staring in marvel as the Dreamling was now a black haze beneath the glass surface. He was trapped inside. Just like he had been all those years ago before he was accidentally set free.

A disorienting wave of relief passed over Selene. Her body sagged and she brought a trembling hand over her face. It was finally over.

———

When Selene opened her eyes, she lay in bed, tucked underneath the comforter. The room was only partially lit, the inexplicable cold no more. A second passed before she pieced together what had happened and where she was. She sat up with a scooch against her pillows and rubbed the sleep from her eyes.

She had really done it; she'd defeated the Dreamling. He was trapped inside the mirror, restricted to his dream realm where he belonged. That thought alone produced a relieved puff of air from her.

Then she saw him. Aiden was collapsed facedown on the floor. The mirror was pressed tightly in his hand. Memory of what had happened to him rushed in at once and she jumped off the bed.

He couldn't really be gone. He couldn't really be dead.

"No, no, no," she cried, rolling him over onto his back with some effort. "Aiden, please. Open your eyes."

"Move away from him right now."

Caught off guard by the sudden voice in the doorway, Selene looked up. Humbolt and Omar looked worse for wear, both bruised with droplets of dried blood on their shirts. Omar clutched his nose while Humbolt's hand hovered over his holstered gun, his steely gaze stuck on her.

"What…I don't understand—" Selene stammered, puzzled.

"I *said*, move away from him right now. Stand up. Put your hands up. Don't try anything funny with those witchy powers of yours."

Her stomach bottomed out and her heartbeat rung in her ears. How did Humbolt and Omar know she was a witch? None of this was making any sense.

"Please, Aiden's hurt. I need to call 911."

"You won't be doing that," snapped Humbolt coldly. "You're coming with us."

Omar released a triumphant laugh, fingers still pinching

his bloody nose. "I really expected more from the *Paranormal Hunters* team. Did you really think I didn't know what you were all along? I told you to your face you were trouble. No matter, though. We'll be making millions off of you and those freak powers. Maybe we can start our own paranormal circus with you as one of the acts."

Witch hunters.

Mrs. Poe's story about Samuel floated to the forefront of Selene's mind. Omar Mhoon and Detective Humbolt must've been witch hunters. Both had made their disdain for her clear over the past two weeks. She should've known it was more than it seemed.

"I don't want any trouble," said Selene quietly.

"It doesn't matter what you want. This isn't up for discussion."

"Where's Phoebe?"

For the first time, Humbolt seemed remorseful. A dark look passed over his face. "I had to subdue her. She refused to let me upstairs. I figured she'd side with a dangerous freak like—"

The large ceramic vase from the hall smashed against Humbolt's head, knocking him out cold. He flopped to the ground without ever finishing his sentence, revealing the person who had struck him from behind. Phoebe dusted her hands off on her leggings.

"You rang, Jude?" Phoebe asked her unconscious ex. "It behooves me why you thought you'd get away with tying me up."

"Phoebe!" Selene gasped with relief. "Thank you! I woke up and these two were here."

"They barged into the hotel, tied me up, and then ran to your room. My own uncle a witch hunter. I'm disgusted, Omar."

The bespectacled man squealed, tripping over his own two feet, falling face first to the ground. "Don't hurt me!"

"You can expect far worse. I've called 911. The police are on their way," said Phoebe.

Selene could hardly pay attention to Phoebe's threats and Omar's cowering. She knelt beside Aiden, checking his feeble pulse.

"Hang on," she whispered frantically. "Don't go. Don't leave me."

As slow tears trickled down her cheeks and she curled over Aiden, his body warmed up. Even if a little. He was still alive. He was holding on. That realization drew more tears from her as she held onto him and counted the seconds as help was on the way.

CHAPTER TWENTY-SIX

Aiden's body ached like it had been raked through a meat processor. He groaned when he shifted in bed and achy throbs rippled across his abdomen. His lids were glued shut, refusing to budge when he tried to lift them. Instead he relied on his sense of touch and smell.

His hand traveled across the wrinkles of the cool bedsheets and he sniffed the clean, chemical scent in the air. If this was waking life or him dreaming about sleep, it was difficult to tell. While everything *felt* real, his last memories were of the dream realm, and that had felt shockingly real too.

He tested his theory with a dry clearing of his throat. Words wouldn't come. Though a few were jumbled inside of his skull, they wouldn't link together to form any real sentences, so he cleared his throat a second time. Then grunted like a caveman.

There was a beeping next to him and a woman's voice occasionally on what sounded like an intercom. She paged a doctor by the name of Jenner to the ICU. His thoughts snailed

along in his fuzzy mind as he put two and two together. He
was in the hospital.

After another minute-long attempt, he finally succeeded
in opening his eyes. The room was a nauseating blur of pale
gray walls and fluorescent lighting. He squinted, the
pounding from his head more prominent now than ever, and
focused on looking around the room.

On his right was an LED heart monitor and a metal IV
stand with saline bags. On his left was a wide window over-
looking the hospital parking garage. Seated next to that
window, slumped in a chair asleep was Selene.

Selene!

His excitement kicked his heartbeat into overdrive and he
tried to sit up. Big mistake, as both his head *and* his body
protested with immediate aches and throbs. He groaned and
sagged back against his mountain of pillows. Selene jerked
awake in her chair, throwing her hands out for her glasses.

She sleepily pushed them onto her face and her warm
brown eyes widened behind the lenses. Either his brain
moved too slow to register her movements or she flew across
the room so fast, she was a blur, because in the next second,
she was hanging off the side railing of his bed, showering
him with kisses.

"You're awake!" she gasped between each kiss. "You're
awake! NURSE SOSA!"

Aiden glanced over to the doorway as a nurse in purple
medical scrubs bustled into the room. She spent the next ten
minutes fussing over him, checking his vitals, drawing blood,
and lecturing him about lying still and getting rest.

"I'll be back with your lunch. You need a meal," she said
with a smiley twist of her mouth.

Selene waited another second 'til they were alone. "You
scared the crap out of me, Aiden. You almost died."

"Sorry. How inconvenient of me," he muttered in his croaky voice. Even his throat ached.

"*This* is how I know you're back. Only you would be sarcastic right now." Selene planted another kiss on his cheek and then straightened up. Her hands were still gripping the railing tightly, the tips of her fingers pink.

He met her eyes and his heart sank. Tears were forming in them. "Selene, I'm alright. Maybe a little banged up. But overall fine."

She gave a shake of her head. "I know, it's just…it's been a rough few days."

Of course it had been. He had left her alone to deal with the fallout. Though his mind was murky, his last moments replayed in his head. He had been pulled under the inky surface. Panic had consumed him as he realized his failure. Then everything had gone black.

His fear had become a reality. He wasn't able to be there for her. He wasn't able to fight by her side like he should've been, and he hadn't been around to support the emotional aftermath. Seeing the tears gloss her eyes and the sad bend of her mouth filled him with a heavy sense of shame. What kind of a boyfriend was he if he couldn't give her what she needed?

"Selene, I'm sorry," he said hoarsely. "I should've been there. You shouldn't have had to face the Dreamling alone."

"It's not your fault. You couldn't control anything that happened. I'm just relieved you're okay. When you fell into that ink…" Selene released a shuddery breath and slid her hand over his. "I thought I'd never see you again."

"This is the part where I'd put my arms around you if I could, but they feel about as heavy as tree trunks right now."

Selene cracked a small smile. "Just get better. Then you can put your arms around me all you want."

"Tell me what happened with the Dreamling. Is that a bump on your forehead?"

"A little one. Fighting the Dreamling wasn't easy. I used the mirror to trap him in his own dream world."

"Hang on a second. Sit." Aiden pressed the button that lowered the side railing. Selene gingerly sat on the edge of his bed and he fought through his achy muscles to pull her even closer. He wanted to know every last detail.

Over the next fifteen minutes, Selene told him. She started from the moment he sank into the inky swamp and ended with how she'd trapped the Dreamling in the mirror. Limb by limb, she scooted closer and he brought his arm around her waist.

"And Mrs. Poe helped me," finished Selene, now curled against his chest. "I woke up and thought it was over, but I was wrong. That's when Humbolt and Omar showed up in my room and tried to detain me. I couldn't understand what was going on. They said something about witch hunting and I was worth millions of dollars. Phoebe knocked Humbolt out. Omar peed himself. The police showed up not long after that and arrested them."

"I should've told you about Humbolt and Omar. I didn't think about them making it to the hotel."

"We were running for our lives from the Dreamling. You were a little distracted."

Though he appreciated her attempt, her light words did nothing to assuage the guilty pit in his stomach. He had failed to be by her side at the most crucial moment of the case and that weighed on him. He had failed her in more ways than one.

"I've never heard of witch hunters before. I didn't realize they were a thing. Apparently they're like bounty hunters, tracking down witches for cash rewards. I guess that's just another reason why witches live in secret," Selene mused aloud. She shifted against him, her hand at rest on his chest. "Are you sure I'm not hurting you? I don't want—"

"It's fine. I like you right here up close and personal. I need my Selene time." He offered her a small smile and watched the spark in her brown eyes pop. She pressed her face into his neck and inhaled a whiff of him, her fluffy coils tickling his face. Though guilt still lurked in his thoughts and churned inside of his stomach, he released a laugh and held her closer, soaking up his good fortune in the moment.

He was grateful for one thing.

The future might have seemed dark, but lying with Selene, it couldn't have been brighter.

———

Aiden woke to an unexpected phone call from Eddie. The two hadn't been close in recent months, much to his dismay. Eddie's absence in his life was part of the negative fallout from their investigation in Brimrock. Any communication they had had since was distant and borderline impersonal.

This phone call differed from the second Aiden answered. It was like old times.

"Bro, what the hell were you thinking?"

Half asleep and groggy, Aiden held his cell phone to his ear and mumbled, "Huh?"

"Every paranormal investigator should know you don't screw around with any kinda creature who can manipulate alternate realms. Do you know what could've happened? He could've done anything! He could've killed you six different ways to Sunday!"

"Just what everyone loves to hear after a near-death experience." Aiden scrubbed a hand over his stubbly, unshaven face, trying to wake himself up. The rest of his hospital room was dim. Only the light from the hall streamed into the room. It must've been late in the night. "It would've been nice if you warned me about creatures who can manipulate other realms before I went into the dream world."

"You didn't brief me beforehand, bro. Since when are we big phone guys?"

That was true. He and Eddie weren't known to be phone call people. They preferred communication via text or some other type of messaging. Their friendship had been that way since they were freshmen in college.

Aiden's hand traveled from his face and into his auburn hair. It hadn't been combed in who knew how long, sticking up at odd angles Selene thought was cute. Raking his fingers through, he found it had grown considerably longer. The first thing he would do when he was released would be a trip to the local barber for a trim, neat haircut. Then maybe he could feel like the old Aiden O'Hare again.

"Have the docs said when you're being released?" Eddie asked.

"I haven't gotten an exact date. They said I'm lucky to be alive. Apparently my heart stopped at some point."

"That doesn't sound good."

"No, it doesn't. But I'm alive. Somehow."

"You've always been lucky with that kinda stuff," said Eddie. "Remember the time you got hit by that driver who fell asleep at the wheel and you walked away A-OK?"

"My car was totaled, but I was glad I wasn't."

"Exactly. Might as well be a bionic man. How's things with Selene?"

Aiden hesitated. Though he was grateful for his time with Selene, he hadn't let go of the nagging thoughts in the back of his head. He wasn't enough for her. He never would be as a regular guy. She was a powerful witch, capable of impressive magical feats. The more they traveled and investigated the paranormal, the more evident it would become he couldn't protect her. The longer their relationship went on, the more apparent it would become he couldn't properly express himself. She deserved both, and *more*.

"I'm feeling guilty, Eddie," Aiden confessed with a difficult swallow. "I feel like I can't give her what she needs. I...I feel like I'm headed down the same road as my father. Some emotionless, detached jerk who only speaks in sarcasm. You should see it. It's pitiful. She opens up to me about things, and all I do is sound like a cyborg."

"Have you tried...*not* sounding like a cyborg?"

"Ed, not the time for smart-assery."

"Sorry, bro. Can't help it. Look, just tell her what you're telling me."

"Don't you think I've tried? I can't even tell her how I feel. Every time I go for it...I start shutting down. Just like my father. He's the same way. We're all the same way."

"Trust me, I'm tracking. I've met your parents."

"But I *do* care about her. I've fallen hard."

"Also trust me, I'm tracking," said Eddie without surprise. "You forget we've been best buds for how many years? I've been around for your dating life. The highs and the lows. Remember that chick you dated in college before Delilah? What was her name? Zadie? I've gotta say, you definitely have a thing for the quirky girls."

"Where are you going with this?"

"I'm saying, I've seen you around other women, Aiden, and I've seen you around Selene. It's different."

Eddie spoke the truth. Things were different with Selene, and it wasn't just because she was a witch. Even in his on-and-off six-year relationship with Delilah, he hadn't felt this way, like he would give his big toe just to see her smile or wrap his arms around her. He had never spent time envisioning what the future looked like, but whenever he did so now, Selene was always there. She was by his side. Partners. Lovers.

"If you're still not convinced," Eddie rambled as Aiden silently mused. "Just look at what's landed you in the hospital. You—a mere mortal nonwitch—traveled to a whole different realm because you thought she needed you."

A slow smile spread onto Aiden's stubbled face. "I'd say I have the bruises to show for it."

"And maybe if you're still having trouble with the feeling talk, show her how you feel. Can't hurt to do something special for her, right? Roses or something? Women like that kinda stuff."

An idea floated to mind, causing his smile to spread further. "I think I know what that could be. Thanks, Ed."

They hung up after switching topics a couple more times. Aiden thanked his best friend again and then pressed his head into his hospital pillow, staring up at the ceiling. He had to figure out the right time to sit down with Selene and talk. *Really* talk about where he was in their relationship. He had to make up for what had happened and make sure she felt special. He mulled over his idea and he glanced at his phone. It would take a few phone calls, but there had to be an auto shop in the area that could do it.

"Time for another check-in," said his nurse on shift, an older woman named Ms. Reba. She dialed up the lights in the room and stopped at his bedside with her carrier of supplies. "You're recovering pretty fast for the banged-up state you were in. Keep going at this rate and you'll be outta here in no time."

"Do you promise?" he asked, shooting her a smirk.

"I'll do you one better. I guarantee," she replied. She drew his blood with a quick pinch of a needle, the warm red liquid traveling through the attached tube and filling up the glass vial. "Your vitals are all looking great. Your injuries are healing up perfectly. *Almost* a little superhuman. You're not Batman, are you?"

"Well...actually, Batman is one of the few superheroes who *does not* have superhuman powers."

The nurse stared at him bemusedly, not taking in a word he said. "Whatever you say. Just don't go speeding off in that Batmobile using that super healing to save anyone. You need your rest."

"But Batman doesn't have super—"

Aiden stopped talking as she walked out, calling from over her shoulder she would check on him again in another half hour. The comic book nerd inside of him would have to let it go. He lay against his pillows and turned his gaze back up to the ceiling. He had to lower his defenses. She deserved to know how he felt. As soon as he was out of here, it was time for some show and tell.

CHAPTER TWENTY-SEVEN

The URide dropped them off outside the Mhoon Hotel and then drove off. Aiden looked at Selene and offered her his hand. She gladly slipped hers between his. Together they plodded up the Mhoon Hotel's front path. He had been discharged from the hospital early with a clean bill of health.

"It feels great to be out," sighed Aiden.

"I bet it does. But I don't get why you insisted we bring Ghost down to the auto shop. Couldn't it have waited?"

"Err, routine maintenance," he answered vaguely. They reached the double doors, pulling them open. "We want him to be in tiptop shape for when we hit the road again, don't we?"

"I guess so."

Aiden frowned at the dark foyer. "It's dark in here for it only being five o'—"

"SURPRISE!"

The shrieks rang through the room as the lights flicked on and the Mhoons jumped out from their hiding places. Selene held on to Aiden, who staggered half a step back. Soon a chorus of laughter broke out at the alarmed look on Aiden's face. Mr. Mhoon was behind the reception desk barking out thunderous laughter while Mrs. Mhoon hovered near the office doorway, hiding hers behind a silky handkerchief. Ms. Coco was by the staircase, wearing a proud smile. Phoebe and Tom were closest as they welcomed them inside.

"I don't know if I should be happy to see you or if this is some twisted beginning to a horror movie," said Aiden. The alarm on his face had gone nowhere.

Selene giggled and eased him along, deeper into the room. "It's a good ol'-fashioned surprise party."

"We're happy you survived," said Mrs. Mhoon with an enthusiastic nod.

"We figured we owe you a big thank-you," added Mr. Mhoon gruffly. "Both of you. You risked your lives to solve our case. The least we can do after my screw up brother and his detective buddy attacked you is throw a small party before you go. By the way, the hotel was featured on the national news today! I was interviewed by award-winning journalist Roger Fairbanks. I've got the video up on the TV in the parlor—"

Aiden turned to Selene, tuning Mr. Mhoon and his starstruck rambles out. "You knew about this?"

She smirked. "*Maybeeee.*"

"That maybe is sounding a lot like a yes."

That was because it was a yes. The Mhoons had approached Selene about the surprise party yesterday. She had agreed after thinking about the difficult last two weeks they had been through. They needed to unwind and let loose.

She linked her fingers with Aiden's and said, "There's lots of food."

"That's all you had to say from the get-go."

The party moved to the dining room. Mrs. Mhoon hadn't

been exaggerating when she mentioned cooking a feast. The dinner table was loaded with an array of home-cooked dishes. All of the classics were included, like baked mac 'n' cheese and a roast turkey so large it could feed a family of twenty. Everyone piled food onto their plates, chatting away as they dug in.

"When is the hotel opening back up?" Aiden asked.

Pride gleamed in Mr. Mhoon's dark brown eyes. "Next week. We figured we'd take this downtime as a chance to do some light renovations."

"I'm spearheading those," Tom jumped in. He aimed a smug look at Mr. Mhoon. "I have *a lot* of carpentry experience."

"Tom is very skilled. Something of a jack-of-all-trades." Phoebe smiled dreamily at her husband.

Selene caught Mr. Mhoon rolling his eyes. Mrs. Mhoon seized the opportunity to regale them with details of the renovations. The parlor in particular was receiving a full makeover.

"The decor is drab," she said. "I'm thinking things need to be brighter around here now that…now that you-know-what is gone."

"Dreamling. It's called a Dreamling, Marie!" Mr. Mhoon grumbled.

Mrs. Mhoon squeaked in shock. "Don't say that word around me! It's not proper dinner conversation."

"I guess some things never change," Aiden muttered under his breath.

Only Selene heard him. She raised her brows and smirked at him. She didn't doubt that for one second. The Mhoons weren't changing anytime soon. In fact, it seemed like now that the Dreamling had been defeated, they were even more over-the-top than before.

Mrs. Mhoon must've sensed Aiden and Selene's sidebar communication. She turned to them, stretching her hand to cover Selene's. "I owe you an apology. I may have been a little too frosty when you two first turned up. I was trying to protect the hotel from outsiders exploiting our family business. That was wrong of me. You were only here to help."

The ham-handed apology wasn't perfect, but it was a start. Selene put on her well-practiced polite smile and said, "That's nice of you, Mrs. Mhoon. We appreciate it."

After everyone had filled up on food, their waistbands tighter, the socializing continued over drinks. Mr. Mhoon had launched into a story about the time he filled in as a volunteer firefighter around town. Tom butted in with another competitive attempt to upstage him. Phoebe daydreamed and offered only occasional input. Mrs. Mhoon chatted Selene's ear off with more details about the decor.

Thankfully, Ms. Coco cut in with the save. "I'm so relieved you babies are alright. I was worried sick when I heard you were in the hospital, Aiden. I should've come clean sooner and told you what I knew."

"We understand. You thought you had put what happened here behind you."

Ms. Coco's eyes scanned the room with the flicker of nostalgia in them, as if every square inch reminded her of when her family owned the place. "I should've known the past always comes back to bite you one way or another."

"No kidding. I think everyone found that out the hard way," said Aiden.

"I suppose it's time I return this. I took it decades ago when grieving over Rhonda." Ms. Coco pulled Mrs. Poe's journal from her purse and slid it across the table toward Selene.

Selene gasped. "So that's what happened to the journal—you've had it all along!"

"You do with it what you want. Let's just hope the future around here is a lot less grim and a lot brighter."

"What's next for you, Ms. Coco?" Selene asked.

"It's back to business at Ms. Coco's Coffee and Cookies. My sixty-fourth is coming up, and I couldn't be more excited."

Though Aiden said nothing, the pink coloring on his cheeks gave him away. Both Selene and Ms. Coco split into loud laughs. Ms. Coco patted his shoulder, wiping away a mirthful tear.

"Oh, Aiden baby, the birthday cake was a joke—though you're both welcomed to attend my birthday party anytime," she simpered. Her eyes crinkled as she glanced at Selene. "Besides, as handsome as you are, you're already taken by a great gal."

Selene swayed on her seat and bumped her shoulder with his. "He's pretty okay. I think I'll stick with him."

"Where are you babies off to after this?" The amusement hadn't faded from Ms. Coco's features.

Aiden caught Selene's eye and he shrugged. "We don't know yet. I sort of made a promise Selene would get to pick our next case."

"You know where." Selene waggled her brows and Aiden groaned. "Why are you so embarrassed about it?"

"I'm not embarrassed. It's just…there's nothing special about it."

"And what's that?" Ms. Coco asked.

"His bachelor pad. I wanna see it!" Selene exclaimed.

"Oooh, sounds like a great next destination."

"This isn't fair. I'm being ganged up on," said Aiden flatly.

Mr. Mhoon picked up on that last bit and cut in, "You better get used to it, Aiden. And remember, you're always wrong. Just swallow the pill and say sorry."

The room rang with everyone's laughter, including Aiden's. He admitted defeat, slipping his arm around the back of Selene's chair and leaning closer to kiss her cheek.

"Well, you two be careful on the road. I'll pack you some snickerdoodles to remember me by," said Ms. Coco once the conversation around the table changed again. "I'm sure you'll make plenty of new memories."

Selene's face brightened, her heart fluttering with a look at Aiden. "I'm sure we will."

———

Later that night, Selene joined Aiden in his hotel room. They unwound together, getting ready for bed. Every few minutes or so, Aiden threw a curious glance in Selene's direction. She pretended not to notice. He had been acting off since his hospital release. If she didn't know any better, he seemed to have something on his mind.

She had things on her mind, too. It had only been a few days since she battled the Dreamling and lived to tell the tale. Aiden had pulled through in one piece. They had banished the horrible creature to his own dream world, where he could no longer prey on the innocent guests at the Mhoon Hotel.

Her first case as a paranormal investigator was a success.

Maybe kind of bumpy along the way, but a win nonetheless. She sighed in satisfaction, staring in the mirror as she twisted her curly strands. She'd spent weeks leading up to her first episode fretting about her abilities. Whether she could fill Eddie's shoes. Whether she could be the investigative partner Aiden needed.

Hell, she'd even worried about herself as an inexperienced twenty-six-year-old braving the world for the first time.
Was she cut out for the big world out there, or was she
supposed to go running to Brimrock, where things were
miserable but familiar?

Her chest felt light as she now knew the answer. Her life
was an open road waiting for her to travel down—and with
Aiden at her side.

Selene finished up twisting her hair in the bathroom and
emerged to find Aiden waiting for her. He patted the spot on
the bed next to him and cheekily said, "Saved you a spot."

"But the real question is, are you going to hog the blanket
tonight?" She lazily strolled toward the bed, letting a flirty
smile form on her lips.

"All the more reason for you to snuggle up to me," he
said. He met her halfway, wasting no time going in for an
affectionate kiss on the mouth. "Just the way I like it too."

Selene clutched the sides of his scruffy cheeks as they
came together for more sweet, short kisses. The balls of her
feet lifted off the ground and she was on tiptoe. Aiden's arm
hooked around her waist and gradually pulled her up until she
left the ground altogether. Kissing Aiden emptied her mind
and a pleasant floating sensation washed over her. She could
spend the rest of the night like this.

"Sorry to interrupt."

Selene screamed, throwing them both off balance,
crashing onto the bed. She sat up and looked wildly around
the room. Aiden was doing the same. The only difference was
Selene spotted the intruder while Aiden saw no one.

Mrs. Poe stood near the doorway in another fashionable
button-up dress and more pin curls. She wiggled her fingers
at Selene in a hesitant wave hello. "I didn't want to interrupt
your couple moment, but I've come to say goodbye."

Selene opened and closed her mouth, overcome by shock. Aiden was frowning. "Selene, what are you looking at?"

"It's...it's Mrs. Poe. She's here."

His gaze followed hers across the room. His lean body tensed up, his posture straightening. "What does she want?"

"To...to say goodbye."

"You can tell him goodbye on my behalf," said Mrs. Poe calmly. "Though I've never said a direct word to him, Aiden seems like a perfect gentleman. I was more so here for you, Selene."

Selene swallowed down her shock. "I didn't expect you. If I'm honest, I sort of assumed you were gone after you attacked the Dreamling."

"Not yet, but now I can be. When you trapped the Dreamling back in the mirror, his hold over me was broken. I'm no longer forced to stay in limbo. After sixty years like this, I can finally pass on," explained Mrs. Poe. "You not only saved this hotel and the people who lay their heads to rest here, but you've set me free. You have no idea how grateful I am."

"I'm happy to hear that, Mrs. Poe. Really, I am. No one should have to suffer like you have."

"My dreams were never realized, but I do hope yours are. Something tells me they will be."

Tiny goosebumps popped up onto Selene's skin. Aiden put his arm around her, warming her up like the doting boyfriend he was. Her gaze was still focused on Mrs. Poe. She smiled and said, "I hope you're right. But I'm still confused. If lunar witches are able to travel to the dream world, does that mean we can manipulate the dreams of others like the Dreamling can?"

"Well, as you know it's been a while since I've been in the lunar witch circles," said Mrs. Poe bittersweetly. "But when I was alive, when I was a practicing lunar witch, there was still much unknown about the link between lunar magic and dream magic. It seems you've gone farther than most lunar witches ever make it. The Dreamling said it himself. You're a very capable witch. Even if you may not realize it yet."

"Maybe I get it from Luna."

"Oh, Luna. She's very proud of you."

Selene tipped her head to the side. "Don't tell me you know Luna. But how? You passed in 1960 and Luna would've only been—"

"All lunar witches know each other. I guess you can say it's a club." Mrs. Poe winked at her.

"Apparently, I haven't been invited."

"I wouldn't say that. I'd say in time you'll see you're a very integral part. But I have to go. As you can see, I'm starting to disappear into thin air." Mrs. Poe held her arms up at her sides, showing off her now see-through form.

"Wait a second," Selene called out. She jumped off the bed and crossed the room. "What about the mirror and your journal? We've been keeping the mirror in Aiden's safe, but we can't keep it in there forever, can we?"

Mrs. Poe gave a sardonic laugh. "Chuck the mirror in a river. We all know he deserves a little more karma. Dump the journal too. Those pages were nothing but misery."

Selene hadn't responded when Mrs. Poe evaporated. She and Aiden were alone again.

"Are you alright?"

Selene nodded. "I'm okay. Confused but okay. She said all lunar witches know each other."

"How many of you are there?" he asked, easing her around so she faced him. "I was under the impression it was just your family."

"I...I don't know. But she knew of Luna and she said it's a club. I couldn't tell if she was joking or not."

"A club, huh? Would that mean there's some witchy coven out there?"

"Maybe," sighed Selene, confusion drawing her brows close. Her mind landed on the sandy beach she had stumbled onto while in the dream world; it had felt *so* real. Too real to only be a dream. "I think I had some sort of vision of a coven. When I was in the dream world I saw these women on a beach. Luna and my mom were with them."

"It was fake, wasn't it? All part of the dream world."

"I don't know anymore. My mom passed away. Her grave is in Brimrock, but Luna? It felt like I was really speaking to her."

"Then maybe you were...wherever she is." The expression on Aiden's face was as puzzled as hers.

"Apparently, I can do dream magic. It's the ability to manipulate dreams."

"Is that how you were able to get to the dream realm without the mirror as a portal?"

"I think so. It would've been nice if my mom taught me about this kind of stuff," said Selene with a frustrated shake of her head. "Instead she taught me to fear my powers. She taught me they were a bad thing and I'd never fit into society if I chose to live my life as a witch."

Aiden matched her frown, sliding a hand to cup her cheek. "Selene, I think that might be the reality. I'm not sure society is ready to accept witches. Except a select few people."

"Like you." She covered his hand on her cheek with her own, eyes softening on him. He had been the solid rock in her life for months now. Ever since the curse in Brimrock was lifted, he had stuck by her every step of the way. "Thanks for being such a great boyfriend."

A look of surprise blinked across his face. "I've been worried I haven't been enough. Sometimes it's like I'm useless. I want to protect you, but then these situations happen that are out of my hands. I'm just some guy off the street. I don't have fancy magical powers or superhuman strength. But I've never wished for them more than when I'm with you."

"Aiden—"

"And," he continued with a deep sigh. "That's not even the half of it. I haven't been good with the emotional stuff either. You open up to me about your hopes, your fears, your secrets. And…and I shut down. Even when I don't want to. It's the O'Hare in me."

"But you express yourself other ways. Remember when you told Humbolt off? I've never seen you more pissed. Let's not even get into how attentive you've been when I told you about the dreams I was having."

"I couldn't sleep well knowing something was up with you—"

"Exactly my point. You make me feel cared for. I get you're not a words guy and you struggle with it."

"I want to be a words guy, though. You make me want to be." He paused and inhaled a breath, the rest of his body tensing up in preparation. "Selene, I'm a goner for you. I can't even picture my life without you anymore."

"Is that your way of saying what I think you're saying?"

"I love you," he finished with a sudden sense of calm, looking relieved it was off his chest. He dropped a kiss on her lips. "And I want you to know that as long as I'm by your side, you'll never have to fight alone again."

Blood rushed to Selene's face, warming her cheeks. She

tossed her arms around him as he pulled her off the ground. For seconds they stayed wrapped up in their smitten embrace until he placed her back on her feet and she smiled up at him.

"I love you too, Aiden."

"You do?"

Selene proved it to him with another kiss. The moment their lips brushed was like its own brand of magic. Her hands clutched his scruffy, badly-in-need-of-a-shave cheeks, and she poured every ounce of her feelings into him. All the hope. All the fear. The sweeping relief and the overwhelming love which often made her heart feel so full it'd burst. Aiden happily reciprocated, kissing her deeply, with enough emotion it was palpable. He scooped her up and dropped her onto the bed. Her laugh was free and uninhibited, as light as the wind as she flounced across the mattress and then patted the space next to her.

"Saved you a spot," she teased, raising a brow.

A peal of laughter left him. "I should've guessed you'd use my line against me."

Aiden jumped onto the bed, the mattress jiggling like jello with his added weight. Selene laid back against the pillows as the long, lean length of his body covered hers and he claimed her mouth in a deep kiss. A warmth was quick on its spread, trickling throughout her body, flushing onto her brown skin. Thoughts about their case and the Dreamling, the mystifying depths of her powers and even Luna's whereabouts, melted away into nothing, replaced by the thrill of being wrapped up in Aiden for the night.

Selene parted her lips for his tongue, moaning when his slicked against hers. Aiden brought out a passion in her she hadn't thought possible of herself. Growing up as a bookish loner, she had rarely felt sexy let alone beautiful, but with him, she was a goddess. He made it known even in his touch as his hands charted a path down her shapely body, slipping under the hem of her robe.

It didn't take him long to catch on to her secret, his palms sliding over her bare, supple flesh. He broke away and choked out, "Jesus, Selene, you're not wearing anything underneath."

She smirked up at him. "I figured it'd be a nice surprise to pull the robe open and be like, *BAM*! I'm already naked."

"Naked is always good."

"But now you've stolen my thunder."

"I see your thunder and raise you a very hard lightning rod."

"Me and him are already well-acquainted. I'd like him inside me now."

They laughed between kisses and wrestling off clothes. Her robe was first to go, followed by his T-shirt and sweatpants. As he tossed both onto the armchair, she propped herself onto her elbows and let her hand creep between her legs, toying with her slick, pulsing sex. Heat warmed in his hazel-eyed gaze when he caught her, enjoying the sight with his own hand blindly stroking his length.

"You are the sexiest witch on the planet," he husked out before descending on her again. His lips found her neck, kissing the column of her throat. Her hand reached between them and took over for his, the weight of his aptly named lightning rod deliciously heavy. Harder than any metal, she worked up and down his veiny, thick length, applying pressure with her grip, making him groan. He buried his face into her neck and said, "You make it so hard to hold on."

"Then don't. Fuck me right now."

Aiden lifted his head at the crass candor of her words, a mildly surprised look on his face. Humor shortly followed, lighting up his features. He took her request to heart, guiding himself to her entrance. Selene pulled him to her mouth at the same time he sank into her. An elated shudder coursed through her, taking him in completely. He withdrew to the tip, the tease too much as her core ached with anticipation. She gasped when he slid inside again, burying himself to the hilt, emptying her lungs with the wonderfully full feeling.

His strokes were slow but deep, each one leaving her breathless. She rolled her hips in tune with his, her fingers tangled in his hair, her mouth agape as her body tingled from sensation overload. Their eyes were on each other, watching the waves of pleasure flicker across their faces. His eyes had turned an earthy brown in the dimmed room lighting, heavily hooded and darkened by desire. Another shudder racked her body under such a piercing gaze—the intensity in them peering through the physical, into her heart, into her soul.

It drummed up an emotion so grand, so encompassing, no words seemed to do it justice. Though she'd spent many nights reading books, tales of fantastical adventures and sweet love stories, she'd never imagined it as her reality. It had never been something she thought she could have. But now she did; the man making love to her, who she was in love with, was real in the flesh. He was who she wanted by her side today, tomorrow, and every day after. The gravity of which hit her in full in that moment as her pleasure kindled and then exploded.

Her eyes pinched shut, and she surrendered to the sweet rush sweeping over her. The tiny shocks radiating from her core, the echoes of her heartbeat in her ears, the dizzy floaty feeling that caused her thighs to vibrate, weak but sated. Aiden was with her, riding out her orgasm with more deep strokes and tender kisses. He came with a husky moan, drawing more shallow thrusts until spent.

Collapsing onto his back, he curled her into his side, their bodies sticky with sweat, but in the most pleasing way. His lids were already lowering shut as exhaustion set in and he mumbled, "God, I am so in love with you."

It reminded her of drunk talk, the drowsiness thick in his tone. He'd drifted off by the time she kissed his cheek, snuggling closer for what she sensed would be a good night's sleep. Her whisper went unheard, but she said it anyway.

"I'm so in love with you too, Aiden. Good night."

CHAPTER TWENTY-EIGHT

Selene poked and prodded Aiden awake. He lay comfortably on his back with an arm bent under his head and the other wrapped around her. He wanted for nothing else as he stirred. How could he? A lazy morning in bed with the woman he loved naked in his arms. Some morning sex was likely on the table along with Mrs. Mhoon's hearty breakfast (whenever they finally crawled out of bed). The moment was perfection.

"Time?" he murmured, eyes still closed.

"Few minutes after nine." Selene wiggled closer, the feel of her warm, silky skin waking his lower half.

"Mmm."

"Mmm, what?"

"Feels good."

"What does?"

He cracked an eye open, peering drowsily at her, but with enough sense to drink in how beautiful she looked in the morning light, a magical glow about her. "*You,*" he said hoarsely. "Just laying here together."

"It does, doesn't it? It's the first time in weeks there's nothing hanging over our heads."

"How are you..." he rubbed his eyes, then slid his fingers in his hair. It was long and unkempt. He really needed a barber. "So articulate... too early..."

"Says the man who's normally a dictionary. You need coffee."

"Everybody keeps drinking mine," he mumbled.

Selene burst into a laugh, poking him again. "You get out of bed and I promise you can have all the coffee you want."

"What about all the Selene I want?"

"Selene will be in the shower. Feel free to join her."

She sat up with her bare back to him, the coke bottle shape of her body an arousing one from behind. He even caught a tantalizing glimpse of side boob that almost made his brain malfunction that early in the morning. He would certainly accept the shower invite.

"Your phone is ringing," said Selene as she passed the desk on her way to the bathroom.

Aiden hopped out of bed and headed for his desk. The name flashing across his phone screen produced a roiling sense of nerves. He hadn't expected Dad to call him out of nowhere, or even at all.

"Hello," he answered uncertainly, slipping on his sweatpants and moving to the window. Mrs. Mhoon was in the courtyard watering the plants. He welcomed the distraction as his hunch told him this conversation would not be a pleasant one.

Dad's familiar timbre was smoky in his ear. "I'm sorry about not calling you sooner, Fin. I've been getting things in order."

"Oh... it's alright. I know you're a busy man. How's the business going?"

"Good, good. We've got new air conditioning units in for the summer. They should be a big hit. You know summer is our best time for business. Nobody wants to be sweating bullets in their home."

"No kidding. New York heatwaves are nothing to sneeze at."

A second passed where Dad blew a heavy breath as though figuring out how to broach the real reason he called. "Listen, Fin, the divorce has been hard on everyone. Cara told me you didn't take the news well."

"I'm not sure there's a right way to take divorce news. You and Mom have been married for over thirty years. It was a surprise to hear."

"I understand… it's an adjustment. It's been different not having her around," he mused solemnly. "Your mother's a good woman—it's my fault for letting her go."

"But you don't have to let her go. You can try to get her back."

"The divorce is happening. No changing it. What's done is done. I know that now."

"Have you even tried—" Aiden cut himself off with a ragged breath. He couldn't lose his composure and go off on some accusatory rant. It would accomplish nothing except driving a wider divide in their tepid father and son relationship. "I wish it could've been different for both of you. I… I wish there was something *I* could do."

"Keep your chin up. Keep doing what you've been doing. I watched a few clips of your show. Might not tell you this often, but I'm proud of you, Fin. I raised my son to be a good man. Better than me. I'll take it."

"Dad, I don't want to make you feel bad. That's not what I'm trying to say."

"I know it's not, but I want you to know not to let this

change you. Don't let it affect how you're living your life. Promise me that."

Aiden nodded, his gaze still on the window. Mrs. Mhoon had moved onto picking apples from one of the apple trees. Aiden turned away from the window as Selene walked out of the bathroom with the shower running. She gave him a quizzical smile, her face glowing, her eyes warm, oblivious to his phone call with Dad. His lips spread in return as he spoke into his phone, "That I can do. Thanks, Dad."

They hung up on that note. Maybe no closer to fixing the issues in the family, but at least on some better level of understanding. Even if by an inch.

Selene dropped onto the edge of the bed, leaning backward with her arms holding herself up. "I didn't realize it was your dad on the phone. Did it go okay?"

"I think so. The divorce is happening, but I think I'm coming to terms with it—slowly, but I am."

"That's really all you can do. I'm proud of you." Selene rose and tossed her arms around him.

He caught her, hugging her close. The tension of the last few weeks lifted from his shoulders as he realized everything had worked itself out. Selene and him were safe, alive and in love. Mom and Dad were still divorcing, but they both accepted the reality of it. They were both moving on. He would have to, too.

"Shower then breakfast?" Aiden asked when he let Selene go.

Her eager nod was like a bobblehead. "About time. The water's getting cold. Plus, my stomach's only been growling for the last fifteen minutes."

———

Their last day in Maresburg arrived, the clouds spreading far across the sky and hiding the sun away. Aiden and Selene loaded up Ghost with their luggage and equipment. His thoughts were already on the long journey ahead. They had agreed filming this episode in Maresburg was rough. They needed a minivacation before conducting another investigation—it was still Selene's pick where.

Aiden stacked the last case with their equipment and slammed the van doors shut. Selene approached clutching two coffees and a brown paper bag. He gladly accepted the warm beverage, looking beyond Selene toward the front of the hotel. Mr. and Mrs. Mhoon stood on the staircase waving them goodbye.

He waved back and said, "I'm assuming a goodbye gift from Mrs. Mhoon?"

"She insisted we take some coffee and dinner leftovers for the road."

Selene moved to hop in the van, then stopped short. Aiden mimicked her movement, stopping beside her. "What is it?"

"What did you do?" she asked, looking from the van to him. She rushed forward and poked her head inside the ajar passenger door. Her mix of a squeal and a gasp made him chuckle. "Aiden, the van—it's been remodeled! The whole interior has changed!"

"Oh, has it?" he asked, feigning surprise. He hovered his much taller frame over hers, poking his head inside the caravan. "So it has. Who would've done that?"

"You sneak!" Selene laughed, twisting around for a look at him. "You said you were taking Ghost in for routine maintenance before we hit the road!"

"That was true. But it just so happened the car repair place does interior renovations."

"You installed a bed."

Selene crawled inside the van with a look of wonder on her face. Aiden put the cups of coffee and doggy bag from Mrs. Mhoon in the front before joining her. He had picked up Ghost from the repair shop last night, but hardly taken a look himself. The inside looked like a different van.

The auto shop had pulled out the old shag carpet and installed wooden vinyl flooring. They had refurbished the interior and installed better lighting. The full-size bed itself was a genius combination of a memory foam mattress and drawers and storage cubbies beneath. They each had a personalized area near the bed; on one side of the van wall were built-in shelves with many of Selene's prized possessions like her favorite books and lunar ritual supplies. Bands secured them in place on the shelves for when they were mobile. They had even installed a kitchenette area near the front with a mini compressor fridge and basin sink and water tank.

It had everything Selene had asked for. Even a touch of home in the fairy lights strung along the ceiling and the soft vanilla scent emanating from the flameless candles. She ran her fingers over her bookshelf and whispered, "You did this for me?"

"Am I allowed to say yes if you like it and no if you don't?" he teased, smirking at her.

"You renovated the entire van for me," she said, louder now, stun laced in her tone.

Aiden moved up to her side, gripping her chin with his thumb and forefinger and turning her face to his. "Of course I did. I wanted you to be happy on our travels. I know how hard it's been for you adjusting. Hopefully now you'll be more comfortable."

"Aiden, this is the sweetest thing anyone's ever done for me."

They sealed the moment with a soft kiss. Any thoughts of their driving schedule fell by the wayside. Aiden pulled her down with him onto the bed. He rolled onto his back and she lay on top, her shapely legs falling on either side of him. One of his favorite places to be: between Selene's legs.

He glided his hands along her dips and curves as their kisses dissolved into an impromptu makeout. Something told him there would be many of these types of moments in the van now that they had a comfy bed installed.

"We should probably get a move on," he said minutes later when they had kissed each other breathless.

Selene's face glowed with a smile. "If you don't mind, I'd like to make two stops before we leave town."

"Say the word and we're there."

The first stop was the Maresburg River, which sprawled through a good portion of the town. Aiden parked off road between trees and bushes. He and Selene hopped out with the crunch of leaves beneath their boots. She carried her leather book bag with her, withdrawing two items from inside.

"What are the mystery items?"

Selene inched closer to the river bank. The water splashed against nearby rocks, its current a fast one. She held up Mrs. Poe's gold-plated mirror and leather-bound journal. "She said to toss them into the river."

"That's one way to get rid of them."

He stood back and watched as Selene first chucked journal and then the mirror into the rapid waters. The current carried them away, the objects growing smaller the farther they were taken. Soon they disappeared from view altogether. He put his arm around Selene.

"I'm glad the mirror's gone," she said quietly.

He squeezed her closer and dropped a kiss on her brow. "Me too. No more spooky dream realm."

"Nothing but sweet dreams in that fancy new bed."

"And other things."

Aiden laughed as she gave him a playful shove and then marched back to Ghost. They buckled in and turned on the heat before he asked about stop two.

"Can you take us to Main Street? I'd like to see Phoebe before we go," said Selene.

The request came as a surprise, but Aiden obliged. In ten short minutes they pulled up alongside a curb on the street and parked. The usual morning foot traffic crowded the small town sidewalks. Townspeople strolled to Ms. Coco's for coffee and headed to the bank or dry cleaners. Aiden and Selene crossed the street and passed through the dangling beaded entrance of Hidden Senses.

Today a smoky haze floated around the new age shop. Aiden waved his hand to dismiss the clouds and scanned the shop room. Selene found her first. Phoebe Mhoon was on a stepladder at the back of the shop, stocking the shelves with essential oils. She didn't pause or turn around for a look at them, but she did greet them.

"You're on your way out of town."

"We are," said Selene, peering up at the seer. "But I wanted to talk to you before we go."

"We've talked about everything there is to talk about." Phoebe climbed down the stepladder and drifted past Selene to the other boxes of merchandise.

Selene refused to be dismissed, following her. "No, we haven't. Because you still never answered my question."

"That would be?"

"The spell book you have—the one with the crescent

moons and the lunar crystal on the cover. That belonged to Luna, didn't it?"

Aiden remained silent, though he paid attention to the subtle change in Phoebe's demeanor. She stopped rummaging in the box and straightened up. Her slouchy sweater slipped off either shoulder and she touched a hand to her beehive hairdo. Her sharp expression was studious as she stared at Selene, as though questioning whether her charade was over.

"If you must know, it's a very real possibility it once belonged to her," she answered. She dusted her hands off on her leggings. "But it's of no real consequence. I've told you things from across the world come into my possession all of the time."

"But you know her name. You know who she is. You've known who I am. That…that I'm a witch."

Silence lingered for a long moment. Aiden felt like a voyeur, hanging in the background as the two women held each other's gaze. Though it might not have been his family business, curiosity swam inside of him. Selene seemed to be onto something.

"She's alive, isn't she?"

"I wouldn't know," said Phoebe.

"The dreams felt so real. Then I learned I can do dream magic. It felt like Luna was in the dreams with me—like we were *really* communicating. There was this part on a beach that had to be—"

"I'm lost as to what you want me to tell you, Selene. I wasn't a part of your dream. I do not know the intricacies of the dream world." Phoebe returned to the box of merchandise, withdrawing more oils. "It's quite possible you were communicating with her. Only you know for certain. Everyone knows Luna's knowledge of magic is extensive."

"Where is she? Why has she stayed away all this time? My entire life…"

"Again, you're asking questions I can't answer," said Phoebe. She sighed, drifting down the aisle stocked with books. She hefted the thick, dusty book into her arms and carried it over to Selene. "I don't know what's fact and what's fiction. There are many rumors floating around. But if you're curious, if you're really seeking answers, you're on the wrong side of the country. Your beach dream might've been more real than you realize. There are many others like you. Head west, drive to the coast. You might find what you're looking for."

Selene quirked a solitary brow. "The west coast as in California?"

"It's warming up in the coming weeks. I hear San Azul Beach is nice this time of year."

"I've always wanted to go to a beach," Selene trailed off.

Phoebe pushed the dusty spell book into Selene's hands. "Take this with you. It's better off with you and it just might come in handy. Just remember, you're not as alone as you think."

Aiden and Selene left Hidden Senses in bemused silence. They stopped on the sidewalk outside and Selene pointed out they hadn't filmed an ending yet. Aiden pulled out his camcorder for a quick snippet.

"Closing out our time in Maresburg. We didn't get much of what happened on video, but it works that way sometimes."

"I just want to point out, I was right," Selene boasted, edging into the shot. "For once, the skeptic was wrong."

"Let's not get into who was right and who was wrong."

"That's what the wrong person always says."

He fought the amusement from his expression, looking

back to the camcorder. "What's important is the Mhoon Hotel is no longer a source of tragedy. However, the truth as to whether other paranormal activity is out there remains to be seen. We'll catch you on our next investigation."

He pressed the button to end the recording, avoiding Selene's gaze. She hugged the spell book to her chest, a gloating air about her. "You almost admitted the paranormal was real on camera. That's some improvement."

He stuffed his hands in his pants pockets and said, "Yeah, well, baby steps. We have a couple weeks before we have to film another episode, and this Mhoon Hotel one needs a lot of editing."

"That's not surprising. A lot happened in Maresburg."

"So where to next? Have you picked a case? Or our vacation spot?"

The morning light sparkled in Selene's brown eyes. She smiled at him and said, "You heard Phoebe. California is nice this time of year. A little warmth will do us some good, don't you think?"

"I hear a lot of paranormal stuff happens out there. I'm sure there's a case in need of solving for our next episode."

"*And* we can find my grandmother, who's playing a game of Where's Waldo? with me."

"That too."

They started for the van in step with each other. Selene's beam had only spread. "Let's not forget what you promised me either."

"Which is?"

"Arizona's along the way, isn't it?"

Aiden groaned, catching on to where the conversation was headed. "You don't want to see it, Selene."

"Your bachelor pad? Are you kidding? Do you know how many times I've wondered what it's like?"

Laughter rolled off their tongues as they reached Ghost and climbed inside. Aiden clicked his seat belt into place and shifted gears into reverse. "Okay, fine. What the witch wants, the witch gets. California and Arizona, here we come."

TO BE CONTINUED…

AUTHOR'S NOTE

I want to take a quick second to thank you for reading *Black Moon Rising*, episode 2 in the *Paranormal Hunters* series. I went into this book excited to write Aiden and Selene working as a team on their first official case. When I say Aiden and Selene are such a joy to write, I mean it. I hope you enjoyed reading them.

If you have a free moment, I'd love it if you could leave a review on Amazon and Goodreads.

You can also visit www.milanickswrites.com for more info on upcoming releases, including episode 3 in the *Paranormal Hunters* series, *Black Siren's Song*.

BLACK SIREN'S

Song

MEN ARE GOING MISSING, AND THEIR BONES ARE WASHING UP
ON SHORE. BUT IS IT THE WITCHES WHO ARE RESPONSIBLE, OR
ANOTHER MYSTERIOUS CREATURE AT SEA?

EPISODE 3 COMING SOON

ALSO BY MILA NICKS

STAND ALONES:

Love's Recipe

Happily Ever Afters

North Star Angel

For Vacation Only (Coming June 2021)

When You Were Mine (Coming Fall 2021)

SERIES:

Paranormal Hunters

Black Witch Magic

Black Moon Rising

Black Siren's Song (Coming Fall 2021)

Wild Horse Ranch

Chasing Wild Horses

Taming Wild Horses

Wild Horses Coming Home (Coming August 2021)

Made in the USA
Las Vegas, NV
01 August 2021